Alien

Vermin

A Novel

By Kevin William Barry

This book is dedicated to my father Patrick, the man who taught me right from wrong, and from whom I inherited enough common sense to understand why it matters

ALIEN VERMIN

First edition. April 23, 2016.

Copyright © 2016 Kevin William Barry.

ISBN: 978-1393777618

Written by Kevin William Barry.

Chapter 1

THREE DAYS BEFORE THE summer equinox, the sky above Tran turned black. Huge thunderheads rapidly built up in the east and rolled slowly westward. The massive clouds roiled and churned, bubbling and swirling like some hellish inverted cauldron filled with boiling, viscous, black oil. Lightning flashed continuously across the sky and peals of thunder rent the air with such volume that the very ground beneath seemed to tremble and shake at its awesome power.

With each deafening crack of thunder a darker, more solid apparition appeared in the tempestuous sky. Then, as rapidly as they'd appeared the thunderheads cleared, and miraculously the sky once more became clear and blue. Seventeen Galaxy class battle cruisers had dropped out of orbit around Tran during the storm, and positioned themselves over the city of Salin, turning day into night with their huge black shadows. Each vessel was over three kilometres long and almost half that wide, and each was fitted with an SRS Twister drive, a breathtakingly powerful machine which could bend the very fabric of space, so that origin and destination were almost in the same place. But the SRS Twister drives had one very real flaw, they could not take the vessel to somewhere that did not exist.

For centuries these massive vessels had waged war all over the galaxy, but recently the visitors had stripped all the armaments from the ships, gutted their interiors and filled the empty voids with up to two and a half thousand stasis units. Each stasis unit was designed to

1

hold the hibernating form of one of the last surviving members of a once great civilisation.

Seventeen thousand and sixty two souls were crammed into the huge cargo holds of the ships. Seventeen thousand and sixty two, the last survivors from a planet which had turned cancerous and imploded, dying not from old age, but from abuse. A world worn out, poisoned and denuded of its once plentiful bounty by the greed and stupidity of the planet's once dominant life form.

The planet Tran was the last in a long line of habitable worlds the armada had visited, and the leader of the convoy, Admiral Vethil Wangan, knew that time and options were running out. Tran was the last known world. Beyond Tran, lay only an uncharted void, and the SRS twister drive could not take them to such a place. An SRS Twister drive needed a destination.

There were no doubt other worlds, other planets which might offer refuge to the seventeen thousand and sixty two, now homeless, refugees. But those other worlds were unexplored. Nothing was known about the planets further out in the cosmos. Not just whether they were habitable or not, but where in the universe they were in the first place. How could they go to a place if they didn't know how to navigate there?

Just three hundred years ago the ancestors of the ship's inhabitants had thought themselves unique. They'd thought that the creatures on their planet were the only living life forms in existence. Even with the naked eye, they could see there were trillions of stars in the sky, and they must have realised that each of those stars probably had planets orbiting around them. Yet they arrogantly refused to accept the simple mathematics of the situation, and chose to deny that the odds against them being the only life forms in the universe, were simply too great to be possible. They'd thought they were the chosen ones. They'd believed they had been created by the Gods, and with an arrogance borne of ignorance, this convinced them that they were extremely special.

With the invention of the SRS Twister drives they soon came to realise that the universe was in fact teaming with life. But rather than revelling in their discovery, the alien's ancestors had embarked on a path of conquest and destruction. Dozens of less technologically advanced civilisations were conquered and enslaved, and for centuries the ancestors waged bloody war across the galaxy.

But predictably not all planets visited were populated by creatures who had barely progressed beyond the stone age. Eventually, the mighty conquerors met their match when they stupidly chose to attack a highly advanced civilisation on the planet they had designated #619. A planet known as Annux.

The inhabitants of Annux were a peace loving species, and as they were totally unprepared for an invasion, they initially suffered heavy losses. But they were creatures of science and their technology was far more advanced than that of their would be conquerors. Within a matter of days they had built an impervious shield which deflected or repelled any weapons fire the invaders could throw at them. Then the people of Annux quickly converted their automated manufacturing plants to the task of building armaments. They produced massive pulse generators, weapons which could hurl unbelievably powerful bursts of energy, half a light year across space. These weapons decimated almost ninety percent of the attacking fleet in less than a day.

Then the inhabitants of Annux retro fitted other weapons to what had once been a cargo vessel and followed what was left of the retreating armada, as it limped back to its home world. The war between the two planets lasted less than a single day.

With a howl like a demented banshee, the Annuxian vessel had erupted from a cloud enveloped vortex, less than a kilometre above the alien planet's surface. It had scorched across the sky, dropping even closer to the ground, swerving left and right as it searched for its first target. Incongruously, rather than midnight black or battleship grey or even silver, the ship had been painted bright yellow, and along its sides were brightly coloured, cheerful looking graphics, which, had anyone on the planet's surface been able to decipher them, told of the wonderful, inexpensive and indispensable products normally contained within. The ship was also bulky and squat, with little or no design considerations given to aerodynamics. So even a child could tell that the ship had been designed as a simple workhorse, a cargo ship, rather than a warship.

But ironically, on that day the only cargo carried by the Annuxian freighter was a cargo of death and destruction. Its hold had been packed solid with thirty seven compression torpedoes, lethal weapons, each one designed to destroy a specific, military target, and each target had been selected so the torpedo would inflict the maximum amount of strategic damage to the planet's considerable defences. The alien's world was under attack.

Suddenly the ship had veered sharply to the left and increased its already breathtaking speed as it powered towards its target. As it raced through the air, the vessel's phenomenal pace set up a huge pressure wave, quite visible in the heavy, smog laden atmosphere, and a deafening sonic boom rattled buildings and shattered the glass of any structure the ship passed by too closely. On the ground people had watched the vessel's trajectory in terror, calling urgently to their loved ones, scooping their children up in their arms, and racing for what little sanctuary they could find.

Seconds later the pilot of the Annuxian vessel sighted the first target through its long range viewfinder. It was the city's main Air Offence Facility, home base to over seven hundred Galaxy Class Battle Cruisers and the crews who flew them. It was also the home to the million strong maintenance personnel, ground control staff and their families. With deft, practised hands, the pilot of the Annuxian vessel quickly entered the facilities coordinates into the targeting computer and sent the first compression torpedo on its way.

It had flown straight and true, impacting the AOF dead centre. But rather than exploding, the compression torpedo had instead instantaneously created a huge and irresistible gravitational field. The field, like a tiny black hole, had sucked everything within its range into its ravenous maw. Whole buildings, some of them multi story sky scrapers, had simply collapsed, compacted into dense balls of rubble which had then disappeared into the evil black whirlpool growing inexorably at the centre of the carnage. People, vehicles, equipment, even the Battle Cruisers themselves, mammoth ships capable of travelling across entire universes and constructed of seemingly indestructible Nelamine alloy, had succumbed to the massive gravitational forces emitted by the compression torpedo. Everything within a five kilometre radius had disappeared into the dark vortex. The devastation had been complete. Only a few bits of twisted or sheered metal, such as the steel girders of building foundations and the like, massive hunks of metal which had been securely anchored into the planet's bedrock, had survived the terrible destruction.

But amazingly the carnage had extended only to the periphery of the facility. Some buildings on the very edge of the AOF had sustained minor damage, but generally all structures outside of the facility had escaped unscathed. Astonishingly, all this had happened in just a matter of moments, and even before that first compression torpedo had struck home, the Annuxian freighter had already turned towards its next target.

The ship had headed north, scything a path across the Fenlat wasteland, a vast, arid ocean of once arable land, now denuded of any living vegetation due to centuries of the over use of fertilisers and the injudicious use of herbicides. As the vessel had sped over the parched and lifeless earth, the ship's pressure wave churned up clouds of the toxic dust, dust which had caked the surface of the wasteland relatively harmlessly for decades, but now it rose up into the atmosphere, obscuring the sun and turning day into night.

The Annuxian freighter had banked steeply to the north, levelled out and taken aim at its next target. On the edge of the Fenlat sat the huge munitions factory bearing the same name. This time however the defence systems protecting the factory had been readied for the attack. A quartet of 'starburst' laser mines had risen up into the air and exploded, sending out a radiating and criss-crossing web of laser beams, blocking the path of the missile. The Torpedo had struck the grid of laser light and been sliced into a thousand, harmless pieces. But even as that destroyed torpedo fell to the earth, the pilot had launched a second and third weapon. The second torpedo had detonated just a few metres before the 'starburst' grid, devouring the four mines and neutralising their protective shield. The third torpedo had shot past a nanosecond later, once again impacting the huge defence facility dead centre. Moments later a second gravity whirlpool opened up, devouring everything nearby in its ravenous maw.

Over the next six hours that single, Annuxian craft had struck thirty one more times. By the end of the day, the entire planet had been left defenceless and nine billion people held their collective breath, waiting for the Annuxians to continue their invasion. An invasion that never came.

The Annuxians took no pleasure in their victory. They were a peace loving race and had been for as long as they could remember. To them, the actions they had been forced to take were reprehensible, and many of those who had either taken part, or authorised the conflict found it impossible to reconcile their actions with their true nature. All were racked with grief and guilt and overcome with despair, a despair which eventually caused the solitary Annuxian combatant to take his own life.

Thankfully the rest of the Annuxians were able to quickly put the war behind them. Certain there would be no further attacks, they decommissioned the force field around their planet, stripped the pulse generators from the hulls of the cargo vessels and recycled the components, using the materials from the once deadly weapons to make benign objects such as personal transport vehicles, and kitchen appliances and even children's toys. Once again peace and tranquillity reigned over their planet.

But on the other side of the galaxy, their former opponents took an entirely different tack. In an endeavour to keep the truth of their reprehensible aggression from the general public, the military claimed that the attack by the Annuxians was unprovoked. That in fact it was the Annuxians who had instigated the war. The military demanded there be a ten fold increase in spending on armaments. The planet need to protect itself from further attacks, the warrior leaders said, and fearful of such an eventuality, the government agreed.

During the next two years, huge amounts of the planets already dwindling resources, were wasted on the production of new, more powerful weapons. Based on a variation of the SRS Twister drive, the military boffins manufactured a vortex canon, a huge, monstrous weapon, which could fire an energy burst that could reach right across the galaxy, pinpointing the Annuxian home world. Best of all, it could do so without the need to ever leave their own planet.

In a rare display of common sense, before launching an all out attack on the Annuxians, the military machine decided to test one of the weapons on a small, uninhabited moon, orbiting a planet just a few million light years away. At the simple press of a button, the tiny moon disappeared in an massive explosion, but then so did the weapon, plus a large part of the area surrounding it. Where the vortex canon had once stood, there was now a huge crater, many hundreds of kilometres across and thousands of metres deep.

Worst of all the gun had created a massive energy pulse which inexplicably began to change the very structure of matter itself on the planet. Over the next few months, the damage from the energy pulse increased exponentially, rapidly turning the whole world toxic. The sea, once the very lifeblood of the planet, grew more and more alkaline until it was so corrosive, it was no longer able to support the sea creatures and plankton which had once been so abundant. The forests died, crops failed, the lakes and rivers became so polluted and clogged with algae nothing could live in them. The planet had reached its tipping point. It was no longer able to repair the damage being done to it by its inhabitants and it began to die.

Chapter 2

THE VIEWING STATION floater hovered around twenty metres above the crater, giving the delegates from Riis city a perfect, birds eye view of the catastrophic devastation wrought upon it by the military's moronic gun. Senator Moodle Dav edged closer to the guardrail and peered over the side into the abyss, wondering not for the first time, if it might simply be preferable to hurl himself over the barricade and end it all, rather than subject himself to the slow and painful death which inevitably awaited him. He and nine million others. They were all going to die.

Even now, eight days after the damn vortex canon had 'misfired' and exploded, the crystallised walls of the crater still glowed a dull cherry red from the heat generated during the explosion.

For years the area around the crater had been barren and desolate. It had once been a mine sight and the ground was already badly polluted with toxic quantities of heavy metals such as Lead, Tin, Cadmium and Copper. Worse, to the north east of the old mine was a tailings dam, or maybe that should be lake, many kilometres in diameter, which was saturated with the deadly chemicals which had once been used in the extraction of the metals from the rich ore. The land was useless and decaying, which was why the military backed scientists had selected the area for their test in the first place.

But now even the few stunted and scrubby trees, the brownish, yellow, rancid mosses and the occasional hardy, wildly mutated reptile or insect which had once inhabited the area were gone. Not even bacteria could survive here now.

Inexplicably the massive energy surge created by the misfiring weapon had changed the very atomic structure of the ground in and around the crater. Now nothing organic could exist there, let alone survive. To make matters worse, the sterile area around the crater was growing exponentially. At first, it was just by a few millimetres per day, then a few metres, then one kilometre, then two, then four, then eight, sixteen, thirty two kilometres each and every day. Now the toxins were expanding through countryside like wildfire at hundreds of kilometres per day, and nothing could stop it.

Two days ago a previously dormant volcano on the the north western continent, on the other side of the planet, suddenly erupted. Like an enormous pustular boil, it spewed forth mountains of lethally toxic lava which, like the rocks and soil around its brother on the other side of the world, killed anything and everything in its path. That volcano was now the centre of a second, rapidly expanding, lifeless wasteland. Just as the geologists had surmised, the toxicity of the ground around the misfiring canon was not only spreading outwards, but like a cancerous melanoma, the poison was also spreading downwards, into the planet's magma bloodstream. Similar eruptions to the one on the north western continent were springing up all over the globe every day.

Dav felt sick. The delegation, ten men and women, scientists, government officials, religious leaders and members of the general public, had banded together to formulate some sort of plan for what the hell they should do next. So far only the two religious leaders had come up with any recommendations. But somehow, getting down on your knees and praying didn't really fill Moodle Dav with optimism.

One of the scientists joined him at the rail. Her name was Lin or Chin or something. She was pale and emaciated, with the bad complexion and arthritic, hunched posture of someone who had spent far too many hours in front of a computer screen. Together they took in the miserable vista of a world inexorably dying, a world choking on its own vomit, and being eaten inside and out by a cancer caused by their own, blindingly stupid actions.

"Latest projections put the tipping point at twenty seven days," Lin or Chin or whoever told him. "If we can't halt the spread before then, there will be no stopping it. If things keep escalating, we reckon the world will become uninhabitable in ninety three days.'

She didn't know it at the time, but she had overestimated by twelve days.

A little over an hour later, the entire group was back in the north wing of the Presidential Palace. President Nillish required an urgent update on the disaster, as did the huge throng of media hounds and concerned citizens milling about outside. They could wait, the President could not.

The room was small and cosy, with a thermo heating unit, complete with 'cool touch' holographic flames, embedded in the centre of the eastern wall and dominated by a long, rectangular, Rhone wood table and eleven matching chairs. At the head of the table sat the President himself. He greeted the delegation, had them sit, and then asked the question no one really knew how to answer.

"So, what's going on?"

The group sat in silence for many long moments, each one looking to the others to take the lead. Eventually Professor Lin got to her feet and addressed the issue. After a few seconds, the President interrupted.

"Uh. If it's at all possible Professor, it might be better if you put it in layman's language, something we mere mortals can understand. If that's at all possible, of course."

Lin stared at the ceiling for a while, trying to remember some basic, school girl physics and chemistry sufficiently simple for the politicians in the room to understand. Of course it was impossible to simplify things that much, but eventually she began again

"Okay. The first law of molecular physics is:- Opposite charges attract, similar charges repel. So, for example, we could have two hydrogen atoms; Hydrogen atoms always have a positive charge. Then we could have one oxygen atom; Oxygen atoms always have a negative charge. So because of their dissimilar charges, the three atoms join together; Hydrogen+Oxygen+Hydrogen; to form a molecule. That molecule's H_2O, good old common or garden water. Add another oxygen atom, we get H_2O_2 that's Hydrogen Peroxide. Add....Oh well, that's not important. What is important is that this atomic attraction is not just possible, it's INEVITABLE. It's certain and it's constant. It always happens and it's the very basis of matter itself."

"But that's not happening any more?" asked the President.

"No... I mean yes. It's just, well, the energy released when the vortex canon exploded, has somehow caused many elements, elements which previously had a specific charge, or were sometimes positive, sometimes negative, to reverse or become uncertain. Sometimes, individual atoms even oscillate from one to the other. For example, in the area we visited today, Hydrogen might not be always positive any more. Which means we might not get that inevitable and predictable molecular reaction I just described."

"So?" This came from one of the religious leaders.

Once again the professor accidentally reverted into technological language, forgetting for a second that the others didn't understand.

The president scowled and Lin reminded herself to dumb it down.

"Sorry Mr President. But to put it simply, if we can no longer rely on the most simple molecular laws of physics, well.... to put it bluntly, we're screwed. Matter itself only exists because of those laws. Solids, liquids, gasses, you, me, everything."

President Nillish leaned forward in his chair and tapped nervously on the table. Suddenly he wished he wasn't President any more. The burden was far too great.

"Do you have any idea what the outcome will be? I mean what's going to become of our world?"

Lin shrugged.

"I can only guess Mr President. I mean we're talking about a whole new branch of physics here. But there is evidence that the resulting atomic reaction is going to be incredibly violent. That's already apparent. We all noticed the incredible increase in temperature displayed by the crystallised walls of the crater today. That's being caused by the huge amount of forming and reforming of new, previously unknown, molecular structures. My best guess, and it's only a guess, is that eventually the world will collapse in on itself. I think we are witnessing the birth of what will eventually become a black hole."

The room was quiet for a few seconds as the ramifications of that statement sunk in.

"So where do we go from here?" asked Senator Moodle Dav. "I have an idea but it's pretty drastic. Perhaps someone else has a better, more workable plan."

"The answer is clear my brethren," claimed religious leader Wan. "The gods will deliver us from our terrible dilemma, but only if we, as an entire species, embrace their benevolence and get down on our knees and beg for forgiveness and atone for our grievous sins."

The scientist exploded.

"You're an idiot," scoffed Lin. "So according to you, we should entrust the very survival of our entire species to the whims of someone's group of imaginary friends. What a moron. Our planet is dying you fool. This time next year not a single cell of what we recognise as organic material will exist on this world. We have to get as many people as possible off the planet as quickly as we can. If we don't, our entire species is doomed."

The meeting quickly descended into a free for all. Lin and Wan nearly came to blows. But eventually President Nillish slammed his hand down on the table with a bang and demanded everyone calm down.

"Senator Moodle said he had an idea," he said. "Perhaps we should hear what he has to say before one of us kills someone."

Senator Moodle Dav rose and waited for the rabble to settle further. He was used to speaking in public and knew all the tricks for getting and holding peoples attention. But the plan he was about to propose was one he had hatched only that morning, and he knew there were many considerations to be made and many details yet to be worked out. It was at best only a plan for a plan, and he wasn't the person to work out all the intricate details on how to make it work. Oh well, he thought, here goes.

"There are twenty three Galaxy Class War Ships sitting in dry dock or orbiting the planet at present. These are the vessels which were off world at the time of the Annuxian's attack and so escaped the devastation felt by the rest of our fleet. My plan is that we strip them of armaments and all other unnecessary equipment and fill the holds with as many stasis units as we can squeeze aboard. I have a little of knowledge of this type of craft from my service in the defence forces and I estimate we could safely transport nearly a quarter of a million people to another location. Once there, wherever that might be, well...we'll just have to start again."

"That's outrageous," bellowed Wan. "Two hundred and fifty thousand people? What about the other nine billion people on the planet. Are we expected to just leave them here to perish? Such a plan is diabolical. You'd be murdering billions."

President Nillish held up his hand for silence.

"I agree, Wan. We'll have to come up with a better solution than just abandoning ninety nine percent of the world's population to whatever fate awaits them. But the Senator's plan has some merit. I recommend we proceed with Moodle Dav's suggestion immediately. Just in case we're left with no alternative.

Chapter 3

IT WAS AT THIS TIME that the government of the once beautiful, prosperous world, a world previously teeming with life, now inexorably and rapidly dying, decided to hold a lottery. Those who were lucky enough to be picked, would be offered a place on one of the twenty three converted Galaxy class cruisers which would shortly leave the planet in search of a new home. Those unlucky souls who were not chosen would be left behind. Sadly the devastation affecting the planet progressed far more rapidly than expected, so just twenty eight days after the drawing of the lottery, the final flotilla containing the hibernating bodies of just twenty two thousand beings left for the planet Soren 6. They'd run out of time and as a result, over half of the stasis units remained empty.

Soren 6 was deemed to be the most suitable of the known worlds to resettle on. It had a similar atmosphere to their home world, its oceans covered a little over sixty percent of the planet's surface and its gravity was comparable. Importantly the planet also had an abundance of life, both animal and vegetable. Conveniently, the most advanced species was a quadruped, with a pair of prehensile tentacles and only a moderately sized brain. These creatures had barely mastered the use of basic language and simple tools, so any resistance from the natives was expected to be minimal.

Decades ago the people from the dying world had set up a moderately successful colony on the planet, and although it had been disbanded a few years later, the scientists who had lived there had amassed a sizeable amount of data about the planet's agricultural possibilities. There was also an abundance of metallic ores and the practicality of converting the planets natural energy resources for manufacturing was good. All of which indicated the resettlement would easily succeed.

The armada lifted off from the surface and took up formation in orbit around the dying planet. Quickly the navigators on each ship entered the navigational co-ordinates into their vessel's computers. Captain Shragn of 'Raptor 3' had been chosen to lead the flotilla. He had the helmsman manoeuvre his huge vessel into position and engaged the SRS Twister drive. Just a few minutes later, screaming like a banshee, the huge ship erupted from the cloud enveloping the end of the vortex, just six hundred kilometres above the surface of Soren 6.

Captain Shragn disengaged the SRS Twister drive and still travelling at nearly one hundred kilometres per second, headed for the planet's surface. The ship had slowed, but still hit the force field surrounding the planet at over one thousand kilometres per hour and stopped dead. The impact crushed the ship like an eggshell, the SRS Twister drive imploded with the force of a dozen nuclear bombs, instantly crystallising the Nelamine metallic alloy of the ship's hull, and vaporising every living soul on board.

'The Warrior Queen' was the next ship through the vortex, following hot on the heels of 'Raptor 3'. Its Captain saw the devastation inflicted on the lead ship and took evasive action. Battling against the vessel's seemingly unstoppable momentum, the helmsman fired the braking thrusters and hauled the helm to the right, banking the ship slowly to starboard. But the manoeuvre was not enough to save the Battle cruiser. It barely glanced off the shield, but even so the impact was still sufficient to tear open the entire port side of the ship's hull. No one survived.

The next vessel through, 'The Huntress', exited the vortex nearly one thousand kilometres to the north. Captain Turook Cank was easily able to miss the force field, but the remnants of the first two ships, now spinning away from Soren 6 at thousands of kilometres per hour, acted as shrapnel and tore into his ship's hull. The Cruiser's SRS Twister drive was irreparably damaged. Even as Captain Turook fought to regain control of his vessel, his ship's communications officer sent out an emergency message to the rest of the fleet, warning them of the danger. His actions saved over twenty thousand lives.

"What the hell is going on?" demanded Admiral Vethil Wangan, the leader of the armada, as he stood on the bridge of the flagship 'War Hawk'. He was watching the images of the devastation sent back from 'The Huntress', now orbiting Soren 6, over twenty seven light years away.

"There's some sort of force field around Soren 6, Sir," answered his tech officer.

Vethil's face turned deathly pale as the dreadful consequences of this news struck home. They'd lost two ships and nearly twelve hundred passengers and crew.

"How do a bunch of uncivilised, stupid farm animals, who've barely managed to develop a rudimentary written language, build a force field capable of repelling a Galaxy Class Battle Cruiser?" he bellowed.

No one knew the definitive answer to that, but the tech officer came up with a possible explanation. "Perhaps the Annuxians built it Sir. Perhaps, as an act of benevolence, they decided to protect their less technologically advanced neighbours from....well, from us, Sir."

Vethil swore. "Has Turook managed to ascertain if the shield can be penetrated with a laser or nuclear torpedo?"

The answer to that question, was it couldn't and because all the heavy armaments had been stripped out to make way for the stasis units, none of the vessels had anything more powerful on board.

Which meant that Soren 6 now had to be ruled out as a possible new home. Using ship to ship communications, Admiral Vethil and the Captains of the remaining twenty Battle Cruisers, discussed their options. The next closest habitable world was 'Balaton 3', a further thirty two light years away. But as far as 'The Huntress' was concerned, where the rest of the fleet was now headed was irrelevant, 'The Huntress' would not be joining them. Without a serviceable SRS twister drive, the ship would have to rely on its manoeuvring thrusters. This meant the vessel would have a maximum speed of just a few hundred kilometres per second. At such low speeds, they would reach Balaton 3 in around four thousand years.

Turook knew there was no way for he and his crew to transfer to one of the other ships without first landing somewhere, and although the others would reach their new home in just matter of minutes, they would not be coming back for 'The Huntress' for at least a year. If ever.

In addition to their sleeping passengers, each vessel carried a crew of ten. There were twenty ships left, and those two hundred crewmen and women were not only responsible for transporting the twenty thousand temporarily hibernating passengers to their new home, they also had to make sure that the new world was able to feed and support them. Crops had to be planted, accommodation built, all the necessary infrastructure had to be organised, and a multitude of other things had to be done before the others could be brought out of stasis and disembarked. Until that happened no vessel or its crew would be available for a rescue mission.

There was also a further complication. With thousands of tonnes of wreckage from the first two ships whizzing around Soren 6, putting 'The Huntress' into orbit around the planet would put it in extreme danger. The chance of a fatal collision with a piece of space junk was almost inevitable. So Turook took the only course open to him. He placed the ship on a heading towards Balaton 3, set the vessel's speed for four hundred kilometres per second and relayed his course and speed to the rest of the fleet. Then he ordered his crew into the spare stasis tubes and activated them. He set a distress beacon to activate in exactly one years time and then climbed into his own stasis tube. As the valgette gas entered his lungs and he felt himself slipping into unconsciousness, he said a silent prayer, hoping against hope that one of his compatriots would return in time to rescue them and that they'd be able to find them when they did. Deep in the back of his mind however, he suspected they wouldn't even bother.

Chapter 4

THE NAVIGATION OFFICERS of the remaining vessels fed the new co-ordinates into their ship's navigation computers, and one by one the fleet moved out. This time however, each vessel laid in a course which would bring them no closer than five thousand kilometres from the planet's surface. The strategy proved extremely prudent. 'Balaton 3' was also surrounded by an impervious force field.

The next planet they tried for was Jana 5, three hundred and fifty nine light years away. 'The Predator' failed to make the voyage. At such vast distances, even the slightest miscalculation in navigation could have a vessel miss its intended destination by light years. The ship was lost somewhere in the universe with little or no way of finding its way back. Predictably Jana 5 was also surrounded by an Annuxian force field.

Hileger minor was their next attempted landing. It is a large moon, nearly 12,000 kilometres in diameter, which orbits around its host planet, the gas giant Hileger major. Fifty one percent of the moon's surface is covered by water. It has a breathable atmosphere, an abundance of vegetation, a liveable climate, a solar cycle which, because of the orbital vagaries associated with its movement around its parent planet, varies between twenty three and thirty one hours, and a six limbed, five eyed sentient life form, which has an exoskeleton comprised of one thousand, four hundred and thirty nine, interlocking silicon plates. The life form has developed both spoken and a basic written language and has developed a simple form of mathematics based around an integer of six. According to the 'War Hawks' computerised records, they had also recently discovered the wheel. Predictably, the Annuxians had installed one of their damned forcefields around their moon.

The fleet dropped into orbit ten thousand kilometres above the moon's surface and considered their next move. The Annuxian forcefield around Hileger minor meant that considering the moon as alternative refuge had, once again, been denied them. They were rapidly running out of options. But Captain Vintent Deng of the 'Leviathan' had an idea.

"I believe the SRS twister drive should be able to open up a vortex with its exit point inside the shield," he told Admiral Vethil. "Once through, the pilot can locate the forcefield generator and disable it. Then the rest of the fleet can land safely."

Vethil, standing on the bridge of the 'War Hawk', listened intently as Captain Vintent's holographic avatar explained his reasoning.

" The shield is not solid matter," he said, "but rather a projected energy field which reacts with and repels solid matter. It stands to reason therefore, that while solids can't penetrate it, other forms of energy can. A clear indication of that, is the fact that sunlight still illuminates and warms the moon's surface."

"So," continued Vintent, "as a vortex created by a SRS Twister drive is also a form of energy, it should be able to create a wormhole right through it."

The idea had a lot of merit.

"Are you prepared to test your hypothesis yourself, Captain?" asked Admiral Vethil. "We don't have a vortex capable probe we could send, so it has to be one of our ships. As the 'Leviathan' is the smallest vessel in the armada and carries just five hundred and thirty nine passengers and crew, your ship is the perfect choice. Are you willing to risk your vessel and its people in what might just end up being nothing more than suicide."

Vintent considered his options and then nodded slowly. The truth was he had grave concerns about the exact nature of the Annuxian shield, and even though, at that range, the navigation computer could place the exit point of the vortex anywhere inside or outside the forcefield with pinpoint accuracy, there was still a huge possibility the ship would crash into the shield when he tried to go through. The vortex was pure energy, a Galaxy Class Battle Cruiser was not. But someone had to try. They were running out of options. They were running out of food, and most urgent of all, they were running out of air.

Four hours later, after extensive research and further testing of the shield's energy composition, and after checking and re checking the navigator's calculations a dozen times, Captain Vintent Deng of the 'Leviathan', broke ranks with the other vessels of the fleet and moved twenty thousand kilometres further away from the moon. That way, the formation of the vortex would not interfere with any of the other ship's orbits. He swung the large, cumbersome battle cruiser around to face directly at the moon and addressed the navigation officer. The Nav' Officer nodded and entered the co-ordinates.

Vintent engaged the SRS Twister drive, and just metres off the 'Leviathan's bow, the black, empty space in front of them, seemed to swirl, as if the void ahead was forming a huge whirlpool in space many kilometres in diameter. The ship's communications system burst into life a few moments later. It was Vethil, confirming that from his ship's position, he could see the exit point of the vortex opening up fifty kilometres inside the forcefield.

'Leviathan's helmsman inched the ship forward slowly until they felt the huge gravitational force of the vortex begin to take hold.

Suddenly there was a tremendous rush of acceleration as the 'Leviathan' was sucked into the wormhole.

Time itself seemed to slow perceptibly, and for a moment or two the entire ship seemed to stretch and twist, as if the whole vessel was being wrung out like a damp cloth. Though everyone on board knew the sensation was merely an illusion, a sub molecular, optical manifestation brought about by the huge gravitational field inside the vortex, and that it was in no way dangerous, everyone on board felt a few moments of panic until the sensation passed. Seconds later the 'Leviathan' burst through into the upper atmosphere of Hileger Minor. The helmsman powered up the anti-grav drives and gently slowed the ship to a complete stop.

"We've made it Admiral," Vintent Deng happily informed his leader. "The ship is safely inside the forcefield. I'm running a complete systems check before we proceed, but it looks as if we made it through unscathed."

That was the first piece of truly good news the fleet had had since leaving their home planet. Of course Hileger Minor wasn't perfect. Despite its size, gravity on the moon was less than eighty percent of their home world and the atmosphere's oxygen levels were only twenty two percent with nitrogen at over seventy. It would take quiet a few months before everyone had acclimatised to the vastly different conditions. Plus there was still those dam Annuxians to worry about. Vethil felt sure they hadn't seen the last of those creatures.

Fifty three minutes later, having completed an extensive integrity check, Captain Vintent gave the helmsman the order to make his way closer to the moon's surface. They had located the origin of the forcefield generator in a heavily forested area in the centre of a large island near the moon's equator. As the 'Leviathan' had no weapons capable of destroying the generator from a distance, Vintent had decided to land the ship on the island and send a mechanoid out, onto the moon's surface to disable it. But first they had to get to the island on the other side of the moon.

The helmsman engaged the anti-grav drive and gingerly edged the Leviathan forward. The first few hundred kilometres flight though any planet or moon's atmosphere was always the most difficult. Numerous factors had to be considered. The minute variations in gravitational strength due to the topography of the surface, plus the mineral composition of the substrata layers of the ground beneath them, and how the anti-grav drive responded to it, had to be adjusted for. The density of the atmosphere also affected the ship's handling, as did temperature variations on the ships hull as she passed from cooler to warmer air and back again. Not that any of these things posed any real danger to the vessel, it was just that without proper considerations of them, the ship would pitch and roll and yaw constantly as the anti-grav drive tried to compensate. It was far better to make a few adjustments now, while the vessel was travelling slowly.

As the helmsman brought the old girl under greater control, Captain Vintent Deng opened Leviathan's forward viewing port and gazed out over their prospective new home. It was not what any of them had hoped for. Below the terrain was rugged and harsh. As far as the men and women on the bridge could see, the entire area was covered with a dense, red carpet of vegetation which swirled and writhed and pulsated, like some huge living, breathing animal. Periodically the otherwise uninterrupted carpet of sickly red foliage was intruded upon by a clump of five or six taller trees, their long tubular trunks spiralling upwards, like giant statues of some hideous serpent reaching towards the pale yellow sun. At the top of these monstrous plants was an ugly crown of red and pus coloured yellow fronds. These plants, if indeed one could call them plants, also seemed to writhe and sway independently of any breeze.

The moon had been visited by Vintent's people before, and that visit had been well documented. From the records on Leviathan's storage computer, Vintent had learnt that the forest below them was in fact made up of millions of individual creatures who were neither vegetable nor animal, but rather a strange hybrid combination. The 'plants' were a weird genetic abomination, an aberration brought about by the unique conditions on Hileger Minor. They were anchored firmly into the moon's mineral rich subsoil, but above the ground they could move quite independently. He'd also learnt that the strange red colour of the foliage was caused by an abundance of a low level radioactive isotope found in the moon's soil. This had mutated Hileger Minor's chlorophyll, so that it now reflected the red light spectrum rather than the more common green.

The Helmsman increased speed to around fifteen hundred kilometres per hour and adjusted his course a few degrees to the north. Seconds later the 'Leviathan' passed over the huge, towering cliffs at the edge of the continent and headed out over the sea. In contrast to the land, the water below them was crystal clear and seemed, at first, to be void of any organism larger than Vintent's fist. He increased the magnification of the viewing port and could see myriads of small, finned creatures, swimming about near the surface. These small fish were obviously feeding on still smaller animals. Suddenly a huge marine monster shot up from directly below the school of fish, its massive maw, filled with multiple rows of viciously pointy teeth, opened wide to catch as many of its prey as possible. As it leapt high into the air, its entire body came clear of the water and Vintent could see it was at least forty metres in length. Its skin was covered in blue and black scales which would have been the perfect camouflage for a predator living and hunting at the bottom of a dark sea. It was shaped like a long tapered dart which allowed it to reach incredible speeds under water, pushed along by its massively powerful, leaf shaped tail.

Vintent had seen enough of the ugly, evil world, and had he any choice in the matter he would have instructed the navigator to work out a course as far away from the miserable moon as possible and to do it as quickly as he could. But they had no choice. Hileger Minor was their only option. No doubt they would adapt, and no doubt they would also do much to remould the world into something more akin to the planet they had once inhabited. But for now, it was the only possible home they had. He instructed the Helmsman to increase speed and head for the island harbouring the forcefield generator as quickly as possible.

The shield generator was a machine, roughly rectangular, nine metres by five metres and four metres high. On its gently sloping roof was a parabolic dish, aimed at the heavens. Next to it and slightly above was a spherical object which floated about a metre above the roof, tethered to an anti-grav sling. As the Leviathan approached from the east, the object suddenly launched itself into the air and headed, at great speed, towards the ship. It was one of the Annuxian's dreaded compression torpedoes, this one obviously an automated defence mechanism designed as back up should the forcefield be breached. On board the 'Leviathan' Captain Vintent and his crew watched in horror as the deadly projectile quickly closed to within three hundred metres. Before Vintent could launch any form of counter attack, the torpedo imploded, setting up a small, dense, powerful and inescapable gravity field. Within seconds the Leviathan began to be inexorably drawn into the miniature black hole generated by the torpedo.

High above the moon, the people aboard the remaining seventeen vessels watched in abject terror as the Leviathan, a ship nearly a kilometre long and weighing several million tonnes, was crushed into a ball no larger than a child's toy and then sucked into the void.

One more ship was lost that day, plus five hundred and thirty nine more people from a species rapidly approaching the critical number required for survival.

Chapter 5

FOR THE NEXT THIRTY two days Admiral Vethil led his armada from one side of the known universe to the other searching for a habitable planet. None were found. At day nineteen they lost yet another ship. The navigation officer aboard 'Firefly' miscalculated the gravitational effects of the asteroid belt near 'Surisi 5' and the second smallest vessel in the fleet came out of the vortex inside the centre of 'Surisi 5's' largest moon.

They had run out of options. They were rapidly running out of food and water. Worse, on all but one of the ships, the air scrubbers were almost totally blocked. The air was tainted and oxygen levels were dropping fast. They desperately needed to do something and quickly.

Finally, Vethil decided to take what he considered to be the only viable option left open to him. If they couldn't find somewhere to settle from amongst the planets inhabited by a lesser species, their only choice was to seek refuge on a world peopled by a more advanced race and ask for asylum. Such a world was Tran.

They came out of the vortex just a few hundred metres above the planet's surface. Vethil immediately sent a message on every conceivable wave band apologising for invading the Tranian's airspace and explaining that as they needed to replenish their air supply urgently, they simply had no other choice. He also sent a second message requesting refuge for the seventeen thousand souls on board. These two messages were accompanied by translations of the same messages, in seventy two other languages. Languages from all over the known universe, which were sent in the hope that the meaning of the Admiral's messages would be made clear.

Once the ships had purged the air scrubbers and recharged their air compactors, the entire fleet rose high above the atmosphere and placed themselves in orbit around the planet to wait for a response from the Tranian government. Nothing happened for three days.

On the third day, a small transporter lifted off from the surface and slowly made its way towards Vethil's flagship. It gradually came alongside and stopped just a few metres from one of the smaller cargo bay doors. Moments later a transfer tube telescoped out from the transporter, latched on to the side of the massive ship covering the cargo bay door completely, and anchoring to the ships hull with magnetic clamps. Suddenly 'War Hawk' was filled with noise as a deafening klaxon sounded, warning the crew of an imminent hull breach. Somehow the Tranian pilot was opening the cargo bay door from the outside.

"Override the door mechanism," commanded Vethil over the intercom from the Bridge.

"I'm unable to comply sir," answered the cargo handler on duty at the time. "They've somehow locked me out."

The klaxon continued to ring out deafeningly. Chief Security Officer Salang Chai, standing next to the Admiral on the Bridge, rushed forward and began furiously typing his security clearance code into the ships computer in the vain hope he might be able override the Tranian pilot's instructions and stop the cargo bay door opening. It didn't work.

"ISOLATE CARGO BAY SEVEN," he yelled.

Over the intercom they heard a loud metallic clang as the internal doors to cargo hold 7 were shut and sealed. Chai knew that while isolating the cargo hold from the rest of the ship would buy them some time, he had just passed a death sentence on the two men working inside. As the door opened, the air in the hold would be expelled in a rush. The immediate drop in pressure would kill the two workers in seconds. They would literally explode.

But that didn't happen. Somehow the Tranian pilot had managed to set up some type of containment field between the transfer tube and the hull of the 'War Hawk'. There was a tiny drop in pressure of less than half of one percent and then the air inside the cargo hold stabilised. The emergency Klaxon eased back to a whisper and then died. A few moments later the face of one of the Cargo bay workers appeared in the communications vidi screen.

"Admiral, the door to the Tranian transport vessel is open. There's no one on board, but I looked inside. It's full of what looks like food and water."

After due consideration, Vethil ordered the crewmen to unload the Tranian ship. "Make sure everything goes through the decontamination process before it's distributed to the rest of the ship. " commanded Vethil. "And make equally sure you and the other man with you are decontaminated as well."

Vethil smiled. It appeared those on Tran had understood his message and had decided to help.

Over the next seven days the tiny unmanned transporter shuttled back and forth from the planet to a different vessel in the fleet. Each time it returned it came laden with provisions, enough to last the conscious crew at least forty days.

But not a word was heard from the Tranian people. Every one on board the seventeen vessels felt they knew what that meant. The Tranians were restocking the cruisers prior to sending them away.

Chapter 6

CHIEF SECURITY OFFICER Salang Chai squeezed himself between the two rows of stasis tubes, reached up onto the top of tube number 50/2/7, and retrieved the tiny Nelamine alloy container which had been hidden there. It had taken him almost an hour to reach the tube, crawling over a quarter of a kilometre through the munitions hold, which had been crammed tight, from wall to wall and almost to the ceiling, with the stasis tubes and their comatose occupants. Fifty tubes across, ten tubes high, fifty tubes deep. Containers for twenty five thousand sleeping souls, all lying horizontally like a huge stack of cylindrical coffins.

Nearly twenty four thousand of the tubes were empty.

They'd run out of time. No one had expected their home planet to collapse quite so quickly. They'd believed they had lots of time left before the toxins reached critical levels and the air became unbreathable. But they were wrong.

Loading the tubes was also very time consuming. Because each row was packed in tightly beside the one next to it, the entire row, five hundred stasis tubes, had to be moved out, filled with its passengers and then slid back into place. Then the next row was dragged out. They got one thousand and twelve people on board before they had to shut the hatches to prevent the air inside the ship being contaminated by the air outside.

Every vessel in the fleet was affected and the loss of three ships had reduced their numbers to what many considered to be a critical level. Seventeen thousand and sixty two was barely enough to guarantee a continuation of the species. Though under the circumstances, that might still prove to be a moot point.

Empty or not, the twenty five thousand stasis tubes still existed, and they were still packed in tight, filling the entire forward part of the former munitions hold. This made getting to one at the very back, a very tight squeeze. Of course Chai could have sent in one of the smaller, automated maintenance drones in and saved himself the trouble, but engineering was trying to keep a lid on power usage, so he'd decided to make the trek himself. Bad idea. Chai was a big man, almost one point four metres tall, which was very large for someone of his species. He was also muscular, barrel chested and broad shouldered and it was this last feature which had made the journey to tube 50/2/7 quite an odyssey. The engineers who had refitted the ship's munitions hold had placed the stasis tubes as close together as possible and had given little consideration to access requirements by broad shouldered Chief Security Officers. There was only one option open to him, get down on his hands and knees and crawl.

The Nelamine alloy container was filled with illicit drugs. Of course the sniffers should have picked that up before the drugs even got on board, but as every first year student of engineering knows, the harmonics of Nelamine alloy will stuff up a sniffer's sensitivity totally. Which was exactly why Assistant Engineer Shillim Del had hidden the shit in such a container in the first place. A chance discovery of the drugs was why Assistant Engineer Shillim Del was now locked up in the brig, and would be until Admiral Vethil decided to let him out. There was a lot to do and the ship currently carried only one maintenance person, so Chai had a feeling that letting him out would happen as soon as Shillim Del stopped vomiting, screaming and defecating uncontrollably due to the horrendous withdrawal symptoms currently racking his body. If he didn't die first.

Chai was deeply saddened by the recent events. Not so long ago, he and Del had been good friends. But Del's drug addiction had put paid to that, not to mention Del's career, financial future, and current freedom. Had they been at war, Vethil would've had Del put into one of the airlocks and opened the outer hatch. But this was supposed to be a mission of peace and more than likely the Tranians were watching the fleets every move. As the Tranians were known to be a peace loving species, Vethil thought it likely that shoving someone out of an airlock would not have been something they would view favourably, so Del was locked up in the brig. Chai was pretty certain that over the next few days, there would be a number of occasions when, in the throws of withdrawal, Del would wish he had been shoved outside into the freezing vacuum of space. At least that way he would have died quickly.

Drugs! Chai hated them, especially the most recent, fashionably chic narcotic. They called it 'Rapture' and as far as Chai could see it was aptly named. That was exactly what it did, gave the user a feeling of rapture, complete euphoria. There were only two problems with the stuff, it made the user so lethargic they were unable to function even at the most basic level, and it was highly addictive. This meant that the user alternated between a state of almost complete torpidity when they were high, and unbridled aggression and desperation when they weren't. The other withdrawal symptoms were also pretty horrific.

What a waste, Chai thought. He remembered a time when Del was not only a good friend, but also a good mentor. In fact, it was Shillim Del who had helped Chai to achieve his promotion to Chief.

In order to progress beyond the rank of Security Officer 1st class, Chai had to sit an exam. The exam covered not only all facets of law enforcement, weapons training, unarmed combat techniques and leadership, but also included basic engineering concepts. The thinking behind this was: if you were going to look after the security on board a Galaxy Class Battle Cruiser, you really should know a bit about how they worked. Chai didn't have a clue. A few days before the exam, he approached his friend Shillim Del and asked him for a bit of guidance.

"Sure," Del had said, as they sat opposite each other in the mess hall enjoying their evening meal. "Let's start with the basic idea of how an SRS twister drive works."

Del dove into the tool box he had sitting on the floor beside him, and pulled out a long length of optic fibre filament.

"Here, " he said, handing Chai one end of the filament. "Take this and stretch it out, see how long you think it is."

Chai walked to the other end of the refectory, feeding out the filament between his fingers as he went.

"I reckon it's about ninety metres long," he called back.

Del told him to drop his end of the filament and come back. Then he took a pencil from his pocket and began to wrap the optic fibre around it. He wound and wound until the entire length of filament was wrapped around the pencil.

"Okay, look at this," said Del. "A few moments ago the ends of the optic fibre filament were about ninety metres apart. Now they're only a few millimetres apart. That's basically what an SRS Twister drive does. It twists a narrow column of space into a tight spiral. What we call a vortex. As long as there's no solid, physical stuff in the way, like an inconveniently placed planet, we can travel millions of light years in just a few moments."

Chai said "Shit!" Then he asked how.

Del pulled a piece of paper out of his top pocket, spread it out on the table in front of them and began to explain the physics and mathematics behind the phenomenon. Chai followed him for a few moments, but then became completely lost.

"Look, I'm pretty sure the maths don't really matter as far as your exam is concerned anyway," said Del. "As long as you can demonstrate a basic understanding, I'm sure you'll be fine."

Chai nodded. "Okay, but from a security point of view, what sort of thing should I be looking out for. How, for example, would someone go about sabotaging the SRS Twister drive on a ship?"

Del held up his fork. "With something like this."

"What? vegetable stew?"

"No smart arse. This.....common old stainless steel. Or for that matter any metal other than Nelamine Alloy. All ships capable of interstellar travel are made out of NA. Any metallic component which isn't, has to be shielded inside a covering of it. If not, the huge magni-grav forces inside the vortex will tear it apart and probably take the vessel with it. The SRS Twister drive is a brilliant piece of technology, but it's the Nelamine Alloy which makes it all possible. If a terrorist secretly replaces even a small component with a fake made from something else, the ships going to go bang."

"Then it's lucky NA's so unique in its appearance. I've never seen anything that has that swirling, iridescence that Nelamine Alloy does. That would be almost impossible to fake."

"Yea. Also the ship's sniffers are designed to sniff out anything potentially dangerous. If it's metallic and not NA or encased in NA, they'll find it." Del put down his fork and leaned forward conspiratorially. "You know that swirling iridescence is caused by the very thing that makes NA do what it does. You see when mixed in precise proportions with various other metals, NA becomes Bi-phasic."

"Bi-what?"

"Bi-phasic," replied Del. "Basically, in lay man's terms, Nelamine Alloy is in two places at once."

Chai was incredulous. "What? How can that be possible?"

"I'll show you."

Del took a small rectangle of card from his tool box and drew a cross on one side. He turned it over and drew a circle on the other. Then he took a piece of adhesive tape and attached the card to the end of his pencil.

"Now watch this," he said."

He placed the pencil between his palms and rubbed his hands together briskly. The card oscillated back and forth rapidly. Suddenly the cross seemed to be sitting inside the circle. Both diagrams appeared to be on both sides of the card.

"But that's just an optical illusion," said Chai. "Everyone knows that. The circle and cross are still on opposite sides of the card. It's just your eyes can't keep up with the rapid movement of the card, so your brain sees them both together. That's common knowledge."

Del put his pencil back in his pocket, placed his elbows on the table and grinned.

"Yea, but what if they weren't? What if by oscillating a solid object at a certain frequency and at a certain speed, it didn't just make it appear to be in two places at once but actually made it happen? Well, that's exactly what Nelamine Alloy does."

"So you're saying the ship will be at both its point of origin, and at its destination at the same time?"

"No! As far as anyone can tell the two planes of existence are just a few microns apart, but it's the fact that they exist at all that makes NA work. Not only does the specific harmonics of Nelamine allow a vessel to travel through the vortex, they make the stuff virtually indestructible. NA is not effected by the enormous amount of heat generated and the magni-grav forces can't destroy it either." Del leaned back in his chair. "Any questions?" he asked.

"Yea. I understand the temperature inside a vortex can reach several million degrees. Yet NA is unaffected. It's super tough. Okay if you hit it hard enough it will shatter, but you can't bend it, stretch it or shape it, and obviously if it's heat proof you can't forge it, So how the hell do they make it into complex shapes like a Galaxy Class Cruiser?"

"You know what a Nanobot is?"

"Yea, of course. Sub microscopic mechanoids. Basically tiny little robots which work at a molecular level.

"That's correct. Well the Nanobots create the required components one molecule at a time."

"Yes, okay, but how? How does a Nanobot extract even a single molecule from a lump of 'indestructible' Nelamine?"

Del smiled. "Argon gas," he replied. Chai hadn't heard of the stuff and told his friend just that.

"It's a rare elemental gas. At least it's rare on this planet. On some, like Relunt 2, it's common. That planet's atmosphere has a concentration of almost three percent. It's harmless to organic matter, odourless, tasteless and completely non toxic. The gas is relatively inert, but it acts like a powerful acid when it comes anywhere near Nelamine. So, they take some Nelamine rich ore, crush it, seal it in a processing container and pump in Argon gas. The Argon breaks down the Nelamine, the Nanobots then collect the freed atoms and combine them with specific amounts of other metals. Then, as I said, they construct the ship molecule by molecule."

Chai said "Wow."

The two friends spent the next three hours discussing Chai's upcoming exam. They also talked about the progression of the current war against some primitive, hapless beings on the other side of the galaxy, the recent catastrophic climate events in the southern hemisphere, and of course, sports. They told crude jokes, complained about their respective bosses and, as the amount of alcohol they consumed increased, wove fanciful tales of exploits they hoped one day to achieve. It was a great night, but eventually, in the early hours of the morning, the two friends parted company and made their way home.

Some time during the evening, Del had given Chai the scrap of paper on which he had scribbled the mathematical equation explaining how an SRS twister drive worked.

"Just memorise it Chai," he'd implored his friend. "Copy it out a hundred times or more, until you remember every section. Even if you don't really understand it, if you can replicate the equation, that should be enough convince the boffins you do."

Chai had taken his friends advice. He passed the exam with flying colours and five hundred and six days later, he found himself appointed as Chief Security Officer on Admiral Vethil's flagship "War Hawk."

He wasn't as proud of that achievement as he might have been. When the job came up, just two years after the Annuxian war, there were only seventeen sufficiently qualified Security Officers still alive.

Chapter 7

BUT THAT HAD BEEN A long time ago. Now Chai's dear friend Shillim Del was a drug crazed addict whose heart might, at any moment, literally explode from the massive strain of the withdrawal symptoms caused by the drug called Rapture.

As it became obvious their home planet was dying and there was nothing anyone could do to stop or even slow it's rapid demise, many others took the same route as Del. Unable to cope with their own imminent death, many of the planet's population choose to spend their last remaining days in self imposed oblivion. Some literally drank themselves to death. Others joined the myriad of suicide groups which had sprung up, ending their lives in mass, ritualistic, communal death, by poisoning, shooting or gassing themselves. Still others embraced chemical narcotics as an escape, and inevitably, 'Rapture' was the most popular intoxicant.

Chai could hardly blame them. He himself had briefly considered ending it all, but then he'd received news that he had been chosen to accompany the crew of the "War Hawk" as Chief Security Officer. Suddenly he had a future and all thoughts of despair had been wiped away by the hope of a new life on a new world. Perhaps for Shillim Del the news came too late and Chai's old friend had already embarked on a massive trip of a different kind. Yet somehow, despite his addiction, Del had made it to the flagship and signed on, but his regular drug use hadn't remained hidden for long.

The crawl back to the front of the munitions hold took even longer than the crawl in. The hard metal floor was punishing poor Chai's knees mercilessly and he had to keep stopping to ease the cramping he felt in his back whenever he had to twist sideways to pass under the cylindrical part of a stasis tube. As he neared the end of his ordeal, he heard someone mumbling to himself at the end of row 56. Someone was waiting for him, and whoever it was, he didn't sound happy.

Chai stopped a few rows from the end and dropped down onto his stomach. He rolled over onto his side and peered under the stasis tubes. He could make out the legs of a single person. He was wearing the dark grey overalls and black safety boots worn by all the maintenance crew and he was dancing around in an extremely agitated manner.

"C'mon, c'mon. Hurry up you bastard," whispered a voice Chai knew well. Somehow Shillim Del had escaped custody and was waiting for Chai to put in an appearance so he could get his drugs back. Chai decided that wasn't going to happen.

He rolled back onto his stomach and slid forward until he was directly below the first row of tubes. He reached into his pocket and pulled out the tiny container of drugs. He opened the bottle, shook out the dozen or so tabs inside, and stuffed them back in his pocket. He transferred the empty container to his left hand and reached down with his right to retrieve his stun whip. For obvious, reasons hand guns were prohibited onboard all interstellar vessels, but occasionally a Security Officer had to use a bit of force to quell a disturbance or even to encourage some errant soldier who refused to do his or her duty. So Chai had a stun whip, a small, handheld device which emitted an electrical charge sufficient to render a man unconscious. Chai had never used the device on another person, but he knew that Del, desperate and running high on adrenalin, would be far more dangerous than he would have been normally, so he was now quite prepared to use it.

Chai waited until Del was facing in the other direction, then hurled the Nelamine container away from him towards the front of the ship. It hit the floor with a loud clatter. Del spun around and saw the container skipping across the floor until it came to rest against the port side forward bulkhead. He took off after it.

It was the oldest trick in the book, but with good reason. It almost always worked. Chai quickly rolled out from under the stasis tubes and sprang to his feet, drawing the stun whip and pressing the trigger. A thin, bright spiral of charged electricity snaked out from its tip. Del spun around at the sound. He held up the Nelamine container and smiled.

Poor Del looked terrible, he was bathed in sweat and was shaking uncontrollably. His hair was lying plastered and drenched with perspiration against his scalp, his eyes were red ringed and bloodshot. There was dried vomit down the front of his tunic. Obviously he was still in the grip of some pretty horrendous withdrawal symptoms. Chai cursed, he was also wearing an earthing harness. An earthing harness was frequently worn by maintenance crew when they were working on the ships electrical systems. It stopped them getting electrocuted. Unfortunately it would also stop Chai's stun whip from having any effect on him. Of equal concern was the impact hammer he held in his left hand. Obviously Del had stopped off at his workshop on the way to the munitions hold and armed himself. The impact hammer had a kinetic head which could multiply the force of a blow ten fold, if Del managed to connect with it, it could easily maim or kill.

Del held the tiny Nelamine container to his ear and shook it. His face changed from smug to totally pissed off.

"Give me my stuff Chai," he demanded.

Chai once again flicked the switch on his stun whip and a flailing arc of electricity curled and writhed from its tip like an angry serpent.

"That's not going to happen Del. You need to put the hammer down and let me take you back to the brig," Chai ordered.

"GIVE ME MY STUFF!" Del screamed. He launched himself at Chai, raising the hammer above his head and screaming like a mad man. Chai lashed out with his whip. He knew that striking his attacker directly was futile, the earthing harness would simply divert any electrical charge directly into the ships hull. But there was a chance the whip could still be useful. If he could make a direct hit on the impact hammer, the electrical charge might fuse the mechanism which increased the hammer's force. It could still do some serious damage, of course, but would not be quite as lethal. The arc shot out, just as Del hurled the hammer with all his strength at Chai's head. There was a bright flash of light as the charge hit the missile, but the weapon kept coming straight at him. Chai ducked at the last moment, the hammer missed his head but still hit him, full force, smashing his left collar bone. Chai felt the bone shatter. But thankfully, the whip strike had done what he'd hoped and the kinetic charge didn't fire. If it had, Chai knew he would not have survived the blow.

Chai sucked in a huge lungful of air and fought desperately to push down the pain. He knew his ordeal was far from over. Del continued to come at him at full pelt, screaming and yelling for Chai to give him his drugs. Chai quickly stuffed the useless whip back into its holster and prepared to meet Del's onslaught. Del launched himself into the air, trying to tackle his former friend to the ground, but Chai was too quick for him. He sprung to his left and then brought his right elbow down on the back of Del's neck. But the blow had little effect. Whether it was a badly timed strike or the adrenalin coursing through Del's bloodstream nullified the effect was unclear, but moments later Del had renewed his attack. He launched a massive round house punch at Chai's head. Chai blocked it, but with only one arm to defend himself, Del's next blow hit him squarely on the chin. Chai retaliated by kicking Del in the stomach. He flew backwards half a metre and toppled to the ground. Moments later Del was scrambling back onto his feet.

Chai's broken clavicle was making it impossible to get the upper hand. His left arm was useless and every time he moved, a bolt of excruciating pain shot through his shoulder. Chai knew it was only a matter of time before Del seriously maimed or killed him. He had to think of another solution.

Del spun around and scrambled towards where his hammer had fallen. Clearly he wasn't as confident of his position over the Security Officer as Chai was. Chai used those few moments to throw himself to the ground and painfully drag himself back under the stasis tubes. He had one chance, somehow he had to climb to the top of the tubes. He stood, and holding a fistful of his tunic up near his right shoulder with his left hand to immobilise his injured left arm as much as possible, he leant back against the row of tubes behind him. Then by placing his feet on the row opposite, he pushed himself upwards, using his good, right arm to steady himself.

He could hear Del trying to clamber under the first row of stasis tubes, bellowing for him to come back and give him his precious 'Rapture', but Chai kept going, moving his feet up onto the next tube, steadying himself with his good arm, pushing himself up with his legs and then doing it again and again until he was nearly at the top. He looked down and saw Del climbing up after him. Chai's injured shoulder was slowing him down considerably and Del was closing the gap rapidly. Del lunged and snatched at Chai's ankle, but the Security Officer kicked out, catching Del squarely on the jaw. Dell momentarily lost his footing and slipped back down a few metres. A few moments later Chai reached the top stasis tube.

Quickly he punched one of the buttons on the tube's control panel and the top sprang open. It was one of the empty ones. Chai climbed inside, pulled out his stun whip and twisted the dial to maximum. Then he pulled out his communicator. He pressed the button for general broadcast.

"I'm in 10/7/16," he told the device. Then he flicked the switch on the handle of his stun whip and sent the electrical charge snaking towards the ceiling. It struck one of the fire detectors and immediately a deafening klaxon sounded the alarm. As Chai closed the lid on his stasis tube, he heard the doors and ventilation system for the munitions hold shut. The automated fire control protocols were coming into effect. As Chai's chamber filled with valgette gas and he slipped rapidly into unconsciousness, Chai knew that outside, the huge room would be quickly filling with Halon gas. The gas was designed to smother any flame. He also knew that unless he hurried, Shillim Del would also be smothered. Del had one chance; he had to climb back down and race to one of the fire exits. There was an emergency button next to each door that allowed anyone trapped inside when a fire broke out to exit the hold.

A wave of nausea briefly washed over Chai as he blacked out, but then he felt nothing until he was rescued an hour later. When that happened, his species numbered one less.

Chapter 8

AS BEFITTING A FLAGSHIP of the fleet, the maintenance drones on 'War Hawk' were the new, ultra, multi purpose, self contained design. They were the eight legged, spherically shaped mechanisms, with a bifurcated top hemisphere, which could perform two separate functions at once. The machine's legs were alternatively fitted with either clamping claws or magnetic feet so that it could access almost any area of the ship, including the outside. There was one of these large drones currently accessing 'War Hawk's' munitions hold.

The mechanoid walked forward on its spindly, metallic, multi jointed limbs to the end of the row of stasis tubes and then dropped down onto the floor. The top half of the drone spun around until its optical sensor caught sight of Shillim Del's body four rows back and one across. A thin silver tendril shot out from the drones' underside, wrapped itself around Del's ankle and dragged his corpse back out into the open. The drone picked up the lifeless body, crossed to the nearest waste disposal chute and dumped the corpse into it. Moments later Shillim Del's mortal remains were reduced to a few grams of ash.

Next the maintenance drone interfaced with the ships main computer and turned off the artificial gravity in the hold. With perfect precision, the drone rose into the air, and using tiny puffs of compressed air, negotiated its way to stasis tube 10/7/16. Once again a tiny silver tentacle snaked out from the drone, this time it tapped the buttons on the control panel of the tube, first extracting the valgette gas and replacing it with breathable air, and then activating the locking mechanism on the lid. The top sprang open revealing the sleeping form of Chief Security Officer Salang Chai.

Gingerly the mechanoid enveloped Chai's weightless body in its tentacles and returned to the floor of the hold. It would be a further two hours before Chai regained consciousness.

Chapter 9

EVERYTHING WAS PITCH black, yet also swirling and tilting in an unsettling, nauseating manner. Plus there was a strange smell, or perhaps taste was a better description, Chai wasn't sure. In the back of his mind there was also a feeling of deep sadness, though at that moment he was unsure exactly why he felt that way. Then it all came back to him.

Chai cautiously opened one eye. He'd never been in stasis before, but he'd heard tales of people waking with blinding headaches, nausea and temporary hearing loss. Thankfully he felt none of those symptoms, well perhaps just a little, and a bit of a dull ache in his left shoulder, which of course had nothing to do with being rendered unconscious by valgette gas.

He recognised the room. He had been there many times before, though not in the usual capacity. It was filled with all manner of medical equipment. The monitors on the wall next to his gurney bleeped regularly confirming what he already knew, that he was still alive. Above him was a large bank of lights, though at the moment they were switched off, and to his left was a stainless steel trolley littered with medical instruments and empty containers which had once held bandages and disposable gloves. He was obviously in the infirmary.

He opened the other eye and gently turned his head towards the sound of someone singing. The singer was female. She was dressed in her usual, pale blue, skin tight, one piece garment all the medical staff wore. The suit covered her body entirely, from the soles of her feet to the top of her head, including her face, like a coat of paint. As far as the woman's figure was concerned, the suit left very little to the imagination. Not that Chai needed to imagine, not when he had an excellent memory.

With her back to him, she glided about the room like a gossamer thread on a gentle summer breeze, collecting her medical supplies and instruments. The reasons for her gracefulness and elegance were twofold: Firstly she was naturally graceful and elegant and secondly, in an attempt to ease the pain of Chai's shattered clavicle, she had turned the artificial gravity within the infirmary, down to around ten percent.

Her name was Doctor Wawa Shan, she was twenty two, dark haired and, at least in Chai's eyes, the most beautiful woman alive. She was also without doubt, the best doctor in the service, and had been hand picked to lead the fleet's three hundred strong medical team. A team which was now scattered amongst the remaining seventeen ships. Most were still hibernating, and would be until the fleet reached its final destination. Wherever the hell that might be!

"Hi!" said Chai, his voice hoarse and creaky from the valgette. Shan spun around at the sound of his voice, raised two fingers in front of her face and swiped from left to right. The pale blue bio-shield peeled back from her face to form a rolled halo framing her beautiful features.

She drifted across the room. "Welcome back Darling," she said smiling, and then in contradiction of all medical rules and protocols, she bent and kissed him on the lips. The kiss was full of passion and love.

"How long was I out?" he asked when his wife finally let him up for air.

"About two hours. Just long enough for me to perform all the necessary, post stasis tests, and inject a full complement of Nano

Meds into your shoulder. They should have your clavicle rebuilt by this evening, but I'm afraid there's not much I can do about the soft tissue damage. Rest and a regular injection of painkillers should have you good as new in about ten days."

Chai gingerly touched the purplish black bruise covering his entire left shoulder. Even with the painkillers Shan had already given him, the arm still hurt like hell. Also, even though he knew it was impossible, under his skin the flesh seemed to crawl and tickle, as if he could actually feel the sub microscopic robots as they scurried around inside his shoulder rebuilding the broken collar bone.

"Now," Shan continued. "You must remember to drink lots and lots of water so that your body can dissolve the excess calcium and expel the Nano Meds as quickly as possible after they've finished rebuilding your clavicle. If you don't, your kidneys are going to let you know big time, and you'll think you're pissing molten steel."

"Yea. Okay. I'll get my wife to remind me. She's a doctor!"

Shan smiled, then suddenly she became very serious. "I'm sorry about Del. I know he was your friend. It's such a terrible loss, especially now, when we need every person we have left."

Chai felt his heart sink. Until that moment, despite knowing there would have been very little chance, Chai had hoped Del had made it out alive. Now he knew for sure that his former friend was dead. It was such a terrible waste.

"Does Vethil know how he got out of the brig? He was locked up tight and barely able to stay upright when I left him this morning."

Shan nodded her head sadly. "Apparently he'd thrown up on the floor. The ship's computer automatically sent for a maintenance drone to clean up the mess. The stupid thing just opened the cell and went in to mop up. Del just walked out behind it through the open door."

Chai groaned. It seemed no one had thought to install any security protocols in the new machines.

"Oh, I have some other news," continued Shan, "While you were out cold the Tran contacted Admiral Vethil. They wish to speak to someone, in person, on the planet, about our request for refuge. They will be sending a transport vessel in two days. They've requested we sent one emissary only. Just one person to put forward the case for what's left of our entire species."

"I suppose Vethil will go himself?" Chai hypothesised.

"Yea, I guess so. I wish I was going. I'm sick of being cooped up here for days on end, and from what we've seen through the observation ports in the mess hall, Tran appears to be a very beautiful planet."

Chai agreed it would be a wonderful opportunity, but although he didn't say so, he didn't want Shan to go. It was too dangerous. There were too many unknown factors to consider. As far as anyone knew the Tranians were a peace loving species, but no one knew for sure. They could be just waiting for someone to land so that they could torture and interrogate them and hold them hostage. Besides, his wife had no training in dealing with an unknown enemy. It would be far better for Vethil to send someone who had military training.

Shan kissed her husband once again, but this time with far less passion.

"I have to attend to my other patient Honey," she told him. I'll come and get you at the end of my shift and we can walk home together Okay?

With a smile, she turned and walked through the open doorway into the next room. As she passed through the door, her petite frame slumped noticeably and her steps became heavier as the full level of artificial gravity took effect. She once again waved her hand in front of her face and the medi-suit sealed shut. Suddenly Chai felt exhausted. No doubt there were still some residual effects present from the valgette gas. He lay back and closed his eyes. Moments later he was fast asleep.

Chapter 10

CHAI AND SHAN HAD BEEN married just one hundred and seventeen days. As is often the case, they had met in work related circumstances.

There had been numerous and frequent sexual attacks on female staff outside the hospital where Doctor Wawa Shan had worked, and the nurses and female doctors were frightened to leave the building alone when their shift finished, especially at night. A friend of Chai's had mentioned this to him, and as he was between postings at the time, Chai had volunteered to teach the women some basic self defence techniques. Shan had been one of the women who attended the lectures and practice sessions. The course lasted for fourteen hours, stretched over seven nights, and after each lesson Shan and Chai had chatted about the lesson, or the government, the current conflict in the western provinces, or wherever the conversation led them.

There was an instantaneous attraction between them, and after the seventh lesson, Chai asked Shan if it was possible to approach her father and request his authority to begin a preliminary courtship. That was, of course, if Shan herself felt such a prelim was appealing. She told him it was. The following day Chai contacted Shan's father and made an appointment for three days hence.

On the morning of that fateful day, Chai made his way from his domicile to the nearby train station and took the public floater train to the other side of the city. He had worn his dress uniform, including his ceremonial brass chest plate, which he had burnished to a brilliant sheen. At his hip he carried his ancestral sword. A weapon passed down to him by his late father after nine generations. The hilt of the sword was decorated with the family coat of arms and the blade itself had been engraved with the names of a dozen Salang clan warriors. Over his shoulder he'd worn the pelt of a Shambok, a large and extremely dangerous feline like creature which had once prowled the mountains to the east, and he had plaited the hair of his lustrous beard, weaving in fine filaments of gold and silver, to form a spectacularly thick rope.

Where he had spent a great deal of time in preparing himself for the meeting, he had also spent a large number of credits on presents for Shan's parents. For her mother he had procured a container of hand made, off world confectioneries, and for her father he'd had a miniature copy of the sword he carried on his hip made and mounted on a timber plaque. He was sure such gifts would impress.

Chai had boarded the floater, taking a seat on the left in the fourth carriage from the front. The train had lifted off and accelerated, silently snaking it's way up and around the soaring, massive steel and glass buildings, up and over the Riis River. Eventually it had levelled out, high above the general hub bub of the teeming streets below. Chai had been filled with trepidation and had looked out of the window at the sprawling city below with unseeing eyes. In just one hour he would meet the parents of the woman he hoped would one day be his wife. Though at the time, Chai was yet to admit even to himself, that such a union was possible. Shan's father was also a doctor and according to his daughter, he did not hold those in the military in very high regard.

Also, even though Chai's family weren't exactly poor, they could never hope to move in the same exalted social circles as the Wawa clan. Those who lived on the eastern side of the city were generally considered by the population of the west, to be a cut above the rest.

There was an abundance of credit associated with 'The Easterners' and it was a rare occurrence indeed when one of them married below their station.

But it did happen occasionally, Chai had reminded himself. Shan had assured him that she had always been able to get her own way with her father. Eventually at least. She was going to do her utmost to convince him that a preliminary courtship with Chief Security Officer Salang Chai was a good idea.

The floater had stopped at a station near Res and a group of matronly, older women had joined Chai in the fourth carriage. They were all laughing and singing, clearly celebrating some important, joyous, occasion. While most had gone to the front of the carriage, one of them, a plump woman with grey hair, wearing a tangerine coloured tunic and with a stylised star tattooed on her forehead, had sat opposite him. The woman glanced at the style of Chai's dress and smiled.

"Someone's a lucky girl," she'd said, indicating Chai's apparel.

Chai nodded. "Not as lucky as I'll be if her father approves of me," he'd replied.

The woman inclined her head slightly in agreement. "Both of you will be lucky, Emissary," she'd said. "Though there will be many times when neither will think so. But always remember Salang Chai, if you lose faith in what must be, the future can change, and returning to the path of the righteous is much harder than to veer away from it."

Chai had been confused at the woman's remarks. "How do you know my name honoured elder, and why do you call me Emissary?" he'd asked.

The woman had closed her eyes and whispered her reply as if she were revealing some deep and dark secret. "I know because it is my lot to know. Soon my young friend, whole worlds will know the name of Emissary Salang Chai."

Suddenly the old woman rose and hurried away, joining her friends at the front of the carriage. Chai had wanted to follow her, ask her exactly what she had meant by her cryptic comments, but he'd known that to do so could have been seen as extremely rude and threatening. There were security cameras all over the train, each one recording every moment of each and every journey. Already they would have shown the woman hurrying away, if he were to follow her and confront her, it might look extremely suspicious.

Besides, in all probability there was be a simple explanation for the woman's strange comments. Perhaps one of Chai's friends was playing a joke and had asked the old woman to help with the prank. Perhaps that friend had shown the woman his image, told her he would be on the Floater that morning, and had her deliver her weird message, meaning it to be taken as encouragement before his meeting with Shan's father.

Whatever the reason for her comments, they at least seemed to be well meaning. Besides, he'd had more important things to worry about, so after a few moments he'd put the strange woman from his mind and concentrated once more on what he would say to Doctor Ni.

The train had again risen above the city skyline, up above the thick smog and pollution into the clear, bright azure sky. Silently it scythed its way across the city to the eastern side, taking a slightly curved track to allow for the curvature of the planet. After about an hour Chai felt his ears pop and realised the floater was once again heading towards the ground. As he exited the train at Eastern Station, he turned back to thank the old woman for her kind words and to wish her and her friends a safe journey. Inexplicably, although the other women were still at the front of the carriage, the woman with the star tattoo was nowhere to be seen.

Chai found the walk from Eastern Station to the address Shan had given to him hard going. The path was predominantly up hill and the sun was already high in the sky, beating down on his head and shoulders. At times he felt he might melt. Eventually he reached Dr Wawa Ni's house.

Chai had felt his heart sink when he first caught sight of the doctor's home. The place was a palace. It was set into the side of a steep hill, an all chrome and glass structure of three interconnected buildings, each of two stories. Each building's roof curved gracefully downwards like the wings of a bird and was tiled with dazzlingly white, silica roof panels. The entire front of the building opened out onto a wide patio, which in turn overlooked immaculately manicured lawns and gardens. Just the portico leading to the front entrance of the house was bigger than Chai's whole apartment.

In front of the main entrance was a curved gravel driveway which led to a garage for Dr Ni's personal transport vehicle. Currently the PTV, a flame red 'Viper', worth more than Chai could possibly earn in his entire lifetime, was parked on the driveway. Chai had felt sick. How could he, a lowly Security Officer, only recently promoted to Chief, possibly hope to gain the approval of such an obviously affluent and influential man?

Things had looked bad and they were about to get worse. Chai had climbed the steps to the front door and presented the palm of his right hand to the ID panel just to the left of the door. Moments later the door swung open. The man who opened it was just a year or two older than Chai himself. He was short and stocky and had a large ugly scar which ran down his left cheek. Whatever had caused the injury had also destroyed his left eye. There was an electronic prosthesis in its place, the iris of which spun in and out disconcertingly as the man tried to focus. He was dressed in a long, dark blue, servants tunic and immediately he saw who was standing in the doorway, he snapped to attention and executed a perfect salute.

"Good day to you Chief. My name is Swinca. The master is expecting you. I'll show you through directly. Please follow me."

The servant swung awkwardly on his heel and took off down the hallway into the main house. He moved with a pronounced limp and Chai was certain he heard the distinctive hiss and click of a mechanised, prosthetic leg. For the first time that morning Chai felt a little easier. Swinca was obviously ex military, probably a veteran who had been injured in the battle with the Annuxians. If the doctor was happy to employ such a man, then his hatred of all things military, couldn't be as deep and inflexible as he had feared. Sadly, all his hopes were soon dashed.

Swinca had led the way into a spacious receiving room. It was a grand and luxuriously appointed space, with soft, multi hued rugs strewn around a floor of highly polished white marble. The walls were covered with art works, a few land and seascapes, but mostly portraits of people who Chai assumed were Ni's ancestors, or family, or beloved friends of the Wawa clan. As with the floor coverings, the furniture too was multi coloured and modern in design. Shan lay on a turquoise Ottoman, her slender body reclining gracefully against the gentle curves of the couch. She had been crying. Her father sat nearby, on a black, high backed chair upholstered in Shambok hide. He'd risen as Chai entered the room and greeted him warmly. He was small in stature, with thick dark hair and piercing blue eyes. Yet despite his small size, he still somehow managed to exude an aura of importance and confidence.

"Welcome to my home Chief Security Officer Salang Chai," he'd said indicating that the younger man should sit. Chai had done so.

Chai had prepared a speech, setting out all the reasons why Shan's father should consider accepting his request. He came from a good family, he had a well paid job, his father, now deceased, had been on the steering committee for the city's education board and he was descended from none other than Salang Wan, one of the city's founding fathers. All this and more he'd intended to relate, but even before he could present his case, Dr Wawa Ni told him he was wasting his time.

"I'm very sorry Chai. I'm sure you're a very nice young man," he'd told him, "but no daughter of mine will ever engage in a courtship with a soldier."

"But why, honoured doctor?" Chai had asked. He'd known that even asking such a question was impertinent and totally against all protocols. To question the authority of a woman's father simply wasn't done. But somehow the old woman on the train's assertion that he should 'never lose faith in what should be' had emboldened him. According to the woman, he and Shan were meant to be together. In fact the old woman had inferred their union was somehow important, not just to Chai and Shan, but to many others as well. Dr Ni had shaken his head sadly.

"Again, I am deeply sorry to refuse your request, young man. I assure you my decision has not been made lightly. But I have seen enough death and destruction to last me a dozen lifetimes, death and destruction, more often than not, brought about by the actions of the military. I'm sure you firmly believe your profession is an honourable one, but I assure you, the world would be a much better place without all the war mongers creating so much misery."

"But honoured doctor, surely the military also do a lot of good. What about the way we repelled the Annuxian invasion last year?"

Shan's father had almost laughed. "You need to open your eyes young man. Stop blindly believing everything you are told and start questioning things, especially when they are so obviously untrue."

Chai was angry at being treated like a fool and wanted to take Dr Ni to task over his assertions, but the doctor had made it clear that the interview was over and Chai was expected to take his leave. Shan showed him to the door. As they walked down the steps and onto the lawn together, Shan suddenly pulled him to one side, dragging him behind some bushes so that no one inside the house could see. She threw her arms around his neck and kissed him, deeply and passionately.

"Don't lose heart my darling," she'd said. "I'll talk to him again in a few days. I'm sure he'll come around in time." She'd squeezed his hand gently and then hurried back to the house.

Chai 's head had been in a complete spin. He was, of course, devastated by Dr Ni's rejection. But then Shan's demonstration of affection for him had far exceeded his wildest expectations. The fact that she had called him 'my darling', kissed him with such passion, and promised she would continue to try to make her father change his mind, left him reeling. Even though they hadn't even begun a serious relationship, Shan had obviously decided she was in love with him. With a jolt Chai realised he felt exactly the same way about her.

Somehow Chai knew the doctor's rejection would only be a minor setback. Despite his assertions that Shan would never engage in a courtship with a soldier, Chai knew that one day she would be his. Smiling to himself, he turned towards the floater station.

Chapter 11

AS SALANG CHAI WALKED through the gate from Dr Wawa Ni's house, the doctor's servant Swinca ambled out from behind one of the huge stone pillars.

"Don't be too hard on the good doctor Chief," Swinca suggested as he fell in beside him. "He has good reason for disliking the Military."

"Obviously not all Military Personnel," Chai had replied, inclining his head towards Swinca.

"Yes, I'm a soldier. Or rather ex soldier." He tapped his leg with his knuckles. It made a hollow, metallic sound as if he was tapping on an empty metal drum. "Got this during the war with the Annuxians, if you can call it a war. Massacre would be a better word. The good doctor fixed me up as best he could, and when I was kicked out of the army he gave me a job."

"Is that what I have to do to have him accept me as a suitable suitor for his daughter's affection? Resign my commission? Become a factory worker or farm hand."

Swinca had reached out and touched Chai gently on the arm. "Follow me Chief," he'd commanded, turning up a narrow track which ran beside the doctor's house. "I want to show you something."

The trail up the side of the hill was steep and poorly maintained. Swinca in particular found the going tough, his prosthetic leg hissing and clicking loudly in protest with every step. Eventually they'd reached the crest. Swinca limped over to a low stone wall overlooking the flat plain on the other side. He swung his legs over the wall and perched on top. Chai joined him.

Below them, in the distance, was a perfect example of the death and destruction Wawa Ni had spoken of earlier. A perfect circle of scorched and blackened earth sat in the centre of a large group of houses. Inside the circle not a single structure had been left standing. In its centre, the gnarled and twisted remains of a once huge factory, jutted out of the now lifeless soil, forlornly pointing towards the sky and the direction from which the Annuxian invaders had come. Perversely, outside the circle, the buildings were all completely unharmed.

"You would have studied the great strategists when you applied for your commission Chief," Swinca suggested pointing at the devastation below. "Tell me what you see."

Chai nodded, he could see exactly what Swinca was alluding too.

"It's a perfectly planned and executed military attack." He pointed to the blackened area below. "That used to be the Res Munitions factory. The Annuxians specifically targeted it to weaken our defences."

"Yes Chief. In fact, they specifically targeted every conceivable military target on the planet. None of their attacks were against civilian targets. Not one. In less than a day they totally destroyed any chance we had of defending ourselves. And then amazingly, they left."

Once again, Chai nodded. "Yea, I know. I've already given that a great deal of consideration. It doesn't make sense. They had us on our knees and then simply retreated. Why?"

"The answer to that question is obvious if you think about it. The Annuxians didn't start the war Chief, we did. We tried to invade their home planet. They repelled our invasion and then made sure we couldn't attack them ever again. That's the reason Dr Ni hates the Military so much. He knows the truth Chief."

Chai shook his head vehemently. He'd heard that rumour before. "That can't be right. We would never attack a planet inhabited by a sentient species, it goes against any civilised concept of right and wrong. It's impossible. Shan's father is mistaken."

Swinca rose stiffly from his perch on the stone wall and stretched his good leg to get the circulation going again. He had been sitting too long and the hard, uneven stones had been pressing into the backs of his leg, restricting the blood flow. He was uncomfortable and the conversation was making him even more so.

"Okay," he said, "if we didn't attack first, how do you explain the fact that Dr Ni had started treating casualties from the conflict two days before the Annuxian invasion."

Chai rolled his eyes. "That's just a rumour started by the bleeding heart anti war campaigners. No one really believes that crap."

Swinca pointed at the tattered remains of what had once been the Res munitions factory on the valley floor below.

"Yea? Well I do. I was one of Dr Ni's first patients. He had me on his operating table exactly two days before the Annuxians destroyed that factory. I lost my leg and my eye during a ground assault on the Annuxian home world, Chai. I was there Chief. It's not just a bunch of peace loving cowards making up stories. It happened."

Chapter 12

OF COURSE CHAI HAD been devastated by Swinca's revelation, but not completely surprised. The reality was, he had already suspected there must have been some truth behind the rumours concerning the start of the war. But his unflinching dedication to his profession had caused him to put such notions aside as nothing more than lies and hearsay. It was all simply anti-war propaganda. Now he knew first hand exactly what had happened. Not only had his own people struck the first blow, they had done so against a sentient, highly advanced society. That was something Chai simply couldn't abide.

It was those actions, by the military, which had resolved Dr Wawa Ni in his determination that his daughter would never engage in a courtship with a soldier. Perversely, it was also the actions of the military, just fifty three days after their meeting, which changed his mind. That was when Marshal Kree, the leader of the planets armed forces, pressed the firing button on the 'Vortex Canon', catastrophically and irreparably damaging their home planet.

When the government announced that the world was dying and there was nothing that could be done to halt its rapidly approaching demise, and then went on to explain there would be a lottery to decide who would go to Soren 6 to establish a new colony (and conversely who would be left behind to perish), Dr Ni knew with the utmost certainty, that the declaration about the lottery was a complete fabrication. There was no way the government would leave such decisions to chance. Each person on board the twenty three ships would be hand picked for their suitability on the new world. To even imagine the government would do otherwise was ludicrous.

Of course as doctors, both Ni and his daughter had an excellent chance of being selected anyway. But Dr Ni also knew that Salang Chai was the Chief Security Officer on the 'War Hawk', the flagship of the fleet, and if Shan was to wed such a man, her inclusion was assured.

So Chai and Shan were married, and now her father was safely ensconced, aboard the 'War Hawk', in stasis tube 37/6/14 and her mother in 38/6/14. Secretly Chai doubted their marriage had anything to do with Shan's inclusion amongst the crew of the 'War Hawk', she was after all a highly respected and admired medical practitioner. But she was by his side regardless, and for him, that was all that mattered.

Chapter 13

AT FIVE IN THE MORNING following Del's death, Chai once again reported for duty. His shoulder was still extremely tender, but the Nano Meds had done a sterling job of repairing his shattered clavicle and he felt confident he was fit enough to go back to work. Besides, Chai detested being idle, especially when there was lots to do aboard the ship. He'd been at his station only a few moments when his communicator burst into life. The call came from the security officer aboard the 'Sabre'

"Chief, I wish to report a possible security breach," the woman told him. "One of our maintenance guys has been trying to repair our secondary air scrubber. I'm afraid we had let it go too long before we could purge it and as a result it was damaged. The thing is Chief, the maintenance guy noticed something strange. Despite the damage to the SAS, the air on board 'Sabre' is actually getting better."

On the vidi screen, the woman leant forward and pressed a switch on her console, sending through an image file.

"Have a look at this," she said.

Chai opened the file and studied the image. It was a high resolution, high magnification picture of a Nanobot.

"That's not one of ours, is it?" he asked.

"Nuh, we haven't got anything that advanced. But that's what's replenishing our air supply. I reckon it came in with that shipment of food and water the Tran sent to us. God knows what else it does. Shortly after I took that image it shut down. Oh and I assume there's more of the little buggers on board. One Nanobot, even one as sophisticated as that, isn't going to replace a seven thousand cubic metre air scrubber."

Chai agreed and suggested she run a complete scan to verify how many of the tiny intruders there were and to ascertain exactly what else, if anything, they did.

"I'll contact the other ships and get them to do the same," he advised. "Then I guess we'd better check all the equipment and machinery to make sure nothing's been sabotaged. In the meantime, just keep an eye on the things. Maybe the Tran are only trying to help. I wouldn't do a purge just yet."

"Yea," replied the woman, mumbling to herself, "not until we've learnt how to hold our breath for a very long, long time."

They discussed things for a while longer and then Chai broke contact. He called the other vessels as promised and then started a diagnostic on the 'War Hawks' computer system to check for anomalies. While the diagnostic ran, he took the transport tube down to the main hold and began checking the priceless machinery and equipment stored there.

The first hold contained the agricultural machinery. Soren 6 was known to be a very fertile planet, quite capable, the science boffins had decreed, of eventually supporting a population of almost three billion people. The plan had been to land each ship on a different part of the planet. In that way no one area would be overtaxed. The ships would land and the ten conscious crew members from each ship would begin to construct accommodation for the other settlers. They would clear an area of land, plant the hybrid, fast growing crops which had been specifically developed for the planet's nitrogen rich soils and begin domesticating any animals they felt might be suitable. Once the area had produced sufficient food, the crew would slowly begin bringing the settlers out of stasis. They would do it one section at a time, progressively waking their sleeping passengers as the food became more abundant. It was expected it would be at least two years before each ship's entire compliment would be awake.

Of course Soren 6 had now been discounted as a possible venue, as had dozens of other planets, but Chai was certain that soon the people on board the ships of the armada would have a new home. Whether that was to be Tran, or some other suitable planet was still to be seen. But wherever it was, the machinery and equipment stored in the holds would still be needed. It was imperative that they reach their final destination, intact and fully functional.

The first machine to be checked was a land clearing mechanism. It was a huge monstrosity, nearly fifty metres long, twelve metres wide and four high. It was vaguely rectangular in shape but with the forward, windscreen section, sloping downwards to a rounded, snub nose to give the pilot greater visibility of the terrain in front. The term pilot was extremely apt, for when in use the machine was designed to hover about a metre above the ground. A series of high temp lasers, spinning underneath, vaporised any vegetation it passed over. Chai climbed up the rungs fixed to the side of the craft, and activated the hatch mechanism. Moments later he was seated behind the controls.

As each vessel in the fleet had only ten conscious crew members, in addition to their own specialised profession, each person had been trained to operate a variety of other equipment. Chai had already been given basic operator instructions on this piece of equipment as well as the planter and the earth moving machine in the next hanger. He quickly ran through the clearer's pre-flight check list and then started her up.

There was a loud hum from the four anti-grav drives and the massive machine rose slowly off the deck. Chai set the variable temperature controls on the lasers to cold and engaged the rotating drive. All around him the walls and floor of the hanger below the craft, were lit up with a pulsating blue light. Gradually Chai increased the temperature until the glow changed to a hotter red and then, before the lasers could do any damage, dialled it back to cool again. He shut down the lasers and then proceeded to execute a series of close quarter flight manoeuvres designed to ascertain the operational precision of the flight controls. Finally, he ran a post flight diagnostic check on the computer system. Everything seemed to check out just fine. He shut the craft down and moved on to the next section of the hold and the first of two seed planters.

It took Chai most of the day to check the seven pieces of equipment on board, rigorously putting each massive machine through its paces until he was sure they were operating perfectly. At the very back of the final hold he made a startling discovery. There, tucked away in the corner, behind a pile of building materials, was something which made his blood run cold. Despite assurances from the government prior to embarking on their voyage that none of the vessels would be heavily armed, 'War Hawk' was not only very heavily armed, it was armed with a small vortex Canon.

Chapter 14

THE CLEANSING ROOM was hot and steamy. Due to the lateness of the evening Chai and Shan were alone and were enjoying a few moments of all too infrequent privacy while they bathed. The water had been filtered, treated and sanitised, and the pulsating jets and micro bubbles cleaned and massaged the couples naked bodies as they floated luxuriously in the large, deep, rectangular pool.

"You're sure it was a vortex Canon?" Shan asked.

"Yea. We've all seen the Vidi News footage of the so called test of the weapon which destroyed our planet. This thing looks exactly like that did, only about a tenth of the size."

"Shit!" said Shan.

"Yea. What the hell is Vethil doing? We were assured that the fleet was basically unarmed. If the Tran somehow learn we've got a weapon which could destroy their whole planet on board, there's not a chance in hell they'll trust us enough to let us settle there."

"That's not what's worrying me, well not just that," replied Shan. "The last time they set one of those things off, it not only completely destroyed a small moon, it blew a huge hole in our own planet. If that idiot Vethil fires that gun, and it does the same thing, it's going to destroy the ship as well."

Chai nodded. It was complete madness.

"I think they must have figured out what went wrong with the first one though," he surmised. "I'm not sure, but this one appears to have been test fired already. The Nelamine alloy barrel has a crystalline coating near the end which could've only been caused by excessive heat. Probably heat generated when it was fired."

Shan thought about that for a while. "In that case, whether the Tran decide to let us settle on their planet or not, might be a moot point. Vethil might just decide to force the issue in our favour with his damn gun."

She was right of course. Things looked bad, very bad.

"I'll ask Vethil about it in the morning. I'll just have to think of some way of bringing it up without appearing to question his authority. You know what the bastards like if he thinks someone's trying to usurp his command," Chai said.

Shan swam closer and wrapped her arms around her husband's neck, then she wrapped her legs around his waist. He backed up to the edge of the bath and supported them both with his arms.

"Chai, do you think we could disable it? Without Vethil knowing I mean." Shan asked.

"No. Not a chance. I checked it out. There's vidi cameras all over the hanger. At least two are directed towards the area where the canon's stored. Also, I'm pretty sure he's rigged up some sort of alarm. If I start fooling around with it, someone's going to notice and Vethil will accuse me of treason and shove me out an airlock.......Though he might do that anyway if he's trying to keep its existence a secret. That way he might finally be able to get you for himself."

Shan scowled. "Now don't bring that up again Darling," she commanded, nibbling playfully at his ear. "Vethil apologised. He was drunk. He told us he would never have made a pass at me if he'd been sober. He has too much respect for us both. We have to forgive and forget. We've all done silly things while we were tanked."

Chai spun them both slowly around one hundred and eighty degrees so that Shan was between him and the side of the pool.

"You're right," Chai agreed, "but I've seen the way he looks at you. With complete adoration and lust. If you weren't married to me, I just know he'd be after you in a flash."

She smiled cheekily. "Of course he would darling. Him and half the population on this ship." She grinned, polishing her fingernails on her naked chest and then admiring them.

She let go with her arms and legs, spun around and pushed herself out of the water. It was too damned hot and she knew if she stayed in any longer she'd start to wrinkle up like a prune. She padded over to the bench where they'd left their drying cloths, laid hers down at the edge of pool, and lay down on her stomach. Her smooth, olive skin glistening with a billion tiny droplets of water. The sublime curve of her neck, back and bottom nearly made Chai groan with desire. She was beautiful and not for the first time Chai thanked the gods for making her his.

She had her face turned away and when she turned back a few moments later, he saw huge tears trickle down her cheeks.

"Honey, what's wrong?" he asked, quickly dragging himself from the water and wrapping her in his arms.

"Oh Chai, what are we going to do if the Tran say no? Where will we go? We can't just wander blindly all over the universe searching for somewhere else. If we don't find a suitable planet within a few months, we'll run out of food and water and air again. What the hell are we going to do then."

Salang Chai had no idea.

Chapter 15

WHEN CHAI BROUGHT UP the existence of the vortex canon in the lower hold the following morning, Admiral Vethil at first adopted such an affectation of surprise, any professional actor who had ever graced a vidi screen would have been profoundly impressed. But there was simply no way he wouldn't have known, so Chai persisted. Then Vethil stammered and looked about himself as if searching for a way out, and this made it all the more obvious that the Admiral was fully aware of the danger stored three decks below. Then, so the other crew on the bridge couldn't overhear, the Admiral invited Chai into his personal quarters next to the bridge to discuss the matter.

"Salang Chai," began Vethil, "I suppose as Chief Security Officer for the fleet, you should have been told of the existence of the canon. But after the tragedy caused by the misfiring vortex gun on our home world, the government decided it best to keep this smaller weapon a secret."

Misfiring canon my arse, thought Chai.

"You said 'this' canon sir, this smaller weapon, am I to assume from your words, that there is only one?"

Vethil considered his response carefully for a few moments. "Yes, no other vessel in the armada is equipped with such a weapon. But we feel it's imperative to be able to defend ourselves should the Annuxians decide to attack again. So one was brought on board the 'War Hawk.'"

Chai could hardly contain his anger. He knew the truth about the Annuxian's attack on their home world, and was certain that unless provoked, there was precious little chance they would ever attack again. Had it gone ahead, the proposed colony on Soren 6 would never have needed to defend itself from anyone. Yet once again the military idiots were ready to needlessly risk the lives of the few remaining people from his home world. Not to mention the lives of anyone else who might get involved.

But just as he had discussed with Shan the previous evening, there was little he could do about the canon's existence. Admiral Vethil vastly outranked him, even questioning the man's authority could have him court martialed, thrown in the brig, or maybe even executed. He had no choice but to bite his tongue and say nothing.

"Of course Sir," Chai said, snapping to attention and saluting. "As I hadn't been informed of its existence and the weapon was hidden in the very back of the hold, I was concerned that it had actually been smuggled aboard by some misguided terrorist group who were going to use it to destroy the rest of the fleet. Please forgive my confusion."

The admiral returned the salute lazily. "Yes, yes I understand. As I said, perhaps we should have informed you."

With that Vethil ushered the Chief from his quarters.

For the next few hours Chai remained at his post, sitting at his computer, conscientiously running and re-running his security tests and protocols to make sure everything was in order. The truth was, the checks were largely superfluous. Nothing was happening. Except for the altercation with Shillim Del three days ago, the only thing of note, had been the discovery of the Tranian Nanobots, and rather than being found to be a threat, they were proving to be a huge asset by keeping the air aboard the 'Sabre' fresh and rich in oxygen.

In fact, a check of the other vessels had found that the Tranian Nanobots had in fact been infused into the entire fleet. The science officer on 'Sabre' had isolated a second Nanobot and ascertained that as far as she could tell, its only function was to restore air quality. In addition, a security detail on each vessel in the armada had checked and double checked to make sure nothing had been sabotaged. So far everything was clear. As far as Chai could see, there was no reason to suspect anything would change in that regard any time soon.

Around midday, he left the bridge and went down to the infirmary. Shan, once again covered from head to foot in her body hugging Medi Suit, was hard at work. She looked up from the experiment she was conducting, and saw Chai standing on the other side of the plastiglass door. She went to meet him, her face shielding rolling back off her face as she came through the door.

"Do you have time for some lunch?" her husband asked. "I'm not due back on duty for at least two hours."

Shan nodded and quickly hurried into the decontamination booth to change her clothes. She had been doing some atmospheric tests on samples of Tran's atmosphere. Tests designed to ascertain the levels and types of pathogens or disease present on Tran which might prove detrimental to the refugees should they eventually be allowed to settle there. So far she had found six viruses and was well progressed with manufacturing antigens for the first four. The tests had been done in an enclosed environment, by remote controlled mechanoids, so there was no chance she had been accidentally contaminated. Nevertheless, protocols were put in place for a reason and Dr Wawa Shan was the last person to circumvent those protocols.

Moments later she re-emerged wearing the short, flowing, gold and green tunic Chai loved so much. Together they walked hand in had down to the mess hall.

When used for the purpose they had been designed for, a Galaxy class battle cruiser operated with a compliment of two hundred and thirty six crew. Correspondingly, communal areas, such as the staging area in the forward hold, the sleeping quarters and the mess hall had to be capable of handling large numbers of people. Because the crew operated on the basis of seven rotating and overlapping shifts, the mess hall was designed to seat a maximum of sixty six people. The room was twenty five metres long by fifteen wide, though this dimension reduced by a metre or so towards the front of the ship due to the shape of the hull.

They were the only people in the mess hall that lunch time, so the couple chose a table by one of the large plastiglass windows, overlooking a breathtaking view of the planet Tran many kilometres below. They'd both sat in a similar position on other vessels before, but at the time they'd been watching their own planet spinning slowly below them. The most striking thing Shan had noticed when she first saw Tran was the planet's colours, realising as she did, that the reason for their depth and vibrancy was the crystal clarity of the atmosphere. On their own planet, a person couldn't see the surface because of all the pollution in the air. From space their planet looked like a great big ball of grey fluff. At least it had done. Now it more than likely looked like a lifeless lump of rock. Or, Shan thought, maybe by now it had already become the small black hole scientist Lin had predicted.

The table and chairs in the hall were made from some sort of hydrocarbon or polycarbonate and were utilitarian in both design and comfort. In the centre of the table was a menu screen with a stylised hand graphic printed in the centre.

"What would you like to eat, Honey?" Chai asked.

Shan placed her palm on the screen to activate it and read the options.

She smiled alluringly. "Oh, I don't know. Why don't you surprise me."

"Okay. I'm pregnant." Chai joked.

Shan smiled at her husbands silly quip, her eyes twinkling. Inadvertently, Chai had provided her with the perfect opportunity to drop her bombshell.

"There's a coincidence," she said, "so am I."

Chai's mouth fell open. "You're kidding?"

"Nope."

"You're pregnant?"

"Yep."

Chai nearly vaulted over the table to get to her. He lifted Shan to her feet and wrapped her in his arms, and smothered her with kisses.

"Are you sure?" he asked, his voice catching with emotion.

"Chai, I'm a doctor. Of course I'm sure."

Chai was obviously ecstatic about the news and for the next little while he could hardly find the words to tell her how pleased he was. They were going to have a baby. He was going to be a father. Eventually, he stopped showering his wife with kisses and let her sit back down.

"This calls for a celebration," he announced, placing his palm on the menu screen. "I'm going to order us a bottle of wine and the most expensive food on the menu. Oh! There's a selection of fruits from Tran available. Maybe we should try those."

Shan agreed with his suggestion. And moments later the screen in the centre of their table slid back and two platters appeared, each laden with strange, multi coloured fruits of the most weird and wonderful shapes and sizes either of them had ever seen. They took the plates, and the screen slid back into place, opening again moments later to deliver a bottle of frosty, ice blue wine and two chilled wine glasses.

Chai opened the bottle and poured the wine. It was cold and crisp, with just a hint of fruity after taste. It was delicious. Shan selected a piece of fruit. It was a deep golden yellow colour, shaped like a tall pyramid. Tentatively, she lifted it to her nose and inhaled its pungent, yet sweet odour. She raised her eyebrows questioningly and carefully sliced off a small section. She touched the exposed flesh with her tongue and let out a husky groan of sublime pleasure. It was heavenly.

She sliced off a bigger chunk, reached across and popped it into her husbands mouth. He chewed, rolling his eyes in ecstasy at the explosion of flavour in his mouth.

"Oh my god," he exclaimed, "that's delicious."

For the next hour the couple worked their way through the two platters, cleansing their pallets with a sip of wine after each different fruit. At the end of their meal Shan had decided that the red star shaped fruit was her favourite, while Chai just adored the little golden pyramids. Both agreed the meal was excellent.

They were still the only two people in the mess hall, so they took the rest of their wine, dragged their chairs over to the huge window, put their feet up on the ledge running along the bottom, and gazed out at the planet below.

When Chai next looked over at his beautiful wife, there were tears in her eyes. He understood why, he was finding the astounding view quite moving himself.

"Are you alright?" he asked.

"Yea." She was quiet for a while, then spoke again. "What if they don't let us stay Chai? What if they turn us away? Where will we go?"

Chai shook his head sadly, reached over and took Shan's small hand in his own.

"I still don't know Honey. But they will let us stay, I know they will. Surely they wouldn't just turn us away knowing that if they do, they might be condemning a whole species to extinction."

That's what Chai said, but even as the words came out of his mouth, he knew in his heart nothing was certain. But where they would go if the Tranian's turned them away wasn't the only question Chai was asking himself. He was also wondering, if the Tranians rejected their request, would Admiral Vethil decide to use the vortex canon sitting in the hold three floors below, to extract his revenge or to force them to reconsider?

But their delicious lunch ended sooner and much more dramatically than either Shan or Chai had expected. Suddenly Shan sat bolt upright, and with a trembling hand, pointed towards the planet.

"Look, there's a ship coming, some sort of small transporter by the looks of it. The Tranian's have finally sent someone to collect the fleet's spokesperson."

She jumped to her feet and together they raced towards cargo bay seven. It was there that the first Tranian transporter had docked with the 'War Hawk', so it was a safe bet that was where the tiny ship was headed now.

They bolted along a corridor. Suddenly Shan veered off towards the infirmary.

"You go on ahead darling. I've got to bring the vaccines I've been working on to vaccinate Vethil. If I don't, he'll get sick within the first few days of his arrival on the planet. I'll meet you in cargo bay seven in a moment."

"No, I'll meet you at elevator six and we'll go up together," Chai yelled excitedly after her.

With that she hurtled down the passage way and disappeared around the corner.

Chai continued down the corridor, turned left into area 'D5' and then right into area 'E5'. He reached the elevator shaft and pressed the call button. Rapidly the circular platform descended its central shaft, slowing a few metres from floor 'E5' and then stopping with a hiss of hydraulics as it reached Chai's level. He turned to wait for his wife, nervously shifting his weight from foot to foot as the moments ticked by. Suddenly he remembered his 'Stun Whip' dangling from his belt and realised he couldn't meet the visitor from Tran carrying a weapon. They were, after all, trying to convince them that they came with only peaceful intentions. He unclipped the weapon and hooked it over the safety rail around the elevator platform. He would retrieve it later.

Shan came hurrying down the corridor, carrying her small medical bag and together they travelled up to cargo bay seven. Chief Security Officer Salang Chai's life was about to change for ever.

Chapter 16

THE CREATURE STANDING just inside cargo bay seven's door was tall, almost two metres tall. She had a small, narrow body with long slender arms and legs. Each arm ended in a trio of sucker tipped fingers and the knees of her legs bent backwards like a shambok's. Her head was shaped like a teardrop, but with the pointed bit facing forward. From the front, her head was a vertical, flattened ellipse, with delicate, trumpet shaped ears and large, almond shaped eyes either side of her face. Chai reckoned she would have to turn her head, side on, to look at something directly, but would probably have an almost three hundred and sixty degree field of vision. Where her slopping forehead met her chin was a tiny, black lipped mouth, filled with small, pointy white teeth. Her skin, her eyes, in fact everything, even the short, sleeveless dress she wore fastened with an ornate clasp at her shoulder, were all a dull silvery colour which seemed to shimmer as Chai watched her. She was obviously mammalian and definitely female.

But the strangest feature of all was the way she moved across the floor. Each time she took a step it appeared as if her whole body was covered with some kind of tiny, crawling insect. Her skin seemed to writhe and swirl as she walked, and though graceful, her steps seemed somehow slow and mechanical. With a start, Chai realised that's exactly what they were. The creature wasn't a creature at all, but a mechanoid, or rather a few billion mechanoids. Her entire body was made up of individual Nanobots, billions and billions of them, each one moving in syncopation with one another to create a moving facsimile of the real creature.

"I am Colopo," the mechanoid announced in a delicate, tinkling, almost bell like voice. "I come to return with the one who will speak for the vermin."

Vermin? Obviously the word had an entirely different meaning on Tran to what it meant on our home world, thought Chai. Admiral Vethil stepped forward and introduced himself. He was dressed in full military regalia, including his polished brass chest plate, ceremonial sword and side arm. The mechanoid barely glanced at him before gliding past. In fact, she passed by almost everyone gathered there, finally stopping before Shan. Chai could have sworn the creature smiled. Gently the Colopo mechanoid reached out and placed her hand on Shan's stomach.

"Boy," she purred.

"Uh, no Dr Wawa Shan is a woman," Vethil assured the visitor. "Like you."

Once again, the Tran mechanoid ignored him.

"Boy well," Colopo sang happily, but only Chai and Shan herself knew what the visitor meant. Somehow Colopo knew of Shan's impending motherhood. They both knew they would have to inform the Admiral of her pregnancy as soon as he returned from his visit to the planet below. But for now there were more urgent things to consider.

Colopo took a step sideways and stopped directly in front of Chai. She turned her head to the side and regarded him closely. With a start Chai realised why she was discounting Vethil and indeed all the other members of the welcoming committee. Apart from Shan, Chai was the only one in attendance who had come unarmed. The fools had thought to impress their visitor with all the military pomp and grandeur. But instead Colopo saw it as threatening. Suddenly he realised what was about to happen.

Colopo held out her hand. "Come", she said.

Vethil tried to intervene. "No, no, we had decided that I would represent our people," he stammered, clearly taken aback. "Chief Security Officer Salang Chai doesn't have the authority to speak on our behalf."

"Come." Colopo said again, making it quite clear that Salang Chai was the only spokesperson she would accept. Vethil considered his options for a few moments and then nodded.

"Just make sure you report in regularly Chief. Every evening. We need to know what's going on," he demanded and then waved dismissively in the direction of the waiting Tranian craft.

Shan hurried after them, threw her arms around her husband and kissed him with all the fervour and passion she could muster. She felt as if her heart was being torn from her body.

"Come back to me my darling," she implored, then remembering the important medical vaccines in her bag, she quickly pulled a hypoderm administer from her bag and held it to Chai's neck. He felt a sharp sting as the antigens went into his blood stream and then Colopo led him to the waiting transporter.

Chapter 17

THE INSIDE OF COLOPO's vessel was unlike any other Chai had ever seen. The floor was covered with a soft, dark blue, spongy material which seemed to cling to his feet as he walked. In the centre of the room was a solitary chair, high backed and upholstered in some sort of black furry fabric. As its shape would be totally unsuitable for Tranian anatomy, Chai guessed it had been built and installed specifically for him. On the port side of the ship was the door through which they had just entered, and on the starboard side, there was a small rectangular hatch, with a swirling, bright red symbol on it. That was all. There were no control panels, no pilots seat, not even a windscreen or viewing port at the front of the vessel through which a pilot could see where he or she was going. Nothing. The whole thing was just a silver and blue, basically rectangular box, with a solitary chair in the middle of it.

The hatch closed behind them and for a brief moment Chai had a vague sensation of movement. The mechanoid called Colopo turned and addressed him once more.

"Please take away all that is not you."

Chai considered her words carefully but was unable to fathom her meaning. "I'm sorry. I don't understand what you want me to do," Chai told her.

"Please take away all that is not you," repeated Colopo.

Chai shrugged. "I'm sorry, I don't understand."

"Demonstration," said the mechanoid. Then she reached up and undid the clasp at her shoulder. Her gown slid to the floor leaving her naked.

"Oh, I see." Chai quickly disrobed, assuming correctly that his actions were required prior to some sort of decontamination process. Suddenly the light filling the vessel turned from white to a deep blue and Chai felt his skin tingle and warm slightly.

"Please make all that is not you to inside this," commanded Colopo, raising her arm. As she did so her hand dissolved into a million tiny, silver dots. The dots hovered in the air for a few moments and then rearranged themselves into the shape of the red symbol on the small, starboard hatch door. This time Chai knew what she meant and stuffed his clothes, shoes and personal communicator through the hatchway. He had a horrible feeling that would be the last he would ever see of them.

Colopo handed Chai a simple blue smock, which he slipped over his head. Once again the light turned from white to blue and once again Chai felt his skin tingle. Clearly the decontamination procedure was a multi step operation.

"Please recline on the comfy seat," said Colopo.

Chai smiled at Colopo's strange choice of words and then complied with her request. To his surprise the chair was indeed comfy, very comfy indeed. But as he sat, the fur covering of the seat rapidly began to grow. The follicles stretched out and quickly wrapped themselves around his body pinning him to the chair. He clawed at the fur trying to get free but his efforts were useless. He was trapped. But was he? Perhaps the fur was some sort of safety restraint, it certainly didn't feel as if it was trying to smother or crush him. In fact, if he just kept still and didn't try fight it, the seats embrace was quite comforting. Moments later Chai was pushed back strongly into the seat as the tiny vessel accelerated away from the 'War Hawk'.

The ship must be a drone, piloted by remote control from the planet's surface, surmised Chai. That's why there's no control panel or pilot seat, the ship doesn't need one. Then he realised that maybe he was wrong. He had been facing the back of the ship, with Colopo between him and the rear bulkhead. But when he'd turned around to sit, facing the front, Colopo had disappeared. Perhaps the Nanobots which had once joined together to form her, were now integrated into the ship. Perhaps even the ship itself, like Colopo, was constructed entirely of the tiny mechanisms.

Then, terrifyingly, the centre of the front section of the transporter seemed to dissolve into nothingness. Like a piece of paper being burnt by the suns rays through a magnifying glass, a small hole suddenly appeared in the centre of the forward bulkhead and grew quickly outwards. The hole rapidly increased in size until the entire front section of the tiny ship had disappeared. Then Chai watched in amazement as the rest of the vessel turned invisible. It was still there, he could still feel the weird, sticky floor beneath his feet. There was no sudden, catastrophic drop in pressure, and he had no difficulty whatsoever in breathing. The ship was still intact, it just wasn't visible any more.

Far below he could see the planet Tran. With nothing between him and the surface, it somehow felt almost close enough to touch. Chai was left breathless by its incredible beauty, hoping and praying at the same time, that this wonderful world would one day soon be his new home. His, Shan's, the new baby's, and the seventeen thousand others aboard the fleet The planet was rapidly growing in size as the transporter plummeted towards its surface, and a few moments later, the ship shuddered as it hit the outer layers of the atmosphere. Now Chai could vaguely see the outline of the ship, glowing bright red, as the outer hull heated up due to the massive friction of the air against the vessels Nelamine skin. The transporter raced towards the city, slowing rapidly as it approached, and then suddenly it banked around to the left and headed for the mountains to the west.

The ship levelled out at around a mere fifty metres above the surface. Below him Chai could see kilometre after kilometre of lush, dense rainforest. To his right was a vast, blue ocean and to his left, a huge expanse of arable land which had been cultivated and planted with row upon row of some form of yellow, flowering food crop.

Between the rainforest and the towering mountain range in front of him, was a series of rolling, grass covered foothills. Scattered over these grasslands were what Chai assumed were herds of domesticated, ruminating animals. The beasts were huge six legged creatures, standing Chai guessed, around five or six metres high at the front shoulder and the same in length. There was a dozen herds of twenty or so animals, quietly grazing on the lush green grass. They seemed oblivious to everything around them save for their need to consume. They had large flat heads with eyes on the ends of stalks which protruded from a dark, horny plate covering their foreheads. Their long flat tails were tipped at the end with a clump of fluffy pale fur. Some were white, some black, some a dark tan colour. Still others were brindle, with patches of all three hues scattered over their hides. Over half also had large, pendulous, milk engorged udders hanging between their back legs, and like their bipedal keepers, their knees bent the wrong way.

The transporter adopted a radically upward tilt as it rocketed up the face of the mountainous cliff ahead. Once it reached the top it levelled out and took a slightly more north westerly track. Suddenly a flock of some sort of avian creature burst out from the canopy below. The creatures were shaped like an upturned, shallow cone, bright purple in colour with a yellow centre. From the middle of that yellow centre jutted a long serpentine neck and atop that neck, was a small teardrop shaped head with a long curved beak sitting between the creatures tiny round eyes. The birds cone shaped bodies seemed to pulse slowly, as if they were some huge airborne jellyfish, swimming through the atmosphere. Chai watched, totally entranced, as the creatures swooped and banked, rising up one moment and then plummeting towards the ground, banking and gilding away at the last moment and then pumping its 'wing' madly once more to gain altitude.

Again the tiny ship changed course and soon Chai found himself flying over the ocean. There were creatures here too, dark largely indistinguishable shapes swimming slowly through the crystal clear azure waters. One shape Chai judged to be over thirty metres in length, and he watched in awe as the massive fish trawled back and forth searching for food.

In the distance Chai could make out a small, white triangular shape in the water at the end of a long churning wake which ran across the surface of the sea. As the transporter grew close, Chai could see it was some sort of ocean vessel. The boat was long and narrow, with two scimitar shaped floats protruding from each side. The vessel's crew, three small Tranian children, looked up at Chai's craft and waved and then scurried about the boat preparing to turn back towards the shore. With a start Chai realised that amazingly, the boys were using nothing more than the ocean breeze to power their tiny craft.

As the transporter neared the shore, Chai could see other Tranians, young children and families, playing on the sand or swimming in the sea. No one had swum in the sea on Chai's home world for generations. The pollution in the oceans was so toxic, anyone foolish or unlucky enough to enter the water would die from the multitude of pathogens within days, sometimes immediately.

The ship flew over the beach and turned a final time, once more heading for the city. Chai felt invigorated by the little tour and was greatly cheered, as he felt sure he was being shown what wonders the refugees could expect to see once settled on their new home.

He was soon to learn he was mistaken.

Chapter 18

FROM THE AIR, THE CITY of Salin was set out as a number of interconnected circles or discs. At the centre of each circle was a tall tower. The buildings closest to the centre were quite low, maybe just a hundred metres or so high. Those in the next concentric row are taller and the next row taller still. In fact each circle's row gained progressively in height, until the buildings near the perimeter of that city circle have achieved an almost stratospheric altitude. In addition, the roofs of the buildings all sloped downwards, each one angled inwards towards the middle of the city circle, and each roof was covered with a highly reflective surface. As Chai's tiny transporter scythed its way across the roof tops of Salin, he suddenly realised the reason for this. The entire city was a series of huge, parabolic, solar energy collectors. The roofs of the city's buildings were catching the suns rays and reflecting them back, concentrating their enormous thermal energy, at a single point at the top of the tall tower in the centre of each disc shaped section. From there, he assumed, the energy was converted from heat into much more useable electricity. Such technology was simple, yet awe inspiring in its execution.

To the west of the city was a multi level structure which was obviously some sort of space port. As Chai watched, a number of transporters, similar to the one in which he travelled, but much larger, took off and headed for the fleet orbiting high above the planet. There was no way of knowing of course, but Chai assumed they were once again carrying food and water to replenish the armada's dwindling supplies. If that were the case, it was very good news. It appeared the Tranians were still in a magnanimous mood and Chai was greatly heartened to know it. His tiny vessel swooped in over one of the landing pads and slowly lowered itself vertically onto the ground.

The female called Colopo was waiting in the docking area when Chai exited the transporter. This time however the creature was flesh and blood, not an imitation made from bits of metal. The real Colopo had a warmer golden colour to her skin and her eyes were a deep, vivid emerald green, and not the lifeless pale silver grey of the mechanoids. She was also much taller, almost two and a half metres tall, yet more graceful than her metallic facsimile. She moved with effortless grace towards him and presented herself to him, the first of his species ever to have visited her planet. He bowed and introduced himself.

"I am Chief Security Officer Salang Chai," he told her, "I'm the newly appointed spokesperson representing the seventeen thousand souls waiting in limbo above your planet."

"I am Colopo," she told him, crossing her long, slender arms over her chest and touching her shoulders in what Chai took to be their way of greeting. "I will speak the words of the vermin so that the Council of Tran will know the vermin's meaning."

Her voice was less mechanical sounding than that of her Nanobot duplicate, but still soft and delicate, and still with that same tinkling, bell like quality to it. Chai copied her greeting pose, crossing his arms over his chest in what he hoped was the accepted manner.

"Thank you for honouring me with your assistance. My name is Salang Chai," he repeated. "When will we meet with the High Council?" he asked.

The Tranian female pondered his question for a while and then answered. "The Council will hear the words of the vermin in eight days." She turned and gestured for Chai to follow.

Eight days? he thought. The Tranians certainly didn't do anything in a hurry. Colopo must have understood the need to elaborate, for she stopped, turned and addressed Chai once more.

"The words I speak are...." she searched for the right phrase, "worthy not enough to understand by the High Council. I study what I get from your computer by little robot sent to me. Not good enough. Colopo and Salang Chai will speak and Colopo will learn much better. Then I will speak the words of the vermin, so the Council of Tran will know the vermin's true meaning. In eight days."

"I understand," said Chai. Hopefully I'll be able to make you realise that the word 'Vermin' obviously has a different meaning on my planet to yours, he thought.

Colopo turned away and walked slowly towards a doorway and a steep stairway leading down to the personal transportation vehicle parking area on the lower, underground floor. Her PTV was a tiny vehicle, with just enough room for a driver and two passengers. Colopo opened the driver side door. There was no seat as such, just a flat padded cushion. She climbed in, folding her feet and legs under her as she sat. The seat in the passenger section was of similar design and Chai was forced to kneel on the cushion with his feet splayed out to the side.

Colopo turned, looked at Chai kneeling next to her, and emitted a tinkling sound similar to that of an avian creature Chai had once heard as a child. She was laughing.

"Legs bend wrongly," she chuckled, shaking her head in amazement.

Colopo pressed a button on the control panel in front of her, engaging the electromagnetic drive, and the PTV moved out of the parking area and turned right onto one of the radial thoroughfares leading out of the city centre.

While the streets were teeming with pedestrians, there seemed to be very few PTVs on the roadway, and those that were, were mostly of a smaller two wheeled variety. Some of these were powered by some sort of electro-mechanical motor, while others were driven by a pair of offset cranking pedals attached to a drive shaft. This appeared to power the back wheel. The two wheeled vehicle's drivers pumped up and down on the pedals and this provided the forward motion. So simple yet so amazing.

As Colopo eased out into the traffic Chai watched, trying to work out just how Colopo's minute vehicle was controlled. There were two levers in front of Colopo's seat and when she pushed the right one forward the PTV turned to the left and when she pushed the left one forward the vehicle turned right. On the top of the right lever was a short, rotating section which when twisted clockwise increased their speed. All quite simple really. But the little car had been designed with Tranian physiology in mind and that made the chance of Chai ever being able to operate such a vehicle highly unlikely. Just in front of the driver's seat was a large flat pedal, which when pushed forward, activated the PTV's brakes. There was simply no way that any being without the Tranian's backward facing knees could contort their legs sufficiently to ever operate that pedal.

But if the PTV was strange, it was nothing compared to the people themselves. All around him, the people of Tran went about their business. Most had the same soft, golden skin of his new associate, but some had a deeper, reddish, copper tone. Occasionally Chai even caught a glimpse of a creature with black skin. Black as midnight but with the lustre of polished ebony. The Tranians were predominantly tall and slender with only a very small percentage showing any sign of portliness. The adult females, some of whom walked around bare breasted, made it obvious the Tranians were mammalian. The males all sported a prominent, bony crest which ran along the centre ridge of their heads similar to some long extinct avian species of his home world.

The Tranian's dress varied from a simple blue tunic like the ones both he and Colopo wore, to extremely elaborate, multi coloured costumes which looked far more like works of art than clothing. Some Tranians, both males and females wore silver and gold tunics with a type of brightly coloured, metallic bandoleer over their right shoulder and across their chest. Chai wondered if this garment was some sort of indication of rank, or perhaps it was some sort of family crest, or denoted membership to a particular religious sect. Colopo must have seen his questioning looks, because she glanced in his direction and offered an explanation.

"These Tranian are keepers of law, as are you Salang Chai."

"They're Police?"

"Police....Yes Police."

So, thought Chai, Tran maybe a peaceful place and it's population may abhor violence, but they still had crime.

Suddenly a group of Tranian males, all dressed in a glossy, skintight apparel, raced past the vehicle, heading back towards the city centre. Chai estimated the runners were reaching speeds of around thirty five kilometres per hour and more.

"Boys racing for prize," explained Colopo as the troop thundered past.

When Chai considered it, the boys speed was hardly surprising. If he remembered the evolutionary science he'd been taught at the academy correctly, the Tranian's physiology indicated that they had evolved from an entirely different kind of animal to Chai's species. The Tranian's tiny mouth, the trumpet shaped ears which twitched and turned constantly as if listening for danger, the narrow head and large, sideways facing eyes which afforded the creature an almost three hundred and sixty degree view of the world around it, plus the backward facing knees all indicated one thing. The Tranians had not evolved from some sort of hunting animal, but in fact the exact opposite was true. In their pre-evolved state, the Tranians had obviously once been prey to a much more dangerous animal. Then he thought of Vethil's damned vortex cannon. Perhaps they still were?

He groaned to himself, remembering the seventeen galaxy class cruisers orbiting the planet. According to Admiral Vethil, no other vessel was fitted with a vortex canon. Chai hoped like hell that was true. But even if there was just one, did its existence mean that if Chai couldn't convince the Tran High Council to let the refugees settle on their planet, would Vethil use it to force them to comply? Was it possible the Tranian's days of being prey to a dangerous, more aggressive creature, far from over?

It took nearly two hours to reach their destination, and during the journey Colopo told her charge a little about herself. Or at least she tried to. As far as Chai could make out, Colopo was a teacher of linguistics at some sort of school. She could speak seven Tranian dialects and four 'off world' languages, including Annuxian, plus a smattering of something called 'Slikina', which appeared to be an ancient Tranian language. A language in fact, that had been spoken by Colopo's ancestors, around ten million years ago.

"I have seven plus thirty students I teach," she informed him. "Six pupils of them I make study of your language. They will help."

They travelled a little further in silence before she spoke again. This time she informed him of some cultural differences between their two species.

"Female on ship, you father of baby boy, Yes?"

Chai was surprised Colopo even knew of Shan, never mind that she was pregnant. It appeared the 'Colopo mechanoid' must have relayed her meeting with Chai's spouse, back to her controller.

"Yes, Shan, the pregnant woman, she's my wife," Chai replied.

"Wife....," mused Colopo. "On Tran male live not with female. Female make ready to mate. Male copulate then go away. Live once more with father and other males. Female live with mother also until mating time passed. Then live with baby."

"How many children do you have?" Chai asked.

Colopo turned towards him and once more emitted her strange tinkling chuckle.

"No babies. Colopo not mate. Mate next year in time before hot time."

Perhaps she means she won't come into season until next spring, though Chai.

At the next intersection Colopo turned left and then left again into a short tunnel which ran under a tall, multi story, square based building. She stopped her PTV inside a rectangle marked on the floor next to an open doorway. They climbed out of the vehicle, then she crossed to a keypad attached to the wall next to the doorway, and selected a sequence of five of the nine symbols displayed. A large mechanical arm extended slowly out of the doorway next to Colopo's waiting PTV. At the end of the arm was a large circular pad which lowered itself onto the roof of Colopo's vehicle. There was a faint hum as the electromagnet attached itself and then the mechanical arm retreated back through the doorway, taking the tiny car with it. It was obviously some sort of automated vehicle storage system.

Colopo then led Chai to an elevator and together they travelled up to the one hundred and thirty ninth floor. They exited the elevator, turned left and walked a few metres to a hallway with eight doors leading off it. They stopped outside the third on the right and Colopo led Chai inside. As they entered the tiny apartment, Colopo sang out a greeting. An elderly female, dressed in a dark purple shirt and skirt, unfolded her thick, heavily veined legs, rose from the mat she was kneeling on, and came to greet them both. She hugged Colopo to her matronly bosom and then bowed deeply to Chai, crossing her arms over her chest as she did so.

"Salang Chai, this is my mother, Silpolo," announced Colopo.

Chapter 19

FOR THE THIRD TIME in as many days, Dr Wawa Shan sat stuffing herself with the delicious fruit the people of Tran had so generously delivered to the ship. Once again she was seated in the mess hall, at a table next to a huge window overlooking the planet Tran. But this time she was seated opposite Dr Wawa Ni, her father. After the death of Assistant Maintenance Officer Shillim Del, and the recent departure of her husband to the planet below, the flagship 'War Hawk' was a bit short handed. So Admiral Vethil had decided to bring a couple of people out of stasis early. That way a full complement of conscious crew were available should they be needed.

Yesterday afternoon, after Chai had been unexpectedly spirited away by the strange mechanoid, the Tranian High Council had suddenly opened communication channels with the flagship. Now, in direct contrast to the previous sixteen days, communications between the ships of the armada and the planet below were frequent. Their first request demanded the medical records of the fleets seventeen thousand and sixty one passengers. Then every man, woman and child's DNA had to be sent to the planet's surface, so that the Tranian scientists could make sure no one carried any disease which might threaten the planet's indigenous population.

Shan had been snowed under before, but now she was simply unable to cope with the impossible workload asked of her. So later in the afternoon, she'd invited Admiral Vethil to join her for a quick, late lunch and requested that her father be brought out of stasis early to help. Vethil agreed and Shan took a walk down to the revamped munitions hold and revived Dr Ni together with a thoroughly unlikeable, weedy little cretin called Skillen Chun. Chun was to replace Del in the maintenance department.

"So have you heard from Chai since they took him away?" asked Ni, sitting opposite.

"Yes, they took his communicator away from him when he boarded the transporter, but returned it to him early this morning. He said it looked as if they'd disassembled it. Maybe to replicate it, which could be an explanation why they've suddenly started talking to us. But it's more likely they've installed a listening device of their own so they can eavesdrop on Chai's report."

Ni looked concerned. "Are they treating him well?"

"Oh yes. He's staying in the home of a female translator. Apparently she's some sort of linguistics expert. She's studying our language so she can translate Chai's appeal to the Tranian Council. He was a bit surprised when the female invited him into her own home. He thought they'd lock him up somewhere until the hearing. But I guess this Colopo creature feels she can keep an eye on him, and get more exposure to our language this way."

She stabbed another heavenly tasting, hexagonal shaped piece of fruit with her fork and stuffed it into her mouth, sighing with undisguised pleasure at the pale blue foods exquisite taste. Her father ate too, but without any gusto. It would be another day at least before his pre-stasis appetite returned fully.

"According to Chai, his first meeting with the High Council will be in seven days time," Shan continued. "They'll take a couple of days to mull things over and then get him back to ask any questions, or voice any concerns they may have. But even then, there won't be any decision made immediately. Chai reckons it could be another thirty or forty days before we know for certain one way or the other.

Apparently the Tranians don't make their minds up about anything in a hurry."

"Goodness," said her father.

They sat in silence for a while, gazing at the beautiful world below and just enjoying each other's company. Emotionally, father and daughter were very close and always had been. One way in which they were similar in personality, was that neither of them ever felt the need to fill in the occasional void in their conversation with mindless drivel. Shan could talk the leg off a chair in a vacuum if she needed to of course, but she was equally happy to remain quiet if the opportunity dictated. Eventually Ni broke the silence, bringing up the question neither of them really wanted to confront.

"Do you think that idiot Vethil will use the vortex canon if the Tranian High Council turns Chai down?"

The existence of Vethil's toy was one of the first things Shan had discussed with her father when she'd brought him out of stasis. The man had been livid, and it was all Shan could do to stop him from marching straight to the bridge and taking the Admiral to task.

"I think it's inevitable Dad. If Vethil believes he has no other choice, he'll almost certainly take matters into his own hands and use the weapon. Maybe not actually use it, but certainly as a threat," she said sadly. "We just have to hope Chai is successful."

Ni leaned forward and lowered his voice to barely a whisper. "Is there some way we might disable the gun before Vethil decides to use it?"

"Hmmm. I'm not sure," she answered, adopting her fathers covert conversational tone. "But according to Chai, despite Vethil's assurances to the contrary, there's a good chance there's a gun on every vessel in the fleet. I've been in contact with all the other medical officers and mentioned, just in conversation like, the possible existence of other vortex canons. Most of the medico's I've spoken to seem genuinely outraged by the existence of the one we've found, but so far no one's actually been able to find another on any of the other ships."

Ni crossed his arms over his chest, scowling as he leant back in his seat.

"We need to mutiny. Take control of each ship and throw Vethil and his cronies in the brig. Don't these fools ever learn?" he snapped angrily.

Shan leant over the table as far as she could. "Keep your voice down Dad," she hissed quietly. "I know this is supposed to be a refugee vessel, but we're still under martial law and I'm sure Vethil won't hesitate to arrest anyone he considers a threat to his authority. We have to watch our backs until we've formulated a plan. Now is not the time to lose our heads."

Ni shook his head in frustration. Shan was right of course. There was nothing to be gained by acting rashly. A cool head was needed now, a cool head and the assistance of at least another seventeen like minded souls, one from each of the other ships, who could search their own vessel for any more weapons. Though each ship had at least one medical officer who was known to them, neither father or daughter thought that it would be easy to find seventeen such people.

"Of course this whole discussion might be moot anyway," Shan continued. "According to Chai, the Tranians know lots about us. So it's obvious they've somehow hacked into our computer system. If that's the case, it's highly likely they already know about the weapon. Maybe the big delay in hearing our request is deliberate. They're stalling for time. Perhaps even now, the Tranians are planning a pre-emptive strike against us, before Vethil has a chance to get his vortex canon on line. Maybe we're on the brink of yet another stupid war, and this time we're not going to survive."

Chapter 20

REPETITION, THAT WAS the key to leaning any new language, repeating the words and phrases over and over again until they were etched on one's memory. Colopo had been doing just that for the past four days. She'd had the stocky, hairy little creature, talk about himself, his planet, and his family, the politics of his planet, religion, in fact anything he or she could think of, almost constantly, since he'd arrived from the vermin space ship. Colopo had repeated every word, emulating his speech patterns, copying the pronunciation and the cadence of his words, then checking their meaning, until she was certain she had at least a basic understanding of the vermin's language.

One of the things she learnt for example was that Chai's people didn't like to be referred to as vermin. He began to explain the word's meaning, foolishly believing that Colopo had somehow got it wrong. She listened carefully and patiently to his definition of the word, but was unable to differentiate between what he thought of as vermin and what Colopo thought. Hadn't the creatures inhabiting the vessels orbiting Tran, infested every world they'd encountered? Hadn't they destroyed countless inferior species, pillaging the worlds and devastating the natural resources of every planet they'd visited, including their own? That certainly sounded like vermin to Colopo.

Eventually she decided, that to avoid any unpleasantness, from now on she would refer to Chai's species as 'The Visitors' or 'The Refugees.'

The truth was, regardless of whatever she called them, from what she had gleaned from the information they'd downloaded from the visitors computers, they were definitely a species to be wary of. She quite liked Salang Chai though. He'd not been the Councils first choice, but when the mechanoid arrived on the visitor's vessel, it had discovered the female Shan was with child. Because of that, the medical woman had to be discounted. Her husband Salang Chai, the only one not walking around armed to the teeth and whose occupation seemed to be some sort of ship bound policeman, was selected to take her place. So far the substitution had proved successful. He was obviously intelligent, quick to adapt to his changed environment, and had shown no tendency towards any unexpected violent or antisocial behaviour. He was also very courteous to both Colopo and her mother. In addition, he was working hard in an attempt to learn the Tranian language, plus he was diligent and always willing to do whatever was necessary to make Colopo's own task easier.

Inviting the visitor into her own home could have caused a big problem, but happily Chai had instantly taken a liking to Colopo and her mother. He had lost his own mother when he was just a child, and his father just two years ago. So whether it was for that reason, or due to the fact that before her retirement last year, Colopo's mother had been a Law Enforcer like Chai was unclear, but his liking for both Colopo and Silpolo was obvious.

In return, the elderly female was enthralled with their new house guest, and questioned him relentlessly on every subject from how his species procreated, to what sporting contests were popular on his home world. Of course this meant every question posed by her mother, and every answer given by the visitor, had to be translated from one language to the other so the other person could understand, and this gave Colopo some excellent opportunities to hone her language skills. So there was no question that, with each passing moment, she was becoming more and more proficient in the visitor's tongue.

In addition to its two inhabitants and one guest, Colopo's apartment was regularly invaded by numerous her students, together with an almost constant stream of neighbours and friends, each one eager to catch a glimpse of the strange creature from the other side of the universe. A consummate teacher, as soon as a new student arrived, Colopo would immediately rope them into helping her in her quest to learn Chai's language.

The constant influx of helpers and busybodies meant that Colopo's tiny apartment frequently became almost claustrophobic, and on one occasion Chai was forced to perch on top of one of the bench top work spaces in the kitchen, just to make some room for the others to stand.

Colopo's revelation that Chai's wife Shan had been the Tranian High Council's first choice as spokesperson went some way to explaining how he'd ended up sharing the language teachers private residence. It would have been much easier, he supposed, with three females sharing than the present scenario, but they managed. The apartment was tiny, but even so, it was bigger than his and Shan's cabin back on the 'War Hawk'. It had just two bedrooms, each one containing nothing more than a small sleeping mat and a cupboard for each female's clothing and personal effects. There was a living area, which was about four metres square and which included a kitchen and food preparation area in the western corner. Finally, there was a separate, tiny shower room and toilet. That was it, not a single square millimetre of wasted space. The entire eastern wall of the apartment was made of glass (or at least some sort of similarly transparent material), and this afforded the occupants a magnificent view of the towering city surrounding them, while also giving the illusion that the domicile was far more spacious than it actually was.

As far as sleeping arrangements were concerned, Colopo had originally intended to bunk in with her mother, sacrificing her own room for Chai's use. But Chai had refused, pointing out he could simply push a couple of the kneeling mats together and curl up on the floor of the main living room.

"I'll be perfectly comfortable," he'd assured them, and indeed he had been.

So far food had not been a problem either. One of the first things Chai had asked about when he first arrived on the planet was, "Apart from the fruit and vegetables you sent to us, what other things do Tranian people eat?"

From Colopo's answer Chai learnt that Tranians were vegetarian, though herbivore would be a more apt description. There was no conscious decision involved, their digestive system was simply unable to process complex proteins. Not that the thought of eating a dead animal held any appeal for them anyway. Luckily Chai loved fruit and vegetables and was happy to refrain from eating meat. At least for a few days.

The trio, plus the multitude of visitors, spent the first three days in the apartment, never venturing outside. But by the end of the third day Colopo's command of Chai's language had improved exponentially. She was talking like a native, well almost. So on the fourth day, Colopo announced they would be going to "The beside of the ocean."

"It will give us more opportunity to interact with other Tranians," she explained.

Her explanation somehow didn't quite ring true, and Chai couldn't help wondering if there was perhaps an ulterior motive to Colopo's kind offer. But, he reminded himself, if Colopo wished him harm, she'd already had ample opportunity to inflict it. So far she and her mother, in fact everyone he'd met on the planet, had shown him nothing but kindness and generosity.

Maybe going to the beach was just another way in which she was demonstrating her naturally hospitable nature.

Maybe not.

Chapter 21

ADMIRAL VETHIL PACED across the floor of his quarters, back and forth, for the best part of an hour. He was angry, livid in fact, beside himself with fury at the way he was loosing control of the situation. Firstly that jumped up, little turd Salang Chai had discovered the existence of the vortex Canon, something Vethil had gone to great lengths to keep secret. It seemed obvious to Vethil the Tranians had every vessel in his fleet under surveillance, but with the canon under wraps, buried in the back corner of a hold full of agricultural equipment, the chance of the creatures from the planet below finding out about it had been slim. But of course Chai had told his wife, who in turn had told her stupid, pacifist father, a man well known for his anti-military stance. Now, according to 'War Hawk's chief communications officer, there had been covert messages sent between either Dr Ni or his daughter and the medicos from every other ship. They were obviously trying to garner support for Dr Ni's half baked plan to sabotage the vortex canon. With communications going back and forth between ships, the likelihood the Tranians were unaware of the weapon's existence was ludicrously small. Of course, they knew.

Secondly, the Tranian Council had chosen to disregard his authority and obvious superior suitability as a negotiator, not to mention his ability to act as an ambassador for his people, and instead had taken Salang Chai to act as emissary. The man had been on the surface for four days and hadn't even had the gumption to demand to see the president or head councillor yet. In his report last evening he'd informed Vethil that today he would be having a picnic with his translator at the beach. What the hell was he playing at? If Vethil had been in attendance, he would have made the stupid, ugly beings on the planet below sit up and take notice. They wouldn't have dared to make such a ridiculous suggestion he spend a day at the beach if he'd been in control.

To Vethil it was obvious they were deliberately stalling while they rallied their defences. Even now they were probably moving their armaments into position, preparing to repel 'War Hawks' imminent attack. They would not have had the chance if Vethil had been there to force them to accept his demands.

He believed he still had the upper hand though. There was no doubt the Tranians were monitoring the fleet's movements, just as Vethil's team had been monitoring theirs. So far his strategists had seen no definitive sign of any mass troop movement. whatever the bastards were doing, they were doing it covertly.

They'd told Salang Chai they would not be considering the refugees' request for at least another four days, which almost certainly meant it would be another four days before they were ready to attack. That gave Vethil another three days to get his vortex canon online, a task which even now was under way.

Of course things might change very quickly if the Tranians were made aware of Vethil's attempts to commission the weapon. The Admiral was certain that Dr Wawa Ni would be watching the hold where the gun was being stored like a hawk, and no doubt he would contact his stupid son in law on the planet's surface the instant the Admiral made a move.

Dr Wawa Ni had to be stopped from taking any action which might jeopardise the success of Vethil's mission. Nothing and no one could be allowed to thwart his plans. He decided he would have Ni arrested on charges of sedition.

But then he reconsidered. Perhaps there was an alternative, more permanent option available.

Chapter 22

COLOPO TYPED HER CODE into the keypad, and the parking centre machine sprang into action, retrieving her personal transport vehicle in just a few minutes. She climbed in behind the steering levers and fired up the electromagnetic drive. Chai folded himself into the passenger seat, and with his knees up around his ears, sat and enjoyed the twenty minute drive out of the city, towards the coast.

The weather was perfect for a day outside. The sun blazed down on the city as they wound their way between the buildings. The sky above was once again a dazzling, cloud free blue. It was simply a glorious summer day and although it was still only mid morning, the temperature had already reached the high twenties. As they approached the outer circle of skyscrapers, Chai noticed that many of the buildings had long tubular cylinders attached vertically to each corner. The tubes were rotating slowly, driven by the gentle breeze blowing in from the ocean. Colopo explained that the tubes were fitted with internal, spiral vanes. As they turned, they sucked in the clean, cool air from the ocean and directed it, through a series of underground tunnels, to the solar generators at the centre of each city circle. The cool air prevented the generators from overheating, and the heated air produced was then channelled around the city. All year round it was used to heat water for bathing and cooking, and in the winter it was also used for heating the populations homes.

"That's amazing!" exclaimed Chai. If only his own people could have been so resourceful!

They reached the outskirts of the city and Colopo turned right towards the east, then veered left and headed north east for the ocean. The road became narrower and rather than being dead flat as the streets of the city had been, the highway generally followed the undulations in the countryside, twisting and turning between the larger hills and mountains and then dropping down along a gentle slope to the beach. The country on either side of the road had been planted with row after row of what Colopo called 'Nago' trees. 'Nago' fruit was the name of the yellow, pyramid shaped fruit Shan had loved so much. Closer to the ocean, where the salt laden air made growing food crops impossible, the vegetation changed to a more arid, scrubby type of bush, and the grass morphed from the lush green ground cover of the inland into course, grey, patchy tufts scattered over the dry, stony earth.

A few minutes later Colopo pulled into a large, flat, paved area and parked her PTV next to a couple of dozen other vehicles. They clambered out, grabbed mats, drying cloths and the basket containing food and cool drinks from the storage area in the rear of the vehicle, and then the Tranian female led Chai down a narrow, winding track down to the beach.

The golden sand was hot, too hot to stand on in bare feet, and after claiming an area of beach as their own, and laying out their mats and picnic basket, Colopo peeled off her tunic, slipped off her shoes, raced across the burning ground, and hurtled herself into the briny, crystal clear water. Chai followed her, but slowed as he neared the water's edge. All around him, up and down the beach, the Tranians, young and old alike, were enjoying the water. Tiny children swam around like fish, splashing and diving and squealing in delight, with the unconscious, unbridled euphoria that only the very young and the very innocent can enjoy. Older Tranians also soaked in the azure sea, floating effortlessly, with barely a movement of their long arms or legs to keep their heads above water.

But even though the ocean was obviously benign, Chai hesitated. On his own world entering one of its filthy, polluted, toxic oceans would have caused severe illness, if not certain death. His planet's oceans had been that way for centuries and subconsciously Chai had difficulty accepting that this was not the case on Tran. Slowly he edged deeper into the water, sucking in air as the shock of the cold water reached his groin. He lowered himself warily into the ocean until only his head remained above the surface. Gradually he began to relax. Of course, he had swum in public swimming pools and cleansing baths countless times before, but the feeling of being immersed in cool salt water was different somehow. Suddenly he realised what it was that felt so odd. Because of the high salt content, coupled with the planet's slightly lower gravity, the Tran ocean was incredibly buoyant. Even without moving his arms and legs, he would pop up to the surface as soon as he lay on his back. In fact sinking was impossible. A concerted effort was needed to swim below the surface.

"CHAI," Colopo called, "swim with me to the floating area," she commanded, pointing to a timber pontoon bobbing on the water about one hundred metres away.

Chai struck out, swimming arm over arm as fast as he could, but he was no match for the speed and power of his new friend and she reached the pontoon before he was even half way there. He climbed out of the water and sprawled out on his stomach. The gently rolling timber deck had been polished smooth by the myriad of bodies who had lain there before him. It felt good against his bare skin and the sun felt nice on his back. He could feel the tingling of the salt on his body as the sun dried him.

"Do you like this beside the ocean place?" asked Colopo, lying on her stomach next to him.

"Yes. Very much."

"Good."

"Colopo?"

"Hmmm."

"When the mechanoid brought me from my ship, instead of coming straight to the space port, she took me on a tour of the countryside around the city." He slowly waved his arm in a broad arc, encompassing the track the transporter vessel had taken. "She showed me the ocean and the mountains, let me see the incredible diversity of your plants and animals and birds and even some amazing sea creatures. Now today you bring me to this beach......I don't understand. If the council is yet to make up its mind about letting us stay.... well, why bother showing me how wonderful your world is? If our request for asylum is granted, then I will have the rest of my life to enjoy your wonderful planet. If not..... Well, wouldn't it be kinder for me to have never known what I'd missed?"

The woman thought for a few moments, formulating her answer before replying.

"The High Council members will ask many questions of you, Salang Chai. One may be, what is the most beautiful thing on our world you have seen? Your answer will help them decide what type of creature you are."

"Oh! So what you're saying is, their decision will not just depend on whether we need to live on your planet, but also on whether we would like living here?"

"Liking our planet or not is one thing, why is something else." Colopo answered. She rolled on to her side, facing Chai, regarding him closely and considering her next comment. After a while she spoke again.

"We have studied your history Salang Chai. The High Council has downloaded all the information contained on the computers from the seventeen ships orbiting our planet. Your history is littered with turmoil, wastefulness, hatred and violence. You have engaged in countless wars, first between different tribes, races and religions on your own world, then, when you discovered intergalactic space flight, you carried your bloodlust and desire for conquest to every corner of this galaxy. Your last battle, the one waged against our friends and trading partners the Annuxians, is well known to us. The Annuxians are a peace loving, gentle species. Your unprovoked attack against them is abhorrent to us."

She sat up, twisted around so that she was facing the beach and curled her knees up under herself.

"But you are a young people," she continued, "both the Tran and the Annuxian's are many millions of years older than you. In our early history, before we learnt the error of our ways, we too had a tumultuous and violent past. But unlike you, we changed our ways before we discovered space flight. We never inflicted harm on other species. It is our hope that if you are granted asylum, with our guidance, your people might learn to live in peace. In four days you and I will present your case to the High Council. But your appeal is more about your ability to adapt to our society than your need to find a new home. We know you have nowhere else to go Salang Chai, that is understood. But it is irrelevant. If you cannot convince the High Council of your ability to integrate into our peaceful, productive way of life such as we enjoy on Tran, your appeal will be rejected."

"I see," said Chai. He turned his face away from her in shame. She was right of course. Nothing she'd said could be argued against. His people's whole history had been marred by almost constant warmongering and waste. They had even destroyed their own planet for God's sake. Now they were asking the Tranians to possibly risk their own world by letting them stay. How the hell could anyone expect the Tranians to welcome them, knowing that in all probability, the visitors would inevitably make them regret their generosity by bringing mayhem and destruction to their planet.

And yet if Colopo's words were true, that was exactly what the people of Tran were hoping to do. Not only make them welcome, but also to act as a sort of big brother and lead the visitors out of the mire and into maturity.

"T...The attack on the Annuxians, Colopo. That was not sanctioned by our government," Chai explained. "The people of my world were deceived. Our military not only launched the original attack, when the Annuxians fought back, they then lied to the people and told them the Annuxian's had attacked us first. Most of the people on board the armada don't know the true story. I'm sure if they did, they would be just as incensed by the war as I am."

Colopo twisted around to look at Chai. He was still getting used to the strange creatures facial expressions, but he was fairly sure her face now showed incredulity.

"Of course the Annuxian war was based on a lie, Salang Chai. All wars are. Even a mad man knows how to sit peacefully unless he is in danger. Therefore, deception is always the opening gambit of all who will lead others into battle."

She slowly unfurled her long legs, bent forward at the waist and raised herself up onto her feet.

"Come my friend. The time for such discussions is in four days hence. Now it is time for enjoyment and pleasantry. Also, it is time for food."

She dove over the side of the pontoon and glided lazily through the water back to the beach.

Chapter 23

THE NEWLY REVIVED MAINTENANCE man's name was Skillen Chun, and as Wawa Shan had already noted, he was a weedy little cretin. He was also irate. He really hated going outside. The safe and warm interior of a Galaxy Class war ship, even one which had ostensibly been stripped of all its armaments and was crewed by minimum personnel, was infinitely preferable to having to suit up in one of those cumbersome, uncomfortable, dangerous space suits and go outside into a freezing, vacuous void. That was why most exterior work on a space ship was normally done by one of the fleets' maintenance drones.

But they couldn't use the robots to do the job Admiral Vethil had charged Skillen Chun with. The mechanoids were controlled by the ships central computer and as it was now obvious the creatures on the planet below were monitoring 'War Hawks' computers, some covert operations had to be done the old fashioned way.

Skillen Chun suited up, entered the large airlock attached to the main cargo hold and waited while the inner door was closed and sealed. The air was purged from the lock with a loud hiss and the outer door opened. Chun activated his magnetic boots and stepped out carefully onto the massive ship's hull. He attached his safety harnesses lanyard to a ring bolt welded to the hull and sent a signal to the cargo handler waiting inside. Twenty minutes later the outer airlock door opened once again, and Vethil's vortex canon drifted slowly out. It too was tethered to the ship with a safety strap.

Chun waited until the canon had reached the end of its lanyard and stopped drifting before he attempted to haul it back in. He knew that out here in space, even though everything was weightless, momentum always had to be considered. The canon had a mass of a couple of tonnes, and if he didn't use extreme caution, its momentum could be powerful enough to tear his arms out of their sockets, or worse, drag him away from the ship. Outside in space, every movement had to be slow and gentle. Every action had an equal and opposite reaction and this had to be considered for possible, dangerous, ramifications at all times. Trying to manoeuvre something without taking the proper precautions, could result in Skillen Chun drifting off into space with no way of getting back.

Chun gently tugged on the canon's safety strap, barely exerting any tension at all, and then waited patiently for the weapon to drift slowly back and settle on the ship's hull. He engaged the magnetic clamps fitted to the base of the canon and the gun attached itself firmly to the hull. Next he unclipped his own lanyard and one end of the one attached to the canon, and walked slowly up the side of the ship until he was standing beside the gun mounting, on top of the bridge deck. He reattached the canons safety strap and then returned to the waiting gun. The other end of the strap was passed through a large diameter eye bolt welded to the base of the gun, and then attached to the ships hull once more. In this way the vortex canon could be slid into position, along the smooth Nelamine alloy surface of 'War Hawk's hull, while still securely tethered to the hull in two places.

Chun disengaged the magnetic clamps holding the canon 'down' and carefully manoeuvred it to the top of the ship. Finally, he bolted the gun in place and then connected the optic fibre 'wiring' which provided power from the ships main generator and controlled the firing mechanism. The task took Chun nearly three hours.

In four days time Salang Chai would be presenting the refugees' case to the Tranian High Council. Admiral Vethil had grave reservations about the outcome of that presentation. With each passing hour, he became more and more certain that the visitor's pleas were not only going to be rejected, the Tranians were using the delay to ready their army prior to attacking the fleet. If that proved to be the case, then Vethil reckoned a demonstration of his lethal weapon on say, the smaller of Tran's two moons, might sway the council's decision back the other way and change their minds about taking on the might of Vethil's armada.

Chapter 24

BY MID AFTERNOON A sea breeze had picked up, thankfully taking some of the bite out of the scorching sun. Both Chai and Colopo had dressed but were still lying on the sand chatting.

As the day came to a close, all up and down the beach, Tranian mothers were packing up their belongings and readying their offspring for the journey back to the city. Interspersed between these family huddles were groups of males. Carefree and unencumbered by any need to look after the kids, the men had spent the day bonding with their comrades, eating and drinking, engaging in beach games, wrestling on the sand, swimming and telling tall tales and jokes which each hoped would increase their esteem in the eyes of their peers.

Chai had come to realise that Tranian society was very matriarchal. Sure, males still often held positions of great importance, but the women held almost all the financial power. Only women owned property for example. Silpolo, Colopo's mother, owned the tiny apartment in which she and her daughter lived. When she died the ownership of the domicile would pass on to her daughter, and then to Colopo's daughter and so on. Men did not inherit property.

The reason for this was readily apparent. Over seventy percent of the Tranian population was female and they generally lived around fifteen years longer than their male counterparts. There was no such thing as marriage, and because a female might take as many as ten different male partners during her breeding life, it was easier to trace someone's lineage through the mother.

There was another big difference, Tranian females only came into season once a year.

"So you and Shan can breed any time you choose to?" Colopo asked incredulously.

"Yes. Our females ovulate fourteen times a year. Though our year is forty seven days longer than yours. But don't misunderstand, it's not just about breeding. On average a woman will have just two or three children during her lifetime. Most of the time we have sex just because it's enjoyable."

"Yes for us too...But it is not necessary to take a partner just to enjoy sex, only to produce offspring."

Chai wasn't sure if that was a statement or a question, so he just nodded.

It was strange to talk about such things with a being from another world. Strange but enlightening. He was learning such a lot about his host and her people. Despite their vastly different physiology, the two species were very much alike. For example, the love of their children and love and respect for one's elders was paramount. Honour and duty was also very important.

Even though the Tranian definition of family was slightly different from Chai's, their sense of family and community was also immensely strong. Giving and sharing were common traits amongst the Tranian people. No one ever had to go hungry on their world. There was always someone willing to share what they had, even in times when it was very little. Elders, especially elderly mothers and grandmothers were held in particularly high esteem. Colopo would never, for example, send her mother off to live in one of those dreadful, community based, aged care facilities. Only men, and those women unfortunate not to have offspring capable of caring for them, went into places like that. Unless Colopo died or became severely incapacitated, Silpolo would be by her side until the day she passed away.

"Are your parents still alive Chai," Colopo asked.

"No they both died years ago. My father died in an accident at work and my mother died a few years later of lung cancer. Probably due to breathing my planet's polluted air." He went on to tell his Tranian friend all about his childhood, beginning with what it was like growing up in the largest city on the planet, his childhood friends, and his early life with his treasured uncles and aunts. But his narration was cut short. Suddenly Colopo's ears started to twitch and she began to look around nervously.

"Mogo!" she hissed in a tone filled with fear, and began hurriedly to gather their belongings.

All up and down the beach, the other Tranians were similarly packing up and rushing back to the PTV parking area, furtively looking around as they ran and calling to their friends and children to make haste. Something was obviously very wrong.

"What's happening," asked Chai, springing to his feet and helping her gather up their picnic hamper.

Colopo answered unintelligibly. In her blind panic she was forgetting that Chai spoke only a few words of the Tranian language.

"Mogo!" she said once again and took off up the beach at a gallop. Chai hurried after her. His short stature and stumpy legs were no match for the sleek and powerful physiques of the Tranians and they thundered past him as if he were standing still. Colopo held back, urging him on, looking over her shoulder every few paces to make sure he hadn't stumbled, and scanning the area for whatever it was that terrified her so. They got to the top of the track and burst out onto the parking area.

Suddenly there was a piercing scream from the northern end of the park. Chai watched in horror as a large black creature leapt out of the surrounding scrub and attacked one of the Tranian children.

The beast was a quadruped, nearly two metres long from snout to tail and standing at the shoulder, nearly as tall as Chai himself. It was an immensely powerful looking animal, with highly developed shoulders and muscular hindquarters. It was covered in sleek, short black fur, had large almond shaped, golden coloured eyes which seemed to glow with hunger, and small pointy, upright ears. It's long tapered snout was filled with vicious, razor sharp teeth. The creature was the perfect predator and it was obvious the Tranian child didn't stand a chance. The beast had the little boy by the ankle and was quickly dragging him towards the scrub. The child was screaming in terror, blood streaming from the horrific wounds inflicted on his tiny leg. All around him the Tranians were racing around in panic, yelling and screaming, desperate to get the toddler away from the Mogo, but without weapons, they were unable to do anything other than try to scare the beast off.

Chai raced towards the carnage, peeling off his tunic as he ran and grabbing it by its four corners so that it formed a simple sack. Without breaking stride he leant down and scooped up a fist sized rock from the roadway and dropped it into the folds of his tunic. A nanosecond later he hurled himself at the beast, swinging his improvised bludgeon with all his strength. The rock hit the creature on its right side and Chai would later swear he could hear the Mogo's ribs shatter from the impact. The beast bellowed in pain, dropped the little boy and swung around rapidly to face his attacker.

The Mogo roared once more and sprang at Chai's throat, its huge dripping jaws snapping at his jugular. Chai swung again, this time with both hands. The Mogo dropped its head at the last moment and the blow whizzed over its skull, missing the beast by mere millimetres. But Chai was prepared for such a manoeuvre and instantly reversed the strike, swinging the bludgeon back the other way. The rock hit the animal in the side of the jaw with a sickening thud and the Mogo fell to the ground and dropped on its side.

An angry throng of Tranian males then descended on the beast brandishing sharp sticks and rocks. They began pelting the animal and stabbing at it with their improvised spears, but their actions were futile. The Mogo was already dead. Chai rushed to where the beast had dropped its prey and cradled the tiny boy in his arms. He carried him a few metres away from the dead animal and then laid him gently on the grass beside the road. The child was crying and hyperventilating, his scrawny leg a bloody mess from the Mogo's vicious teeth. The wound was bleeding steadily, but not profusely, so Chai was fairly certain the animal's bite had missed any major blood vessels. But the bleeding had to be stopped and stopped quickly, or else the boy would surely die. Chai ripped a strip of cloth from the hem of his tunic, tore it in half and then one of the pieces in half again. These smaller bits of cloth he folded into two thick pads and placed them over the bites on either side of the boy's ankle. He wrapped the remaining strip of tunic tightly around the leg, holding the pads in place. The bandage didn't stop the blood loss completely, but it slowed it sufficiently to stop the boy dying before help arrived.

Someone in the group of onlookers must have had a personal communicator handy, for less than three minutes later, a Paramedic Dome sailed silently over the tops of the surrounding trees and descended towards the prostrate form of the injured boy. As the dome dropped, the others stepped back out of the downdraught from the pulsing anti-grav generators and retreated to a safe distance. The centre section of the dome's base, the section directly over the little boy, opened up like the iris of a huge eye and the dome dropped to the ground, encapsulating the Tranian child.

The dome was a transportable Paramedic Station. It was around six metres in diameter, with a clear spherically curved wall above a solid, white floor, the centre of which had just opened up to accommodate the tiny boy. Inside the dome were three medical officers and a plethora of what was apparently essential medical equipment. Immediately they had the boy inside they raised him up on an operating platform and began to repair the dreadful wounds on his leg. One of the Tranian Paramedics, a tall male dressed in a bright, red, one piece medi-suit similar to the one Shan wore, unwrapped the blood soaked bandage from the boy's ankle. He peered through the transparent wall of the Dome, searching inquisitively. When he saw Chai standing nearby, now once again dressed in his ripped and blood stained tunic, the medical officer crossed his arms over his chest and bowed deeply. Then he turned back to his patient and concentrated on the tiny boy's leg.

Suddenly a female, a short woman (well short for a Tranian) wearing a gold skirt and with some sort of flamboyant, multi coloured headgear, threw her arms around Chai, hugging him to her considerable bosom. She was sobbing and jabbering unintelligibly.

"She is the boy's mother," Colopo explained. "You have saved her son's life, first by heroically fighting off the deadly Mogo and then by stopping her son from bleeding to death. She is telling you she is thankful for your courage and strength, and for your quick thinking."

Chai nodded and gently extricated himself from the blubbering woman's vice like grip, held her at arms length and looked up into her eyes smiling.

"Please tell her how happy I am that her boy is okay. I hope he recovers quickly from his terrible ordeal."

Colopo complied.

After a while one of the paramedics left the dome and came over to speak to the boy's mother. They spoke for a while and then the medic led the woman back into the Transportable Paramedic Station. Shortly after it lifted off and soared away, back over the trees towards the city.

"The boy will be fine," Colopo told him. He will spend three or four days in..." she searched for the correct word....Uh!"

"Hospital?" offered Chai. "That's a place where they take the sick and injured to be treated and made well again."

"Yes, hospital. The boy will spend three or four days in hospital, then he will return to his home to be with his mother."

That night, after dinner, Chai powered up is personal communicator and called Shan. He wanted to tell her of his day at the beach and of how he had saved a young boy's life from an attack by a terrible beast, but he never got the chance. As soon as his wife's avatar appeared before him, Chai could see she had been crying. She was distraught, sobbing her heart out and she was barely able to tell Chai her terrible news before she collapsed in tears and couldn't go on.

Chapter 25

ADMIRAL VETHIL SEETHED with anger as he sat behind the locked door of his personal accommodation at the rear of 'War Hawk's bridge deck. The Admiral was livid. Once again, that annoying bastard Dr Ni was interfering in matters which did not concern him.

Ni had discovered that the vortex canon was missing from the main hold and had concluded that the gun had somehow been moved to the outer hull and installed ready for use.

He had stormed onto the bridge, ranting and raving about how the military had already destroyed their own planet, and then claimed it seemed they were intent on destroying another. What utter shit! The man was delusional. Vethil had no intention of destroying Tran. That would be suicide. The canon was only there to add a little bit of extra influence, a bit of additional persuasion, should the Tranians decided not to let the seventeen thousand and sixty one people on board the fleet settle on their fucking planet. It was also there as a way of defending the fleet should the Tranians decided to attack. Vethil had to make sure things went their way. If not, well that could well mean the end of their entire species. Couldn't Doctor Wawa fucking Ni see that?

The Admiral had had the doctor arrested on the spot and thrown in the brig. He couldn't have such gross insubordination on his ship. Such mutinous behaviour had to be quashed immediately. But that action had caused problems which Vethil had not foreseen. Ni's daughter had taken it upon herself to inform the rest of the fleet of her father's arrest, and while the captain of each ship was under Vethil's direct command and would never question his authority, most of the other crew members were civilians, or at least non combat military. The civilian personnel on the other ships were now demanding Dr Ni be released immediately. Some were even suggesting that Vethil be relieved of his command.

Of course had this been a proper military campaign, Vethil's next more would have been obvious. Make an example of the bastard. Have him formerly charged and brought before a military tribunal. He'd be found guilty and summarily executed. Fear of further reprisals against any of the other insurgents, would quickly bring everyone back into line.

But Vethil couldn't just execute the troublemaker. Dr Ni's daughter Shan, a woman for whom Vethil had secretly once held romantic aspirations, had far too much sway with the other non military personnel scattered throughout the armada. According to his spies, Wawa Shan was quite capable of stirring up a great deal of dissatisfaction amongst the others if she wanted to. It was even possible she might lead a mutiny against Vethil's authority. So he had to keep her on side as much as possible. Also, if he were to have her father executed, Wawa Shan would no doubt refuse to continue as ship's doctor. 'War Hawk' would be without a medical officer, and as no one other than her husband had been inoculated against the numerous Tranian pathogens and diseases, that put everyone at grave risk. Vethil included.

But there was, as they say, more than one way to skin a Shambok.

Vethil had Wawa Ni released from prison and brought before him for a stern dressing down. The Admiral left Ni in no doubt exactly who it was who called the shots and promised him, that if he ever questioned his authority again, he wouldn't see the outside of a prison cell for at least two years. Then he sent him back to work.

"Oh and not that I have to answer to you Dr Ni," Vethil snapped as the medico turned to leave, "but for your information, the reason the vortex canon isn't in the cargo hold any more is because the damn thing's power cell started to leak and it was becoming unstable. At this moment it's hurtling towards Tran's sun where it will be harmlessly destroyed before it can do any damage. I suggest you get your facts straight before you come in here making wild accusations."

Wawa Ni made his way back to the infirmary, where he rejoined his daughter. He told her of Vethil's claim the vortex canon had been destroyed. Though the Admiral's claim was impossible to disprove without someone going outside and inspecting the hull of the ship, neither of them believed it for a second.

Ni led Shan into one of the larger isolation rooms. Inside there were no vidi cameras or listening devices, and once the isolation field was activated, there was no way anyone could sneak up on them with out the containment breach alarm going off.

"But what are we going do about things now Dad?" Shan asked, once they were safely inside. "Even if there was some way of ascertaining whether the canon has been installed ready for use rather than destroyed as Vethil claims, there's no way any civilian personnel can get outside to disable it."

Ni nodded. Shan's assumption was correct. No non military person on board knew how to operate outside.

"I'm sorry Dad. You were right. We should have made an attempt to disable it while it was still on board. Now we've lost any chance we had to stop this insanity."

Ni put his arms around his beautiful daughter and hugged her close.

"No. It's not your fault, sweetheart. The only person responsible is that madman Vethil. We need to bring him down, take control of the fleet away from him. That's the only way we can make sure he never uses that gun."

Shan agreed. But how? If only Chai were here, she thought, he'd know what to do.

For the next two hours they discussed various, possible ways of achieving Vethil's removal. Unfortunately, none of their ideas held even the remotest possibility of success. Eventually they decided that the only course of action left was to attempt to enlist the assistance of others they felt could be trusted, and hope that one of them could come up with a workable plan.

"I'll be talking to Chai tonight," Shan told her father. "No doubt Vethil will be monitoring our conversation, but if I'm careful, I might be able to let Chai know what's happening. He'll come up with something. I'm sure."

"Okay. Good idea," her father replied. He thought for a while and then continued.

"If you tell me what time you'll be speaking to him, I'll visit the Admiral at that time and keep him busy so he can't eavesdrop on your call."

Shan agreed. Then, as they'd both spent far too much time away from their important medical duties, they went back to work.

Later that day, toward mid afternoon, an edict was posted to everyone's personal communicators. All crew members were to meet in the mess hall in one hour to discuss preparations for moving the 'War Hawk' to a more secure orbit. Originally the navigator thought 'War Hawk's landing on the planet below would only be delayed for a couple of days. So he'd just placed the ship in a temporary orbit. One he felt would be good enough, as long as it was only for a short time. Because of the vagaries of Tran's two moons, the ship's current orbit was starting to deteriorate. Slowly but inexorably, the ship was moving closer and closer to Tran's atmosphere. Now, as it appeared the inhabitants of the planet below were in no hurry to make up their mind, the ship had to be moved to a new, more stable location.

Everyone on board knew that manoeuvring a Galaxy Class ship under turbo jet power alone, was in many ways, more dangerous than flying to the other side of the galaxy using the vortex drive. In a vortex, there was no need to concern oneself with inertia. Acceleration was instantaneous, but as the ship and everything inside and outside it accelerated at the same rate, there were none of the problems normally associated with rapid acceleration.

Under turbo jet power however, G forces could be astronomical. The computers controlling the ships internal environment would of course compensate accordingly, exponentially increasing 'War Hawk's artificial gravity's 'pull' towards the front of the ship to counteract the 'push' towards the rear as the ship accelerated. Even so, everything had to be made secure just in case something went wrong. All loose items had to be strapped down with magnetic clamps or stowed away securely, and every crew member had to be strapped into their transit seats before the vessel began to move. The maintenance drones would do the bulk of the work, but then everything had to be manually checked by one of the crew to make doubly sure everything was shipshape. Even a tea spoon or someone's pen could become a deadly projectile if not properly secured. The meeting was to be held on the bridge in one hour so Vethil could delegate which crew member would double check which section of the ship.

"Okay everyone," Vethil announced at the end of the meeting. "You all have your designated duties to perform. We will be relocating the vessel in exactly two hours. I want everyone back where they should be, strapped into their transit seats, at least ten minutes before launch. Okay? you're dismissed."

Predictably, Shan had been given the infirmary and other medical facilities to secure, while her father was charged with checking cargo bays twelve and thirteen.

The cargo bays were situated on the fourth floor, towards the rear of the ship. Ni made his way there, travelling down to the fourth floor, walking along the narrow passageway around the ship's main power-plant, and then crossing to the port side via a Nelamine mesh bridge. The bridge passed directly over 'War Hawk's massive SRS Twister Drive, linking the four cargo bays situated either side of the main engineering workshop.

Both holds twelve and thirteen contained huge stores of grain seeds. Had the fleet been able to settle there, these seeds would have been planted as a food crop on Soren 6. Now the grain's future was as uncertain as the entire fleet's crew was. Even if the Tranians agreed to let the refugees settle on their planet, it was doubtful they would entertain the idea of allowing the introduction of alien plant matter. Without its natural environmental restrictions, the grain could become a highly invasive weed, destroying vast tracts of indigenous vegetation. In all probability, if the Tranians agreed to accept the refugees, the grain would have to be destroyed. But in the meantime, all the storage bins, and all the associated conveying equipment and grain augers had to be checked to make sure they were properly anchored down.

The first hold, number twelve, was over three hundred metres in length, forty metres wide and fifteen high. The grain itself was stored in specially designed, climate controlled, rectangular Nelamine containers, each one holding around five tonnes of grain. The containers were packed in tightly, stacked one top of each other, ten high, eight deep and in rows of twenty two. Each of these containers was magnetically anchored to those around it and the whole block was then anchored to the floor in the same way. Ni walked down the rows, making sure that the power indicators on each magnetic anchor was illuminated. Just this simple task took him over an hour.

Next he moved on to the conveyor equipment. Once the grain containers themselves had been removed from the ship, these conveyors would be used to unload them. The conveyors were large diameter Nelamine tubes, which used a column of spinning air to suck the grain out of the containers and blow it into the hoppers attached to the mechanical planters.

Checking the conveyors and the rest of the equipment took Ni around fifty minutes, which left him with ten minutes to spare before he had to be back in the infirmary, and strapped into his transit seat. He reported to the bridge, informing Vethil that all in the two holds was in shipshape order and then made his way back to the infirmary.

But when he reached the exit of hold number thirteen, he was surprised and somewhat concerned to find the door locked from the outside. He reached over and slapped the emergency override button, but it had no effect. Once again he punched the button and got the same result. He pulled out his personal communicator and called the bridge. The device hissed white noise and the vidi screen displayed an 'inoperable' message. He tried another waveband, but again all he got was static. He tried yet another band, but his efforts were futile, the thing was dead. He banged on the door, using the useless communicator as a hammer, trying to alert anyone outside who might be passing. But there was no one there. He was trapped.

Ni was concerned, but not alarmed. Being strapped into a transit seat wasn't a necessity of course, it was merely an additional precaution. The artificial gravity would largely cancel out the G forces created by the ship's massive acceleration. Even so Ni thought it prudent to make his way to the rear of the hold and lie on the floor, hard up against the rear bulkhead, just in case the force proved to be unexpectedly excessive. He managed to make it a couple of hundred metres towards the rear of the ship, then Vethil turned off the artificial gravity in holds twelve and thirteen.

Suddenly Ni was floating, drifting slowly towards the ceiling with no way of propelling himself to the back of the hold. He tried to grab hold of the nearest grain container, but its sides were too smooth and devoid of any handholds. Ni began to panic. He quickly checked his chronometer, he had less than three minutes before the turbo drive engines fired up. He had to get to the back bulkhead. With the artificial gravity disabled, the G forces would be almost unbearable. He would almost certainly be rendered unconscious, but providing he could brace himself against the back wall, he would survive. But if he couldn't get there, well Ni didn't want to think what would happen then.

Suddenly he had an idea. Everyone who had ever contemplated going into space and expected they might to have to deal with a zero gravity situation, knew the law of physics which stated, 'Every action has an equal and opposite reaction.' Ni pulled his useless personal communicator out of his pocket and hurled it towards the front of the ship. As expected his action had an equal and opposite reaction. Ni started to drift slowly towards the back of the ship. But after about thirty metres the friction of the air against his body started to slow him down. He was still at least seventy metres short. He took off one of his shoes and threw it forwards. This time he twisted his body so that he was facing the rear of the ship and positioned himself as if he was diving into water, trying to reduce his friction through the air as much as possible. He hit the side of one of the Nelamine containers and grabbed hold of its corner. Dragging himself forward with his arms, he propelled himself along the corridor between the containers. He reached the edge of the next container and once again dragged himself forward. Now he had less than forty metres to go.

"This is Admiral Vethil," announced the intercom, his voice echoing around the massive hold. "All personnel are to immediately strap themselves in. We will be igniting the turbo jets in just a few moments. Launch will be in one minute and counting."

"Shit," Ni still had nearly thirty metres to go. Desperately he scrambled along the sides of the containers, grabbing hold of each box's corner and hauling himself as fast as he could towards the safety of the rear bulkhead. Moments later he heard the unmistakable hum of the turbo jets as they ignited. He had only twenty metres to go.

With just seconds to spare he reached the back wall. Quickly he swung himself around the corner of the final container, pulling himself into the gap between it and the bulkhead. He braced himself with his legs, his back against the wall and his feet pressing firmly against the huge, five tonne, Nelamine box. He'd made it.

Then as the sound of the turbo jets filled the hold with a deafening roar, the anchor light on the container his feet were pressed against, blinked out.

Chapter 26

HER FATHER'S MURDER, and Shan had no doubt in her mind his death had been murder, left the poor woman totally distraught. Vethil himself delivered the news, pretending to be terribly upset by the tragedy, but failing dismally. The bastard was almost gloating.

He informed her there had been a malfunction of one of the magnetic anchors holding a grain container in place. The container had slipped during the ships re docking manoeuvres and Shan's father had, unfortunately, been crushed. Why the doctor had not returned to his transit seat as ordered was unclear. Perhaps he hadn't heard the two minute warning delivered over the intercom?

A half hearted inquest into the good doctor's death revealed nothing out of the ordinary. The security footage of cargo hold thirteen, showed Dr Wawa Ni methodically checking each container anchor of the outer row, and then disappearing into the space between the last container and the rear bulkhead. The time signature showed him entering the space only moments before the Turbo Jets fired. Although Shan couldn't prove it, she was certain the footage had been taken earlier and Vethil had changed the time signature.

Everyone who knew Chief Security Officer Salang Chai, knew him to be a compassionate, caring man, and his obvious love for his wife made him doubly so. But when Shan first told him of Dr Ni's death, nothing he could do or say eased her suffering one iota. She was inconsolable.

"Please ask your translator to have the Tranian authorities send you back to the ship," she wept, barely able to catch her breath between heart wrenching sobs. "I need you here with me darling. Let one of the other crew meet with the High Council..... I can revive Senator Songren Del, he's had years of experience in diplomatic dealings with alien species. We can send him in your place."

But even as she begged her husband to come back to her, she knew it would not be possible. It was highly unlikely that the Tranians would agree to a change of Emissary at this late stage. Besides, from what Chai had told her previously, he had made some wonderful inroads into establishing an excellent rapport with the female acting as his translator as well as many others. Shan was not sure what sway these people might have with the Tranian High Council, but it seemed likely that some of them might have to answer questions about Chai's behaviour over the last five days. Having them onside had to be a boon.

It broke Chai's heart to see his wife so distressed, but he too knew returning to the ship at that time was impossible.

"I'm sorry darling," he told her, "but I'll be back in another seven days at the most. Colopo says the meeting with the council will take about three or four days. They won't make a decision immediately, but hopefully I'll be able to return to the ship while we wait."

On screen, Shan nodded, wiped the tears from her eyes and smiled bravely. They spoke some more about Dr Ni, about the wonderful life he'd lead, the huge number of people he had helped, both as a doctor and as a person, and of the amazing memories Shan had to remember him by. She would miss him terribly.

"I suppose I'll have to ask Vethil if I can revive my mother. I still need help with producing vaccines and antigens for the Tranian diseases I've identified, and even though she's not a qualified doctor, she's helped Dad and me out on a number of occasions. She would be a great help to me now." Her hand shot to her mouth as she realised she would have to tell her mother of her father's death.

"Oh God, Chai," she cried, once again bursting into tears. "What am I going to do? My poor Mum will be devastated."

Chai had no idea, but he knew what he was going to do once he was back on board. Admiral Vethil was a dead man, he just didn't know it yet.

Chapter 27

"BUT WITH RESPECT HONOURED Ambassador, we owe it to our friends the Tranians to offer them protection in every way possible. These so called refugees have already proven themselves to be extremely volatile and dangerous as we well know from our own painful experience. We must offer the Tranians assistance. After all, it was we who placed the forcefields around Soren 6 and the other habitable planets in the first place. So in a way it's our fault they find themselves in this predicament. If we hadn't installed the shields, the vermin would have settled on one of those other planets instead of going to Tran. Besides, the Tranians have been good friends and trading partners with the Annuxian people for centuries. We must support them. We must rearm our ships as soon as possible and make our way to Tran."

Ambassador Iwar ran the long, slender 'fingers' of its 'hand' through its luxurious beard while contemplating the treasured colleague's words. The two friends had been debating Annux's next move for the last four hours and Iwar hoped it would not be too much longer before they finally reached consensus.

"I understand your concerns my learned friend," Ambassador Iwar replied, "but the Tran aren't like the young, recently evolved, sentient life forms to be found on Soren 6. The Tranians are quite capable of looking after themselves, are they not?"

Volot, Guild Leader of the Trader Clan, shook its furry head vigorously and waved its four arms above its shoulders, expressing in the Annuxian way, the complete but polite rejection of the Ambassador's assumption.

"In theory yes, honoured Ambassador, but in practice....they are more likely to issue a sternly worded rebuff than take any truly meaningful defensive action. And knowing the Tranians as I do, I wouldn't be surprised if they took ten days to draft it."

The Ambassador smirked at the younger Annuxian's joke, knowing there was a lot of truth in what Volot was saying. The Tranians were notorious all over the known galaxy for procrastinating.

"The vermin have begged to be accepted as refugees, Volot," Iwar said. "They are claiming that they have seen the error of their ways and that during our encounter with them last year, they had been misled by unscrupulous war mongers. In reply, the Tranians are considering, and at this stage it is merely a consideration only, offering them a new home. Not only that, they are also thinking about offering them guidance and instruction on how to live a better and more peaceful life. Personally I can't think of a better species to give that guidance. Can you?" asked the Ambassador.

Volot nodded its head in agreement, its large, leaf like ears bobbing up and down with the movement.

"Of course, honoured Ambassador," Volot replied bowing deeply in acknowledgement of its colleague's superior knowledge on the subject. "I agree we should give both parties time to work out a peaceful solution to this dilemma. But perhaps then, the Trader Clan Guild might be allowed to arm just one or two vessels so that we are prepared for any eventuality. That way we can speed immediately to our friends assistance should the need arise."

Ambassador Iwar considered young Volot's offer of a compromise carefully before replying. The truth, over their entire history, the vermin had consistently demonstrated a penchant for violence, in addition to a complete inability to be trustworthy. If

Iwar had been a gambler, it would have happily staked its entire life savings on them eventually doing the wrong thing again.

"Your offer is unacceptable my young friend. But I will confer with the other members of the government and ask them to send directions to the new factory in East Plags at once. We will request they tool up for the immediate manufacture of seventeen compression torpedoes, one for each of the vermin's ships, should they be needed. If it appears the vermin are about to attack, these weapons will be loaded aboard just one of your trading vessels. Once this has been accomplished, we will have the Captain of that vessel move to within eight million kilometres of Tran and stand by to offer our assistance, should it be needed."

It was something, Volot supposed. The Guild Leader of the Trader Clan, thanked the Ambassador, bowed deeply, and left.

The walk through the ancient city's streets, from the Ambassador's offices to Volot's home on the eastern perimeter of Plags, took nearly an hour. Of course Volot could have requested a levitation vehicle and completed the four kilometre journey in just minutes, but the young Annuxian was feeling more and more uncomfortable about its rapidly shrinking purse and felt it prudent to save credits by walking. Besides, Volot felt almost light-headed from distress, and walking in the wonderful spring sunshine did much to dispel its sense of foreboding. Of course Ambassador Iwar wasn't a fool and had obviously guessed that Volot's intentions in arming a few of the guild's vessels was not purely altruistic. Doing so might also result in considerable profit. Profit which Volot now needed desperately.

Last night, lying restlessly in bed, unable to sleep, Volot had felt as if its life was coming to an abrupt end. The recent arrival of the vermin near the planet Tran had severely affected the share price of the Trader Clan stocks. The Tranians had immediately closed their borders to all other visitors, and they would remain closed for the duration of the discussions with the vermin's spokesman. In addition, the shareholders had surmised that the vermin could possibly cause a huge upheaval to peace in the area, and this would almost certainly bring major and long lasting disruptions to trade between Tran and Annux. The price of Trader Clan shares had plummeted and Volot, Guild Leader of the Trader Clan and a major shareholder in his own right, had lost a small fortune over night.

But being a shrewd business person. Volot knew it wasn't the threat of war which had the other shareholders worried, it was the uncertainty. In fact, although the thought of war filled its mind with dread and made its stomachs roil, Volot was nevertheless quite certain a war would be good for business. Not that such a deplorable event could ever be condoned.

Thankfully this time, despite their deplorable track record, the vermin actually seemed to be serious in their request for asylum. Nearly a complete quarter lunar cycle had passed and the vermin hadn't issued a single ultimatum. There had been no threats, no posturing or displays of military might, not even a single angry communique. They were just sitting quietly, waiting for the Tranians, the worst procrastinators in the entire galaxy, to make up their minds.

But that meant the uncertainty prevailed and the Trader Clan share prices continued to ebb.

But if Iwar had approved the arming of a few Annuxian ships, and more importantly, ordered Volot to place them close to Tran, such a manoeuvre would have had one of two possible effects. One: The vermin would see the Annuxian's arrival as a threat and run away, or Two: The vermin would see the Annuxian's arrival as a threat and retaliate. And then the Annuxians would blow them out of the sky. Either way, the problem with the share prices would be removed. The Trader Clan stock would return to its former value and Volot and the Guild would end up very rich. Very, very rich. But there was another reason Volot wanted the vermin out of the picture, a reason it hoped Iwar would never learn.

Volot arrived home and paused briefly at the enormous house's entrance while the security systems DNA sensors checked its identity and opened the door. A servant, one of the six on staff who Volot could no longer afford, came scurrying up the grand marble hallway, retrieved Volot's outer garment and hung it on the Rolupan bone coat rack, just inside the door.

"A pleasant and fruitful morning I hope, Guild Leader Volot?" inquired the servant in that nasally whine, seemingly adopted by all in the Servant Clan Guild.

"Very, thank you Illmag," Volot answered. "How are the children?"

"All six eggs are comfortable, Guild Leader. The nurse rotated them about an hour ago, adjusted the thermostat slightly and checked the function of the monitoring systems. Everything is in order. Soon you will be a new parent, Guild Leader. The time of their hatching approaches quickly. Cook is already well advanced with the preparations for our celebrations."

Volot smiled and preened its large ears in pleasure.

"Wonderful, I shall visit the hatchery directly, then I will take my afternoon libations in the east library. Please have cook prepare something light." (And cheap Volot hoped.)

Illmag nodded and hurried off to deliver the Guild Leader's orders, leaving Volot to make its way, through the house's massive entertainment area, along the main eastern corridor, past the office and on to the hatchery.

The hatchery itself was at least ten degrees warmer than the ambient temperature of the rest of the house and was strictly controlled. The boffins at the reproduction academy had deduced that an exact temperature of twenty eight degrees during the final twenty nine days of gestation, caused up to an eight percent increase in brain development in pre hatched Annuxian offspring.

The room was kept only slightly illuminated, just enough to make the as yet unborn Annuxian children feel safe and secure. It was small compared to the other rooms in the house, only about five metres square and with a low ceiling, so that Volot had to duck slightly when walking around the room, admiring the beautiful eggs.

Volot's beautiful eggs.

Annuxians were hermaphrodites, neither male nor female and yet both. Volot had not needed to take a partner to produce these six, wonderful little creatures. In fact the thought of such a thing was repulsive. Lesser species had two genders, not Annuxians. Volot was filled with a sense of awe at what was soon to come. Pride and love filled its heart and sheer unbridled joy washed over it at the thought of the wonderful future they would share together. At least they would if the Trader Guild share prices went back up.

Volot was certain it was only a matter of time before the Vermin reverted to their aggressive ways, and when that happened the Guild Leader was going to be in the perfect position to take advantage.

"My financial worries will be over soon, and then nothing will jeopardise my families future ever again," Volot whispered quietly to the six unborn children.

Silently, Volot slipped out of the hatchery and made its way to the office. The Guild Leader sat at the huge old antique desk which dominated the centre of the room and turned on the communicator. Moments later the Guild Leader was speaking to its esteemed colleague on Tran.

"Are we ready to give these Vermin a bit of a nudge my friend?" the Tranian asked.

Volot cursed. "No. That fool Iwar has vetoed my request. I can do nothing unless the Vermin attack first. That is if they attack."

"Well then I guess it's up to me. I'll have to convince the High Council to refuse their application. If that doesn't work, well let's just say I've had a thought or two on ways we might push the Vermin into action."

Chapter 28

SALANG CHAI SAT IN the darkened room, gazing out over the sparkling city of Salin spread out before him. Colopo and her mother had already retired for the evening. Both females were exhausted from the intense review and critique they had been giving Chai's upcoming address to the Tran High Council in two days time. Eight times Chai had read out the desperate words he had written, and eight times the two women had listened patiently, trying to gauge his audience's probable reaction, helping him polish his clumsy words, until they felt his appeal was as close to perfect as possible.

Regardless, Chai now suspected deep in his heart, that his plea would more than likely fail. Everyone he had met since his arrival on Tran had been incredibly polite and friendly towards him, and initially this had led him to believe the Tranian people would be accommodating. But recently he had come to realise their actions were more than likely just a part of their nature. They were polite and courteous to everyone, but of course they were still quite capable of refusing a request if it suited them to do so. They were just incredibly polite and apologetic when they did.

But the uncertainty wasn't what was causing Chai's insomnia. Finally, after days of pushing it to one side, burying himself in his work, and concentrating on the upcoming appeal, Chai's grief at the recent death of his father-in-law, the destruction of his home planet and the annihilation of almost nine billion of his species, was beginning to take its toll. Perhaps it was the added stress brought on by the imminent meeting in just two days time, or perhaps it was the knowledge that the fate of his entire species now rested squarely on his shoulders, but Chai felt decidedly unwell.

He suddenly found himself barely able to breathe. Despite everything he tried, a feeling of complete panic and despair washed over him, leaving him unable to think of what he should do next. He was assailed by a sense of complete uncertainty, even about what he had already done. Had he remembered to tell the Tranian High Council of things he and his people could bring to the planet? Things like the thirty six seed planters and vegetation removers now secured in the holds of their ships. Or for that matter, had he remembered to mention the multitude of maintenance mechanoids and mountains of machinery they had? Or the medical expertise Shan and the other doctors, nurses and associated medical staff might bring to Tran? His mind swirled and churned from one disastrous, imaginary scenario or problem to the next. He sat in a pool of sweat, staring vacantly and unseeingly out over the glistening lights of the nocturnal city as the panic inside of him rose to a crescendo. Eventually, around midnight, he rose from his spot on the floor, crossed to the domicile's tiny kitchen and poured himself a glass of water. He noticed as he lifted the glass down from the overhead cupboard that his hands were shaking, that his heart was pounding and that he felt uncomfortably hot and clammy. He also felt itchy, incredibly itchy. Suddenly his vision began to dim and lose focus, and Chai felt the world tilt and swirl as the floor suddenly rushed up to meet him.

Colopo heard the crash of broken water glass and then a loud thump as Chai collapsed in the kitchen. Quickly she slipped on a robe and rushed out of her room into the main living area. Chai was lying inert and unconscious on the kitchen floor, his squat little body twisted awkwardly, and jammed between the food preparation bench and the sink. There was a pool of water on the floor next to him and bits of shattered glass strewn everywhere. Gingerly, Colopo threaded her way through the minefield of razor sharp shards and placed her fingers on Chai's neck just below his jaw line. She had studied her visitor's physiology and knew that she should be able to feel a pulsating throb in that area which was caused by the beating of Chai's heart. The pulse was distinct and strong. Carefully she extricated her comatose house guest from between the food prep bench and the sink and carried him over to his sleeping mattress. She lay him on his left side, bending his weird knee up and tucking a pillow under it to stop him rolling onto his face. Then she checked to see if he was breathing, placing her trumpet like ear next to his mouth and listening for the rhythmic hiss of his breath. To her unpractised ear, Chai's breathing seemed scratchy and shallow. It was regular, but laboured, and he appeared to be struggling to get enough air into his lungs.

"MUM!" she yelled, "come quickly, Chai has collapsed."

Silpolo stumbled into the room, trying to fight her way out of the fog of deep sleep her daughter had woken her from.

"What's wrong Sweetheart?" she asked, hurrying over to Chai's prostrate form and squatting down beside him.

Colopo shook her head. "I'm not sure. I heard a crash and came out to find him lying in a heap in the kitchen. He must be ill."

For a few moments they discussed what they should do. Silpolo wanted to call a paramedic team, but Colopo thought that would be pointless. Tranian paramedics would have no knowledge of their visitors physiology. At best, all they would be able to do was take a stab in the dark at a diagnosis and treatment, and Tranian medicine might do more harm than good to an alien life form such as Chai.

Colopo jumped to her feet and raced over to where Chai kept his belongings. She rummaged through the small bundle of clothes and the written notes he was compiling, and found his personal communicator. Chai had shown her how it worked a few days ago and now she turned it on, located the symbol which connected the device with Chai's wife, and pressed the button.

"His female is a doctor," Colopo reminded her mother as she waited for the call to be answered. "Perhaps she will know what to do."

Suddenly the device emitted a vertical cone of bright light. Colopo placed the device on the floor, face up and waited until the holographic image of Wawa Shan formed in the air above it. She was fully dressed in her medical suit. Apparently, despite the lateness of the hour, she was still working.

"Oh! Hello," the image said. "You must be the Tranian female translator who is helping Chai. You're Colopo, is that correct?"

Colopo confirmed the doctor's suspicions and quickly went on to explain the reason for her call. But if she had been concerned that Wawa Shan would react badly to her husbands plight, she needn't have worried. Shan was used to dealing with medical emergencies and although it was obvious she was extremely concerned for Chai's safety, she didn't let that interfere with her professionalism.

"So tell me his symptoms," she commanded.

Colopo did just that.

"Does his skin feel hot to touch?"

"Yes"

"Right. Can you open one of his eyes and see if his pupils react to light."

Colopo asked her mother to fetch a portable light source from the cupboard in the kitchen and rolled Chai onto his back. Gently she pulled up the eyelid of his left eye and shone the light into it, watching as she did so to see if the pupil reduced in size to accommodate the increase in light.

"Yes, his eyes react readily to light."

"Good, that's good. Did his eye close again after you released the eyelid."

"Yes."

"Good." Shan went on to ask Colopo to perform a number of other, simple tests in an attempt to ascertain what exactly was causing Chai's condition. He appeared to have been accidentally poisoned. But the most likely scenario was that he had succumbed to one of Tran's endemic diseases. They would have to get him back to the ship as quickly as possible so that Shan could treat him.

Then Silpolo noticed something.

"His face is swollen and puffy around his eyes and lips," she told her daughter.

Colopo translated her mother's comments for Shan.

"Oh!......Can you check his skin? Lift up his shirt and see if there are any red spots or welts," begged Shan.

"Yes, his chest and stomach is covered with red spots and large, swollen red patches on his skin."

Shan's avatar nodded knowingly. "He's having an allergic reaction to something. Has he eaten anything different today? Something he hasn't eaten before?"

Colopo hadn't heard the word 'allergic' before but guessed it's meaning. Chai's body didn't recognise something he had eaten earlier and was reacting badly to it.

"Yes, tonight we had some Silick. It is a root vegetable. It is this which is making Chai sick, yes?"

Shan nodded. "Hold on. I'll check the manifest to see if any of this Silick stuff has been sent to us with the shipments you've sent to us."

Shan's image stepped away for a few seconds and disappeared from the room. Moments later she reappeared with some sort of digital screen in her hand.

She nodded. "Yes. Some Silick came through with the food shipment which arrived today. I'll get some from the cargo hold and run some tests. I should be able to come up with an antidote for the toxin within a few hours."

"Please hurry friend Shan," Colopo implored, "Chai is very ill. He might not last a few hours."

Colopo could tell Shan was fighting to keep her emotions in check. She was obviously distraught at the thought of her husband's life being in peril and was trying desperately to keep herself together. Shan signed off, telling Colopo she would contact her as soon as she had an answer.

Chapter 29

FOR THE NEXT HALF HOUR Colopo and her mother watched over their guest, helplessly watching his condition slowly deteriorate, and distressingly, finding themselves unable to do anything to help. Colopo explained the details of her conversation with Shan, most of which her mother had guessed anyway.

"Chai is allergic to Silick?" she asked. "Like Dillip is to Fragel weed."

The younger female looked questioningly at her mother. "Who's Dillip?" she asked.

Her mother rolled her eyes. "Dillip! You know Dillip sweetheart, Talopan's son! He and his mum live in apartment 763, two floors down." She went on to describe the young boy and his parent. Dillip was studying intergalactic navigation at the very same university Colopo worked at. He was a tall, lanky boy who always wore a black tunic and a silver crest plate on his forehead. He had one of those new, two wheeled PTVs with the extra wide wheels and a solar recharging power plant that never needed replacing. Or at least that's what the manufacturer claimed.

"His mum works at the Annuxian Embassy. She's a bit big, like me, but a lovely woman."

Colopo recognised who Silpolo was talking about. Yes, she did know both mother and son, but she had been unaware of their names.

Now Chai's skin seemed even hotter to her touch, so Colopo rose and went to the kitchen. She took out a clean hand towel from the drawer under the sink and dampened it under the cold water tap. She wrung it out and brought it back to Chai, placing it on his forehead. Amazingly his skin felt even hotter now than it had just seconds before. She desperately hoped the cool towel might help to bring his temperature down.

But a few moments later Chai suddenly opened his eyes and began to gasp for breath. His allergic reaction to the Silick was getting worse. The swelling in his throat was closing off his oesophagus and he was suffocating. Silpolo suddenly leapt to her feet and bolted out of the apartment.

"I'll be back in a moment sweetheart," she called to her daughter. "I have an idea."

Colopo heard her mother's footsteps as she thundered down the steps to the seventh floor. Then she heard loud banging on one of the apartment doors and her mother's voice calling urgently and loudly. There was silence for a few seconds and then came the sound of a door opening and the hushed tones of people talking hastily late at night. Seconds later Silpolo burst through the door back into to her own domicile. Hard on her heels was a short, dumpy Tranian female dressed in a floral nightdress and a slender male youth wearing black pyjamas. The boy was carrying a large, evil looking, intravenous injector. He rushed into the room but pulled up short when he saw Chai lying on the floor gasping for breath. Though he had seen images of an Annuxian before, Chai was the first alien he had ever seen close up. Even so, Dillip considered his next move for only a nanosecond. Then he rushed to the visitor's assistance. Quickly he began to prepare the injection.

"But..." Colopo began to protest and then fell quiet. Her mother's plan was obvious, Dillip was going to inject Chai with the medicine he used when he had a reaction to Fragel Weed. Colopo had a vague recollection of reading somewhere that all allergic reactions, regardless of what caused them, were treated the same way. Chai had to be given a massive dose of antihistamine and adrenaline. They had to keep him alive until the medicine had worked sufficiently to keep him out of danger. But to treat an alien life form with a drug developed for an entirely different species was madness. More than likely the Tranian antihistamine would kill him.

But then what choice did they have? Chai was fighting for his life and it seemed unlikely his female was going to get back to them with a cure in time. They had to do something, and they had to do it now.

Dillip rolled Chai over onto his stomach, lifted up the hem of his tunic and stabbed the intravenous injector into the man's right buttock. Then he rolled Chai back onto his side, sat back on his haunches and together with the three females, waited hopefully for the medicine to weave it's magic.

Chapter 30

THE NEXT MORNING, DR Wawa Shan sent an edict to all the medical officers on the seventeen ships orbiting the planet Tran, that all Silick root crop was to be disposed of immediately. It was extremely poisonous to non Tranian life forms, she told them. In fact, she said, it had nearly killed her husband, Salang Chai. He had survived, but according to the translator woman, it had been touch and go for a while. Amazingly the Tranian antihistamine they'd given him had had no adverse side effects and had begun to work almost immediately. His breathing had returned to normal within just a few minutes and the swelling and itching had also quickly abated. Now Chai was up and about once more and working hard in preparation for the next day's crucially important meeting.

Within hours every gram of Silick had been ejected out through the ship's garbage disposal system. Every gram that is, save for the half kilo of Silick Wawa Shan had hidden in her medical laboratory.

Shan told herself that she was keeping the Silick so she could conduct further medical tests and hopefully develop an antidote. But deep in the back of her mind there was a much more sinister plan hatching. A plan, which at that moment, Shan would not allow herself to even admit she was considering.

Her father was dead, murdered by the very man who was supposed to be protecting him and the other passengers and crew aboard the 'War Hawk'. It was obvious to everyone on the ship, that the so called accident in cargo bay twelve hadn't been an accident at all.

Assistant Maintenance Engineer Skillen Chun had run a diagnostic check on the anchoring system holding the cargo containers in place and found they should have operated perfectly. The fact that they didn't, could only mean one thing. The power to the magnetic locks had been deliberately turned off. Of course anyone on board could have done such a thing, but only Vethil had the authority to wipe the computer records which would have shown such a heinous act had been committed. In Skillen Chun's opinion the computer records had definitely been wiped.

Vethil was guilty of murder, of that Shan had no doubt, but there was no way of proving it. Also, as Vethil himself was at that moment the highest ranking authority on board, the point was probably moot anyway. Were Shan to take Vethil to task, he would no doubt just discount any accusations against him as mutiny, and ultimately that would result in her own death.

But Shan couldn't just let the bastard get away with murder. The fact that the victim had been her much loved and admired father made it doubly impossible. Something had to be done. Carefully she began to prepare a concoction of Silick extract.

Wearing her isolation suit to protect herself from the toxic vegetable, she placed 500 grams of finely chopped Silick pulp and 20 millilitres of distilled water into a centrifuge and set it for 15 minutes at 10,000 rpm. The resulting liquid was then placed into a molecular separator which extracted the toxins. These toxins, enough to kill a dozen people, were combined with a single dose of the vaccines Shan had developed to combat all Tranian diseases she'd felt might be harmful to the refugees. She used this highly toxic concoction to charge one of the hypoderms, which she then marked with a blue stripe. She didn't want to accidentally give it to the wrong person.

Next she made a concoction of mild laxatives and other ingredients which, though relatively harmless, would cause stomach cramps and nausea. This she added, together with the vaccines, to another three of the hypoderms. Her plan was to administer the vaccines to all the conscious members of the crew in preparation for their eventual trip to the planet's surface. Vethil would get the Silick enriched dose, three others would get the anti-viral drugs plus the stuff which would make them ill but not kill them. The rest would get just the anti-viral. Besides Vethil, three others would also become ill following their injections, and this would make the Admiral's death look like he was just unlucky. It would appear to everyone else like he'd unfortunately had a particularly violent reaction to the vaccine, something which was both unforeseeable and unavoidable.

Shan placed the ten hypoderms on a stainless Nelamine tray and covered them with a clean white cloth in preparation for the crews' inoculation in two days time.

Chapter 31

FOR TWO DAYS THE NANOBOTS had worked ceaselessly preparing Dr Wawa Ni's corpse. Of course they could not bring the great man back to life, that was impossible even when working at a molecular level, but they could repair the damage done to his lifeless body by the massive, crushing impact of the runaway storage container. That way, even in death, he could at least appear as he had when he was alive.

The doctor's corpse had been placed in a tank filled with an embalming fluid which preserved his body while the tiny robots worked. Deep inside the tissue and bone of his body, they slowly rebuilt his skeleton, repositioning each tiny fragment of crushed bone in its proper place and then stitching them together with a calcium filament just one atom in diameter. Gradually Ni's face and body once again began to resemble the man he had been in life. The extensive soft tissue damage, at least that damage which could be seen, was repaired by removing any mutilated, sub dermal, flesh and then replacing it with a polyester, semi liquid filler of the correct volume which was then shaped as required. Finally, his cuts and abrasions were covered up as successfully as possible with thick make-up. There wasn't sufficient time or resources to repair his whole body, but the nanobots did what they could in the limited time available, and when the day of Dr Ni's funeral arrived there was no visible evidence of the violent way in which he had died. The corpse lying in his coffin looked for all the world as if Ni were simply sleeping.

The service was held in the mess hall on board 'War Hawk' and was attended by nearly one hundred and fifty people, though most of them were in reality, only present thanks to the mess hall's powerful and elaborate holographic projecting system. Of the one hundred and forty seven mourners, only eight were actual flesh and blood, the others were merely avatars, holograms projected directly into the mess hall after being relayed from each ship in the fleet. Even so it was a huge mark of respect and an illustration of the esteem in which Dr Ni had been held, that everyone who could attend did so. Had it been possible to physically transfer people between ships, Shan had no doubt that most of the people attending would have come in person.

The mourners filed in just before lunch and one by one presented themselves to the great man's grieving daughter. Shan sat on one of the mess hall's hard, moulded plastic chairs, next to her father's coffin. The highly polished, silver grey casket had been positioned on a gurney, directly in front of one of the huge windows overlooking the beautiful planet Tran. Stoically, Shan accepted the condolences and heartfelt sympathy of the procession, but refused to give Vethil the satisfaction of seeing how distressed she really was. Later Admiral Vethil gave a short speech, telling the people assembled there, how much Dr Ni's friendship, advice and medical expertise would be missed. Shan herself delivered a heart rending eulogy and then stepped forward and placed her personal communicator on the floor in front of the coffin. She pressed a button on the control panel, and seconds later Salang Chai's 3D image rose up to greet them.

"Over the past two years we have lost nearly nine billion of our brothers and sisters. So I suppose it's a bit incongruous that we even bother to gather here today to celebrate the passing of yet another," Chai's image told the congregation. "But Doctor Wawa Ni could never be considered just another victim. For me, his greatness transcended that of all but a select few, and it would be a crime not to mark his passing without saying a few words."

"The day I met Dr Ni for the first time, was the same day I met another great man. His name was Swinca, and he was in the employ of the good doctor as a valet. Swinca was a returned serviceman, a soldier, like many of us here today. Swinca was a man of just twenty nine years, who had fought in the first Annuxian battle. The one we started. The one the government didn't tell us about, until people like Swinca and Dr Ni began making waves. Swinca had been grievously injured during the conflict. In fact his injuries were so severe he had not been expected to survive. But then they brought him to Dr Ni. The doctor worked tirelessly in the operating theatre for over twenty three hours, desperately trying to keep Swinca alive. Eventually, through skill and perseverance, Ni managed to stabilise his patient's condition, and over the next thirty six days, slowly brought Swinca back from the brink. Doctor Ni replaced Swinca's heart with a fusion powered prosthetic device, his left leg and his right eye were similarly replaced, plus Ni conducted numerous other life saving medical procedures. So how did Swinca, a lowly foot soldier, manage to pay the tens of thousands of credits this medical care should have cost him? The answer is; he didn't. Doctor Wawa Ni waived his own fee and picked up the tab for the rest of Swinca's care himself. That was the type of man Doctor Wawa Ni was. Despite his vehement opposition to the military, Doctor Ni had always been ready to offer assistance to any one who needed it."

"He has been an inspiration to me. He has taught me that even when you vehemently disagree with someone's religious beliefs, philosophy or political ideology, you must always treat them with respect and be prepared to put your prejudices behind you. In the future I shall aspire to do my utmost to emulate Dr Ni's actions and follow the path of tolerance and understanding just as he did."

Chai then proposed a toast to the good doctor and after everyone had raised their glasses, Shan stepped forward once more and retrieved her communicator.

She crossed over to the window overlooking the planet below and sadly watched as the mechanoids wheeled away her father's remains. Minutes later his coffin was placed in the airlock of cargo bay nine and sent on its first and final voyage towards the huge flaming orb of Tran's sun.

Chapter 32

DILLIP, SON OF TALOPAN and student of intergalactic navigation, hurtled down the hallway, his long, skinny legs striding out like an Annuxian land crane. Of course, running in the hallowed corridors of Salin University was prohibited, but youthful exuberance was sometimes impossible to contain, and as such, transgressions of that nature were both frequent and just as frequently ignored.

"Halinop, Halinop," Dillip called as he hurried towards the elevator. The literal translation of his words being "I am urgent, I am urgent," but which in turn really meant "I'm in a hurry, get out of the way."

He skidded to a halt just outside the elevator and pressed the call button. Seconds later it arrived at his floor. He squeezed himself into the already packed cabin and pressed the button for the ground floor. The elevator dropped rapidly to the next floor, which was the eighth. A few passengers alighted, a similar number got on, and the box plummeted downward once more, stopping at each of the next seven floors during its descent. Eventually Dillip reached his destination and scrambled through the door out into the marble and glass foyer of the university's 'Education of Navigation' building. He hurried outside, raced to where he'd parked his Personal Transportation Vehicle, keyed in his pre-set identification number, climbed aboard and headed for home.

Dillip had owned the PTV for just thirty four days. It was blue, had a large carry box between the seat and the control handles which was large enough to hold his text discs and an electronic writing tablet. Plus it had extra wide wheels for improved traction. Also, since just its second day of ownership, Dillip's PTV had had its speed governor disabled. Which was, unsurprisingly, the most common modification (and the most illegal) done to PTVs owned by teenagers all over Tran. Now, instead of being limited to just 30 kilometres per hour, Dillip's bike could quite easily reach twice that speed. This transgression happened just as frequently as running in the halls at the university, but it was never ignored, at least not by the cops. So Dillip kept a sharp eye out for any Law Enforcers lurking on the roads between the university and his home. Thankfully there were none.

He stored his bike in the building's automatic parking station and took the elevator to the ninth floor. Seconds later he was knocking urgently on the door of Colopo and Silpolo's apartment. The younger woman answered almost immediately.

"I've discovered an alternative planet for Chai and his people to settle on," he explained excitedly.

Colopo invited him in. Chai was sitting on the floor, studying for tomorrows meeting, with reams of paper strewn across the floor in front of him. Dillip wasn't sure, but to his inexperienced eyes, even though he still exhibited some slight swelling around his mouth, the hairy little alien looked a lot healthier than the previous night when he'd seen him. The man stood, stepped closer to Dillip and crossed his arms in front of his chest in greeting in the approved manner.

"Health and peace may follow you, Dillip," the alien greeted him in perfect but heavily accented Tranian.

"It may you also," replied the student.

Dillip turned to Colopo and asked that he might use her vidi-screen to show them what he'd found. Colopo nodded, turned towards the large window overlooking the city and placed the palm of her left hand on the glass up near the top left hand corner. Suddenly the window turned black and a series of characters from the Tranian alphabet began to scroll across the screen. Dillip moved forward and began to manipulate the letters and numbers by placing his fingertips on each icon and moving them to another position on the screen. As he worked, he explained what he was doing. Colopo translated so that Chai could follow his reasoning.

"Today in school we learnt how a navigator can locate an L1 class planet, that's one capable of supporting life such as ours, by accessing earlier travel logs and cross-referencing them with desirable planetary features. For example, I did a search of planets with a mass less than 6 x10^{24} kg which have been visited by Tranian expeditionary forces over the last fifty years. I came up with over ten thousand possibilities."

He swiped the screen from left to right and a list of just eleven planets appeared on the screen.

"These are the ones from that list which have a suitable abundance of fresh water. Then I modified my search by atmospheric considerations."

Seven of the eleven disappeared.

"Finally I discounted any planet which already had sentient life forms."

Only one name remained. Colopo translated the hieroglyphics into something Chai could understand,

"Mogo 3. Never heard of it." said Colopo.

"It's the third planet in the system," he said, bringing up a graphic showing a beautiful blue/green planet revolving slowly in dark space. "It's 149,600,000 kilometres from the star at the system's centre. The planet is 12,756 kilometres in diameter, with a mass of 5.97237 x 10^{24} kilograms. That's about 3% heavier than Tran. Most importantly, around seventy percent of the planet's surface is covered by water, and although most of it is heavily laced with sodium chloride, there is also ample fresh water. Dry land has an area of around 149,000,000 square kilometres, which is about thirty percent of the planet's surface."

"That sounds perfect," said Chai. "And there's no pre-existing sentient life forms?"

"No," Dillip answered, guessing the reason for Chai's concern. "There is an abundance of both plant and animal life however, but even the most advanced animal is a very primitive primate. It has no language, hasn't developed even simple tools or fire, and still lives by scavenging for fruit in the trees. I see no reason why the Annuxians would have erected a force field around this planet."

The trio discussed Mogo 3's suitability for the next two hours. Dillip didn't have answers to all of Chai's questions but what he didn't know, he quickly discovered by searching on Colopo's computer. It all sounded wonderful.

"There is something which worries me," exclaimed Chai. "The planet is called Mogo 3, yes? Well if I understand correctly, a Mogo is one of those deadly predators, like the one which attacked that young boy near the beach the other day. So why did the Captain of the ship who discovered the planet, decide to name it after a dangerous animal? Also, if it's such a wonderful planet, why hasn't someone else colonised it already?"

Neither Dillip nor Colopo could come up with a definitive answer immediately, but eventually they discovered Mogo 3's one devastating weakness. Colopo noticed it first.

"Damn. The atmosphere has almost a one percent concentration of Wrillin gas."

"And that's poisonous?" asked Chai.

"No, not to living animals. In fact it's harmless to all organic creatures, but it's highly corrosive to the alloy they make vortex ships out of."

"Shit!" cursed Chai. "We call it Argon. At a one percent concentration it would completely destroy the entire fleet in a matter of days. We'd be stuck on the planet, unable to get off again."

Both Dillip and Colopo agreed. But the destruction of the ships wasn't the only problem. The Argon gas would also make the possibility of settling on Mogo 3 extremely difficult, if not impossible. Dillip pointed out, that at one percent concentration, the ships' integrity would be compromised within a matter of hours. Once the hulls of the ships had been breached, the gas would be attacking the ship from both inside and out. That meant they'd no longer have the luxury of bringing people out of stasis progressively. Within a matter of days everyone on board would have to be evacuated, including the passengers in stasis. Within a month not a trace of Nelamine alloy would be left. There'd be no machinery or equipment, no building materials, not even basic tools. Everything would have corroded away to nothing and the settlers would be left to fend for themselves with nothing more than their bare hands and whatever tool they could fashion out of stuff they found on the planet. The chances of them surviving such an event were slim at best. Devastatingly, Mogo 3 had to be discounted as a possible new home.

Chapter 33

"HOW IS THE ALIEN NOW?"

"He is recovering from his allergic reaction to Silick at my home as we speak, honoured councillor. I am confident Salang Chai will be fully recovered and able to present his case before the tribunal during our meeting tomorrow morning," Colopo stammered in reply, nervously picking at a loose thread from the side hem of her silver tunic as she did so.

"Good. So, we are now ready to receive your interim report translator, please proceed if you would be so kind,"said High Councillor Fillipon, the tall, broad, elderly female who had taken it upon herself to lead the High Council tribunal.

Colopo took a deep breath and tried to calm herself, not an easy thing to do when addressing members of the Tranian High Council, and especially so when within the very hallowed precinct of Salin's Government offices. The meeting room she now found herself was in part of one of the oldest buildings on the entire planet. It was literally dozens of centuries old. The offices were near the centre of Salin, part of the ancient city, which for the past eight hundred years had been buried deep underground. Colopo now found herself many metres below the more functional structures which currently made up the modern city of Salin. The room had been constructed of opaque limestone. It was at least one hundred and fifty metres square, with a polished marble floor and a lofty, ornate, black granite ceiling supported by twenty four massive gold plated pillars, each one representing the supporting hand of one of the twenty four ancestral mothers of federated Tran.

The eight High Councillors sat patiently, a metre above her, seated in a row behind a massive white marble altar, the front of which had been decorated with images in gold leaf and red and blue enamel of Tran's history. Or at least they depicted the events as they had been interpreted centuries ago, by the twenty four ancients. Every student of history knew the foremothers had seldom reached consensus on any subject, let alone remembered an occurrence in exactly the same way as her sister. Tranian history, as with almost every civilisations' history, was a mixture of fact, conjecture and utter make believe.

But accurate or not, the mythology surrounding the ancient building was palpable and Colopo was understandably awestruck at finding herself addressing such a distinguished group in such auspicious surroundings. Squirming uncomfortably, she cleared her throat, briefly crossed her long graceful arms across her chest in greeting and began her report.

"I will preface my comments by stating that I have grown to consider the alien known as Salang Chai as my friend. Despite what we have been led to believe about the aliens, I have found Chai to be honest, genuine, gentle and with the exception of one particular incident, which I will elaborate on later, in no way aggressive. He is always ready and willing to do his share of any task, he is polite to everyone he meets, and is industrious and dedicated in everything he undertakes."

Colopo paused and helped herself to a sip of water from the goblet on the bench in front of her before continuing.

"But I wonder if all of Salang Chai's species are so pleasant and accommodating? In truth, to me the alien's very existence is an enigma. From the little I understand of evolutionary science, the whole species should have died out in infancy."

"Please elaborate," pleaded Lead High Counsellor Fillipon

"Well, they are quite small in stature, yet unlike other bipedal primates, they are neither agile nor quick. In fact Salang Chai, who I believe is considered physically strong and fit by others of his kind, has great difficulty in matching even my elderly mother in either stamina or speed. His eyes are weak, his hearing poor and his skin is so fragile, even a blade of grass brushing against an unprotected arm or leg might to draw blood. He possesses neither tooth nor claw to protect himself from predators and...well I'm sure you understand my meaning honoured Councillors, when I say the aliens are extremely ill suited to natural life in general. How they managed to survive as a species for so long is a miracle."

"And yet here they are, a species which we know once numbered in their billions. How do you explain that?" asked Councillor Balopop, the youngest and only male member of the eight adjudicators.

Colopo nodded, considered her answer carefully and then continued.

"I believe their success is due to two things. Firstly, they have an almost continuous breeding cycle. Females who have achieved maturity can get pregnant at any time of the year. Not only that, but they resume ovulation almost as soon as they have given birth. Copulation occurs almost continuously during adulthood, frequently just for enjoyment, and not necessarily for the purposes of propagation. But even so pregnancy is frequently the result of such encounters. Hence, they are prolific breeders. My postulations are substantiated by their obvious rapid growth in numbers.

"And your second hypothesis."

"I firmly believe their success as a species is also, if not mainly, due to their almost insatiable lust for violence and aggression. I imagine that even during their evolutionary infancy, their intellect allowed them to fashion weapons and tools with which they could fight off their predators and defeat their enemies."

"Which I assume, is why you claim to be unsure if all of your guest's people are as pleasant and accommodating as this Salang Chai creature," suggested Balopop

"Exactly. Their very success as a species relies almost totally on their ability to kill those other creatures, and even members of their own people, who might otherwise threaten them. This genetic predisposition towards aggression and violence has been reinforced with each successive generation, until only the strongest, most aggressive and most ruthless remain."

"So we take it then, that regardless of your obvious affection for the alien known as Salang Chai, your recommendation is to refuse the alien's request?" asked Fillipon.

Colopo stepped forward hurriedly and looked up at the eight counsellors in horror.

"No, certainly not," she implored. "I firmly believe the aliens have turned a corner in their evolution. Salang Chai has told me how his people were misled about the circumstances leading up to the attack on their planet by the Annuxians. Very few people were aware at the time, that it was the aliens themselves who launched the initial, unprovoked attack against a previously peaceful species. According to Chai, when the truth came out, almost the entire planet rose up in protest against the military rulers of the day. They were incensed at their stupidity and found their actions deplorable."

As she spoke she became more and more agitated and began to pace back and forth in front of the counsellors, waving her arms demonstratively to illustrate a point whenever she felt the need.

"I have studied their history and it seems to me that almost every aggressive incident was preceded by a period of manipulation of the general public, by a small but powerful and influential group who wished to further their own agenda by starting the conflict. Salang

Chai now firmly believes that the vast majority of his people wish for nothing more than to live in peace and tranquillity and never go to war ever again. With our guidance, I believe they can achieve that goal."

"Well, I guess that is yet to be seen," said Councillor Balopop. "Personally I think the sooner we send these creatures away the better."

Chapter 34

INITIALLY CHAI HAD been impatient and couldn't understand why the Tran High Council were taking so long to convene the all important tribunal. Now that the day had finally arrived however, he couldn't help wishing he had a little more time to prepare, perhaps just a few more hours to polish his all important speech. But it was not to be.

When Colopo and her mother rose shortly after sunrise, they found Chai already up. He had showered, breakfasted and dressed himself in the elegant silver tunic he had been presented with by Colopo and her mother especially for the occasion. He was pacing the floor of the tiny apartment, rehearsing his speech in a mumbling monotone that only he could understand. Clearly he was deeply concerned about the upcoming ordeal.

An hour later, after Colopo and her mother had washed, dressed and attended to their own dietary requirements, the three squeezed themselves into Colopo's Personal Transportation Vehicle and headed for the Salin Government Offices. As they drove, Colopo explained that the meeting would be presented in four distinct sections. Firstly Colopo, on behalf of Chai and the other alien refugees, would make a formal request that they be granted asylum. Tradition dictated that this be done in the formal form of the Tranian language, which meant it was imperative the request be presented by someone who spoke the correct dialect. Once this submission had been tabled, Chai would be asked to present his case on behalf of his people. Comments from other interested parties would be called for, and then Chai would be questioned at length about his request. The final decision on whether the Tranians would grant the aliens refuge or not, would not occur for another three or possibly four days. Colopo went on to explain that she would act as principal interpreter, but that a further four, young men and women, all students of hers from her university, would be on hand to assist if needed.

The trio finally made it to the offices. Colopo parked the vehicle and they crossed to the elevator and travelled down to sub level 4.

Chai was immediately struck by the grandeur and opulence of the historic chambers. The massive gold pillars, towering upwards to the ornate, cathedral type ceiling were most impressive. The walls were adorned with paintings, each one depicting the face of an important person from Tran's history or a defining event from the past. In the centre of the huge entrance was an ancient sculpture, in dazzlingly white marble, of one of the massive winged beasts which had once plied the skies of Tran. Now, Colopo told him, the huge avian was extinct. Although no one was sure, it was widely believed to have been wiped out by a deadly virus almost two thousand years ago.

They passed through the main foyer and entered the offices of the tribunal to find the auditorium packed to the rafters with Tranians eager to see the strange, hairy little creature from across the galaxy. Of course everyone on the planet knew of the refugee's plight. Their story had been beamed out over the news services almost constantly since their arrival. In fact, it had headlined most of the media's daily reports. The refugee's story only being usurped yesterday, with the news of a discovery of huge Nelamine ore deposits on an asteroid in the Nastalin quadrant. Now everyone wanted to catch a glimpse of one of the weird little aliens who begged to share their home. Many rose from their seats when Chai,

Colopo and her mother entered the room and crossed their arms over their chests in greeting. Chai took this as a good sign.

Then his blood ran cold and a feeling of nausea washed over him. Towards the front of the courtroom, to the right of the centre walkway, was a group of other off-worlders. They were tall, bipedal but with four, tentacle like arms. They were covered in a soft golden fur, short around their triangular shaped torsos, but longer and denser on their faces, heads and powerful looking legs. They had broad square shoulders tapering to an extremely narrow waist, large heads with upright ears and small, golden, almond shaped eyes which seemed to bore into Chai's very soul. They were Annuxians.

Silpolo took a seat at the rear of the auditorium and Colopo led Chai to the front where they sat together at a long rectangular table facing the eight councillors.

High Councillor Fillipon rose, crossed her arms across her chest in greeting and called the amassed audience to order. Gradually the general hub bub died down, and then the woman addressed the court.

Although Chai couldn't begin to understand the High Councillor's formal style of speech, it was obvious she was requesting Colopo to begin her address. As the translator rose and stepped forward, one of her students slipped into her place next to Chai and haltingly began to translate Colopo's speech into Chai's own language.

Her address was long winded and, at least to Chai's ears, terribly convoluted and wordy. She told the assembly of the trials and tribulations of her ancestors, of how her great, great, great grandmother had travelled from the other side of the ocean to settle in the city of Salin. She told of the way her ancestor had gained the trust of the city's inhabitants and eventually came to serve the people of the city as a Law Enforcer. Her grandmother too served in this way, Colopo told them, as did her mother, here today in support of the alien's appeal.

Then she spoke of Tranian history, delicately reminding everyone present that it had not been that long ago, that they themselves had stood at the crossroads of enlightenment. They had seen the error of their ways and embraced a life of peaceful harmony. Now the aliens had come to a similar stage in their development. They too had had an epiphany. They too were now ready to live a peaceful and harmonious existence.

Next she spoke of the many creatures who had once roamed the Tranian landscape but were now extinct. Some, she reminded the tribunal, had been hunted to extinction by their own ancestors, while others had simply died out from natural causes. Such events were a tragedy and the entire universe was poorer for their passing Colopo reminded them.

Finally, she spoke of the peaceful and harmonious life the people of Tran now enjoyed.

"This is the type of life the visitors from across the galaxy seek. We are in a position to afford them such a life. Please find it in your hearts to grant them refuge." Colopo concluded. Then she returned to her seat next to Chai.

Chai guessed Colopo's speech had lasted almost an hour. Now it was his turn. High Councillor Fillipon again rose and called Chai forward. With his heart in his throat he dragged himself unsteadily to his feet and walked to the front of the auditorium. In clumsy, heavily accented Tranian, he thanked the tribunal for granting him the privilege of speaking with them and then reverted to his own language and launched into his address. Colopo translated his words.

"People of Tran, I stand before you as one of the last remaining members of a once prosperous and vibrant people. A people who now find themselves on the very brink of extinction."

"Our rapid and possibly fatal demise is purely and wholly of our own doing. We have stupidly waged war against every race and species we have encountered, even our own. At every opportunity, we have constantly tried to assert our will upon others. We have murdered many and enslaved many more. We have been thoughtless in our actions, selfish in our greed, uncaring and aggressive in almost every undertaking. Now, unless you help us, we have foolishly condemned ourselves to a bleak if not hopeless future. Or rather should I say, perhaps no future at all. We have nowhere else to go, honoured Councillors. If you do not offer us sanctuary, we will surely perish."

Chai leaned forward and placed the palms of his hands on the table in front of him. He looked pale and weary, both from his recent illness and from the mammoth effort he had been putting into the preparation of his speech. He knew with stomach churning certainty that whatever he said over the next few minutes would undoubtedly mean the difference between life and death for the seventeen thousand and sixty people aboard the fleet orbiting the planet.

"Honoured Councillors," he continued, "you may find it strange that I begin my desperate appeal to you by admitting such heinous acts. But my people have come to realise that, if we are not able to admit to the mistakes of the past, we will never be able to move forward into the future. I could attempt to deny our deplorable history, or try to explain away our actions by telling you we have been misled. That, for example, during our recent conflict with the Annuxians, certain members of our military elite lied to us and tricked us into taking steps we would not have normally taken. But you have studied our history and you know that our war with the Annuxians was not an isolated incident. Our history is peppered with such shameful events, and to try to gloss over them would be an insult to your intelligence and an affront on the sanctity of this tribunal."

"Our only hope therefore, is to throw ourselves on your mercy, assure you that we have finally seen the error of our ways and pray that you might take pity on us and allow us to settle on your beautiful planet, if not permanently, then at least until we can find a new home world of our own."

Changing tack, he stood and adopted a less consolatory attitude. He understood that the Tranians would not make a decision based purely on what his own people required. Now he needed to tell them what the refugees would bring to the deal.

"Among the seventeen thousand people currently in stasis aboard the crafts orbiting your planet, are doctors, scientists, engineers, farmers, and experts in the fields of animal husbandry. There are also our most famous artists, painters, sculptors, writers, dancers and musicians. All people, who will contribute greatly to your society. To further ensure we will not be drain on your valuable resources, we also bring a great deal of machinery and equipment. We have land clearing machinery, planters and harvesters, and mechanised maintenance drones to maintain them. We even have prefabricated buildings to live in. In fact much more than we need to be merely self sufficient and independent. If allowed to settle, we fully intend to be productive members of Tranian society. In addition, we also bring the seventeen Galaxy class ships currently orbiting your planet. These we will make available to you whenever you need them, for transporting people or freight to and from anywhere in the universe.

We are not asking the people of Tran for charity, only for a place to live in peace and safety."

He stepped around to the front of the table, took a few paces closer to the eight High Councillors and looked up at them, regarding each one in turn, in what he hoped they would recognise as a look of complete sincerity.

"Finally honoured women and men of the tribunal, I pledge that my people will at all times do their utmost to integrate ourselves seamlessly into your society. We wish to become part of the Tranian world, not set ourselves apart from it. We promise to uphold your laws, respect your customs and follow your guidance. But most of all we promise to renounce the foolish ways of our past and live alongside you in peace and harmony. With your help we will be able to enter our next phase of evolution. Please give us that chance. Without your help we are surely doomed."

In reply Councillor Balopop gave a loud snort of derision.

Chapter 35

TO CHAI'S SURPRISE and delight the other members of the tribunal showed a great deal of displeasure at Balopop's outburst, as did a great many of the public. It appeared Chai had the majority of the board onside already. Or maybe they were just being polite. That was something he had quickly learnt during his visit to the planet. The Tranians were all so incredibly polite.

High Councillor Fillipon once again called the assembly to order, and when she had achieved silence, requested members of the public to make submissions in support of or opposition to the motion.

The first person to step forward was Silpolo. For the first time since her retirement, she wore her Law Enforcer's bandoleer over her silver and gold uniform. She carried herself with dignity and pride as she made her way forward. Law Enforcers were obviously held in high esteem in Tranian culture, for many of the audience rose from their seats as a mark of respect for the position formerly held by Colopo's mother.

She crossed to the front of the auditorium and stood at attention before the eight councillors. She saluted them, crossing her arms across her chest and then thrusting them out and up before dropping them to her sides. She spoke in a clear and powerful voice, telling the tribunal how her new friend, Salang Chai, had been a most pleasant, helpful and polite house guest. She told them of his efforts to learn their language, his willingness to embrace their customs and his interest in Tranian history. Not once during the past eight days, she told them, had she had any reason for concern. If they were all like Chai, she said, then she had no hesitation in recommending that the tribunal accept the alien's request.

Dillip, the young man who had almost certainly saved Chai's life two nights ago, then stepped forward. For some reason Dillip had decided he too should offer his support. Colopo whispered to Chai that she guessed Dillip felt some sort of kinship with him because they'd both shared a common ailment. Whatever the reason, Chai was grateful for his efforts.

Dillip greeted the tribunal and then began his carefully prepared speech. Although he didn't have to, like Colopo, he delivered his address in formal Tranian. According to Colopo, he did an admirable job of mastering the difficult dialect and this no doubt added weight to his comments.

He explained that he didn't know the alien well, but had found him to be a most charming and amiable person. Chai had told young Dillip a little of his life on his home planet, he explained, and based on that account, felt sure the alien's culture would integrate well with that on Tran.

Next a female Tranian approached the tribunal. She was a portly woman and, quite short for a Tranian, who moved slowly to the front of the room, nervously looking around at the others as she made her way forward. She looked vaguely familiar and as she passed Chai, he noticed she was holding the hand of a small boy. The boy's left leg was heavily bandaged and he hobbled slowly by, limping painfully. The woman stopped before the councillors, lifted the tiny child into her arms and held him up for everyone to see. Then she turned and placed the boy in Chai's arms.

"This man," she began, her voice trembling with fear and emotion at the enormity of the situation she found herself in, "this man who some call vermin, saved my child's life. With no assistance from anyone else, and completely unarmed, this wonderful, courageous man, fought off a large Mogo. The animal attacked my little boy, had him in his jaws. My boy was as good as dead. Then, with no regard for his own safety, the alien Salang Chai threw himself upon the beast and killed it. My son owes this man his life. I owe him my life as well."

The woman threw her arms around Chai's shoulders and hugged him until he nearly passed out from lack of air, then she lifted her precious child from his lap and strode out.

Chai felt quite moved by the woman's emotional declaration, and very happy she had made the trip to the tribunal to give him her support. He felt things were going exceedingly well so far. Except for councillor Balopop, everyone seem to be on his side.

Then one of the Annuxian's rose and made his way forward.

Chapter 36

AS WAWA SHUN HAD ALREADY concluded, Assistant Maintenance Engineer Skillen Chun was a weedy little cretin. At just over a meter tall, weighing only 35 kilograms and having arms and legs which looked like they could have been fashioned out of lengths of electrical cable with knots tied where the elbows and knees should have been, meant the first two adjectives of that description were more than adequately justified. But it had to be said, the term cretin was a little unkind. Certainly his pale complexion, bulging eyes, narrow beak like nose and weak chin were all features one might attribute to a cretin, as was stupidity. But Skillen Chun was anything but stupid. In fact Assistant Maintenance Engineer Chun was highly intelligent. Some even considered him brilliant, though others felt a more apt description would be 'technically gifted but socially awkward.' Sadly for Chun, it was that last character trait which drove most people away.

But whether he looked like a terminally ill Hobbit or not, it was Skillen Chun's intelligence, along with his tenacity, which resulted in the discovery that the 'War Hawk's' power consumption was 32% higher than it should have been. AME Skillen Chun could always be relied upon to do his duty, and part of that duty was to ascertain everything onboard the flag ship 'War Hawk' was running at one hundred percent efficiency. He'd checked the power consumption a dozen times and each time he came up with a similar answer. The vessel was leaking power like a sieve.

He checked it once more, manually adding up the amp hour consumption of every conceivable device, gadget or piece of equipment on board which was active and in use. Once again, he came to same indisputable conclusion. 'War Hawk' was chewing thorough far more power than it should have been.

Perhaps a less conscientious man would have just put it down to an anomaly, simply some glitch in the system which would probably right itself once the maintenance mechanoids ran their periodic systems check and re-boot. There was, after all, no reason for immediate concern. In fact even with the unexplained phenomenon, the ships power-plant was running at barely sixty percent capacity. So there was certainly no danger of overload or load shedding. It was just.... well it was just annoying that he couldn't find the leakage.

He began to isolate sections of the ship from the equation, looking at each area in exclusion rather than the vessel as a whole. It took nearly two hours, but eventually he found the source of the problem. The munitions hold, the huge area now housing nearly twenty four thousand empty stasis tubes was bleeding power at almost twice what it should have been. Something was dreadfully wrong. He grabbed his tool kit and a portable systems analyser and made his way down to the stasis tubes.

The munitions hold didn't look any different to how it had looked seven days ago after Dr Shun had revived him early from his slumber. The forward part of the hold was still filled with fifty rows of stasis pods, each row ten pods high and fifty pods long. The first two port side rows were the only ones occupied.

AME Skillen Chun carried his tool box to the first row of pods, placed the box on the deck at his feet, and opened the lid. He extracted his AG belt and a small, spherical portable systems analyser. He fastened the belt around his waist and turned it on. A circle of light lit the surrounding floor. Everything within that circle was now affected by a column of artificial gravity generated by the belt. Next Chun aimed his remote control device at the holds control panel nestling against the starboard side wall, and turned off the holds own artificial gravity. Then he turned on the portable systems analyser and held it outside his AG belt's field of influence. The analyser was the size of his fist, with a series of angled vanes arranged around its centre which rotated independently of the main structure. Its surface was dotted with sensors which could detect the smallest variation in temperature, illumination, electrical charge, polarity, and a myriad of other, all the important tests and checks, which Chun had to perform during the execution of his duties.

The analyser hovered in mid air for a few seconds and then, with Chun controlling it with his remote, it rose up on tiny jets of compressed air and made its way to pod number 1/1/1. It drifted slowly over the stasis pod's control panel and then lowered itself into position. Chun observed the readout on his remote as the device went through a complete diagnostic of the pod's systems. As expected the stasis unit was operating at peak efficiency and drawing just 75 milliamp hours. The test unit disengaged itself and moved on to stasis unit 2/1/1with ostensibly the same result.

In fact every unit Chun tested came back with an almost identical reading. None were outside normal operating parameters. So why the hell were tests showing that there was a massive energy leak occurring in the munitions hold?

Chun sat cross-legged on the floor and racked his brain, trying to come up with a plausible explanation for the anomaly. He knew there was something he was missing, something which was staring him in the face, but he just couldn't see. It took over an hour before a possible solution occurred to him.

He remembered how he had been loaded into his own stasis tube just before the 'War Hawk' left their dying planet. He remembered thinking it was weird how the exercise had been undertaken. Because the tubes were packed in tightly together, to load them, one complete row, fifty long and ten high, had to be rolled forward, away from the others. Then the stasis pod's occupant climbed inside, and when the row was full, it was rolled back into place and the next row dragged out. Chun remembered wondering why they didn't roll out two rows at a time? Not rows next to each other of course, the second row would block access to the first, but why not opposite rows. Start with both rows 1 and 50, fill them and then roll out 2 and 49, 3 and 48 and so on. Of course rows 25 and 26 would have to be filled separately, but not every single row. With so many people trapped outside being slowly poisoned by the rapidly building toxins in the atmosphere, why the hell hadn't they sped things up with such a simple, common sense approach?

There was only one possible answer to that question, an answer that Chun really didn't want to even consider. He retrieved his portable systems analyser and crossed to the other side of the munitions hold. Then he sent the test unit to stasis tube 1/50/1. The result all but confirmed his worst fears.

But he had to be sure. He had to check out the pods himself. He crossed to the end of row 50, grabbed hold of the grab rail to stop himself drifting away and turned off his AG belt. Weightless, he quickly climbed to the top of row fifty and straddled the first pod, 1/50/1, holding himself in position with his knees. The indicator lights on the pod's control panel were dark and the dial indicating the level of valgette gas read zero, just as one would expect with an empty stasis tube. But the analysers read-out read 76 milliamp hours power draw, and that could only mean one thing. The gauges on the pods had been tampered with. Working quickly, Chun vented the chamber to the atmosphere. There was an audible hiss and the distinct odour of valgette gas assailed his nostrils. The cylindrical lid slid open and there inside was the comatose form of a soldier. He was dressed in his battle uniform, complete with side arm and laser rifle. The insignia on the soldiers' epaulette indicated he was from Admiral Vethil's own brigade.

Pod 2/50/1 also contained a sleeping, heavily armed soldier as did every pod in the rows 49 and 50. Despite the governments decree that the exodus was to be a non military exercise, it was apparent that Vethil had brought along his army.

Chapter 37

THE ANNUXIAN GLIDED across the marble floor of the courtroom on legs which seemed to somehow lack any discernible joints. They were more like the tentacles of some strange, invertebrate sea creature than actual legs. It turned to face the audience and uttered a few words in Colopo's direction.

"Ambassador Iwar wishes for me to act as translator, my friend," Colopo advised Chai. "You need to be aware that Annuxian protocols dictate I must translate its words exactly. Annuxian speech patterns are unique and you will have to follow its words carefully if you wish to understand its true meaning."

Colopo rose and joined the Ambassador and another of her students took her place besides Chai.

The Ambassador's voice was low and guttural, in some ways almost bestial. Colopo translated its words quickly into Tranian and her student, a willowy female with skin the colour of alabaster, translated Colopo's words for Chai. For the first few moments, Chai wondered if the girl sitting next to him was adequately qualified. Very little coming out of her mouth was in any way comprehensible.

"Ambassador Iwar says. 'Time great sadness for Annuxian endure death before. Alien vermin come, death come before. Now no more. Alien vermin home no more. Time great sadness again. Now alien vermin make new home planet of Tranian people. Annuxian say yes and yes. No more death please. No more suffering please. Time of sadness no more. Time of recrimination no more. Time of peace come. Annuxian and Tranians join welcome new friend alien now."

The Ambassador bowed deeply to the eight members of the tribunal, turned and glided back to its seat.

Chai felt tears well up in his eyes. He'd never felt so ashamed. Without any provocation, his people had attacked the Annuxians, slaughtered thousands if not millions of them, and yet here was a representative of their government offering their support for his appeal. Was this what it was like to achieve true enlightenment? To forgive even the most heinous crimes and then ask that even your most despised enemy be given a second chance? Chai wished he could speak to the ambassador directly, throw himself at its feet, thank the Annuxian for its magnanimous gesture, beg its forgiveness and tell it how utterly ashamed he and many others aboard the fleet felt.

But he also felt like cheering. Surely now there could be no question about his people's fate. Surely the eight councillors would find in favour of Chai's appeal.

Councillor Balopop had other ideas.

Chapter 38

VETHIL HAD TO BE MADE to pay for the murder of Dr Wawa Ni. Somehow, something had to be done and the weedy little assistant maintenance engineer, sitting opposite her in the isolation ward, had just given Shan yet another reason to act.

"Almost ten thousand troops?"

"Yes Doctor Shan. I have had others, loyal friends who I know to be people not answerable to Vethil, check the stasis pods on the other seventeen ships. All of them have found the same thing. Many of the supposedly empty stasis tubes actually contain soldiers from Vethil's army. A quick tally based on each ship's previously unexplained power drain, indicates the total number of soldiers to be nine thousand and seven hundred troops; give or take 3 percent."

"Shit! And you believe Vethil is intending to use these troops to declare war against the Tranians?"

"Yes... No.....I'm not sure. Though of course, as our original plan was to settle on Soren 6, I suspect his initial intention must have been to use the troops against us. That is, those not under his direct command. I believe he intended to set himself up as a military dictator of sorts. Install himself as supreme leader over all the survivors."

"What about his vortex cannon? Do you think with all those troops behind him, he will still need to use it?"

"I'm afraid military strategy is not one of my strong points Doctor, but my guess would be, if they reject our request for asylum, he'll do something like use the vortex cannon on a small city or town, and then threaten to destroy Salin or some other similarly sized metropolis unless the people of Tran bend to his will. Once he has their surrender, his troops could then be deployed as his own personal army and he would appoint himself as ruler. Uh or something like that..... I guess."

"Mmmmm, yes that makes a lot of sense, Chun. What the hell are we going to do?"

Skillen Chun shrugged expansively. "As far as I can see, our only option is to get rid of Vethil. If we can somehow arrest power from him, lock him up in the brig and prevent him from reviving his troops, he won't be able to cause any more trouble."

"Yes, but what then? We can't keep nearly ten thousand troops on ice indefinitely. We'll have to bring them around sooner or later."

"Of course, but if we can keep them in stasis until we have established ourselves on Tran, without Vethil around to command them, they'll almost certainly look to our elected leaders for direction. Hopefully those elected leaders won't be a bunch of war crazed mongrels like Vethil."

"But what do we tell the Tranians? Oh! by the way, we made a mistake, there's actually twenty seven thousand of us, not just seventeen thousand."

Skillen Chun thought for a long moment.

"Why not. We can just say it was all a mistranslation. Tran is a big planet. They have room for a million more people if they choose to accommodate us."

Shan nodded. She felt such a ploy had little chance of success, but what choice did they have? As she'd just said, they couldn't keep the troops in stasis forever. Sooner or later the truth would come out. Besides, at this stage the point was moot. Today was the first day of the tribunal. No decision had even been made yet.

Skillen Chun seemed like a man who could be trusted, but even so, Shan wasn't yet ready to discuss the half baked plan, still simmering in the back of her mind, about another way in which they might deal with Vethil. So for the next two hours they discussed ways in which they might simply usurp Vethil's authority. But whatever plan they came up with, all had one major flaw. They were of course, committing mutiny, and as such, if Vethil somehow managed to retain his iron fist authority, they were both as good as dead. Plus, how would the Tranians react when they learnt there had been a mutiny aboard the armada's flagship. Such actions could not possibly be considered the actions of a peaceful species.

Of course for Shan there was another solution, perhaps one Skillen Chun had already considered as well. Vethil had to die.

When the assistant maintenance engineer left the infirmary later that day, Shan once again replaced the ten, pre-charged hypoderms on a stainless Nelamine tray and covered them with a clean white cloth. Tomorrow she would inform Vethil that she had finished preparing the vaccines and ask him to gather the crew together so she could administer them. She guessed Vethil would last about thirty seconds before going into cardiac arrest.

But first she had to talk to Chai and tell him about the discovery of the ten thousand troops and ask him what he thought what she should do about them.

Chapter 39

IN CONTRADICTION TO normal Tranian behaviour, Councillor Balopop railed against the refugees request to the gathering of his fellow High Councillors and concerned citizens in the strongest possible terms.

"These monsters have been responsible for the death of millions of people," he declared. "Ambassador Iwar may be able to forgive such heinous transgressions, but we Tranians must not. Not now, not ever. Their history is awash with bloodshed and destruction. They have destroyed their own planet and now they aim to destroy ours."

There was a loud murmuring of descent from amongst the crowd and Balopop rudely slammed his hand down hard on the bench in front of him to quieten them. The blow echoed around the auditorium, silencing the protestors for a few moments.

"They have nowhere else to go!" proclaimed a tall dark skinned female timidly. "We can't just send them off to die, to starve to death or run out of air, lost and alone somewhere in the galaxy."

"WHY NOT?" snapped Balopop. "They have left many to die on the battlefields without any consideration or regard for what they have done. Send them away with all haste, I implore you, my fellow High Councillors. Send them away, before it is too late."

Then the tribunal descended into mayhem. People called out, some in support of Balopop, but many more in support of Chai's plea. Eventually High Councillor Fillipon was forced to call a halt to the proceedings and adjourned the tribunal until the following day.

"We shall all meet here again tomorrow morning. I will then call on the alien to answer questions from members of the High Council and later, questions from the public," she said. Then added sternly, "I must remind you all of you of the enormity of this occasion. We are here to consider, quite possibly, the very survival of an entire species. I will not, cannot, allow this tribunal to descend into anarchy. Members of the public are therefore requested to behave appropriately. If they do not do so they will be ejected immediately."

As Chai, Colopo and Silpolo made their way home, they discussed the day's exciting events.

"It went even better than I had ever imagined," said Chai excitedly. "Almost everyone seemed to be on our side. Only Balopop was opposed to our request."

Colopo nodded in agreement as she piloted her tiny personal transportation vehicle towards their home. She was silent for a few minutes as she negotiated a sharp right hand bend and then slowed for a group of school children making their way home from school. Finally, she spoke.

"Yes, hopefully the other members of the council will be able to convince him to change his mind. We need all eight votes for the motion to be passed."

Chai was incredulous. "What? All eight? Surely we only need a good majority?"

"No my friend. All eight votes are needed to carry the motion. Without a unanimous decision, your people will not be granted refugee status."

"Then I have failed," he said dejectedly. "Balopop's mind is obviously already made up. There's no way he's going to change his mind, that's clear from today's tirade."

Sitting quietly on the vehicle's rear seat, Silpolo then piped up with a comment.

"My mother says to tell you that all is not lost. The Annuxians have shown support for your cause, and Ambassador Iwar is held in very high esteem by the Tranian High Council. Because of this, the other seven councillors will tonight lobby Balopop relentlessly in an attempt to achieve a unanimous result. You see if the tribunal cannot reach consensus, many Tranians will feel that we have lost face before our friends the Annuxians."

Chai hoped like hell Silpolo was right. Unfortunately he had no way of knowing that the whole debate would soon be rendered moot anyway.

Chapter 40

AFTER HE, COLOPO AND her mother had finished their evening meal, and Chai had placed the dirty dishes and cutlery in the recycler, he excused himself and went into the other room. The two Tranian females understood this was the time of day their house guest chose to speak with his mate, so they gave him some privacy.

Chai placed his communicator on the floor and pressed the receive button. Moments later Shan's beautiful countenance appeared before him. She looked worried, very worried. But even though she obviously had something important on her mind, the first words out of her mouth were to ask him about his meeting with the Tranian high councillors.

He told her about his day, enthusing about the incredible support he had received, but warning his wife that they still had a seemingly insurmountable hurdle to navigate before any final decision could be expected.

"The Annuxian Ambassador actually supported our request?" Shan asked incredulously. "I can't believe it."

"It's true. I nearly fell off my chair when Ambassador Iwar said the Annuxians felt we should be allowed to stay. To show such compassion after all we've done to them is simply breathtaking."

The couple discussed the tribunal for a while longer and then moved on to what was so obviously worrying Shan. She told Chai everything, starting with the discovery of Vethil's army and progressing to the Silick toxin she had prepared and her plan to use it. He was quiet for a while and then gently told her what he felt about her terrible plan.

"It's not what your dad would have wanted Shan," he said. "Your dad was a great man sweetheart, a great man and a great doctor, but most of all he was a man of peace. He wouldn't want you to kill Vethil, Shan. In your dad's eyes, doing so would make you no better than he is."

Chai's beautiful wife began to cry. She knew he was right, her dad would have been horrified she was even contemplating such a deplorable act. But if she didn't stop Vethil, what the hell were they going to do? Someone had to do something.

"We can't let him get away with it Chai, we just can't, she sobbed, "and what about the troops and that damn vortex canon. What are we going to do about that?"

Chai considered his answer carefully before replying. The truth was, he didn't have a clue what the solution was. He needed time to think, and after the day's events at the tribunal, his head was already swimming. Eventually he came up with the only possible way out of the predicament he could think of.

The last thing he needed right now was Vethil stirring things up. Unfortunately High Councillor Balopop would revel in the news that the fleet orbiting above Tran was not only armed to the teeth, but had approximately ten thousand troops waiting to strike. But there simply wasn't any other way. If there was any chance at all of the tribunal agreeing to let them stay, Chai had to be honest and truthful with them. If he told Colopo the whole story, asked her to arrange a one on one meeting with High Councillor Fillipon, explain that these events were all due to the actions of just one man, and that the rest of the people aboard the fleet condemned Vethil's actions outright, there was a good chance they would understand. No, that wasn't correct. There was a slight chance they would understand.

There was a good chance they would give them five seconds to get the hell out of their airspace before they blew them out of the sky.

But then he thought of another possible solution.

"I'll talk to Colopo and her mother," Chai told Shan. "Silpolo used to be a Law Enforcer and has a good grasp of Tranian law. Perhaps the Tranian cops can invite Vethil to the planet and arrest him on suspicion of sedition or terrorism charges once he gets here. If we can get him locked up, away from the War Hawk before he can fire the canon or revive his troops, we'll neutralize him before he can cause any trouble."

Shan was filled with enthusiasm at Chai's suggestion. Of course, she thought. It was the perfect plan. Not only would having the Tranian Law Enforcers arrest the Admiral get Vethil safely out of the picture, such actions would lend weight to Chai's argument that the rest of the refugees were dead against the violence perpetrated by others in their name.

"Okay," said Chai after they had discussed the plan further. "I'll talk to Silpolo, get her opinion and call you back in about an hour. With any luck that mongrel Vethil will be out of our hair by this time tomorrow."

Chai signed off and went into the other room to talk to his host's mother. Later she called on one of her old contacts to see what could be done. The following morning at dawn, six Tranian Law Enforcement officials made an arrest. Unfortunately Admiral Vethil was not the one charged.

The Tran sun was just rising when the door to Silpolo's domicile suddenly smashed open. There was a loud bang and the light alloy structure flew off its hinges and crashed into the wall before falling to the floor. Six heavily armed Law Enforcers rushed into the main living room and dragged the befuddled Chai out of bed. Hot on their heels came the young, pale skinned student of languages. The girl who only yesterday, had assisted Colopo with translating the words of Ambassador Iwar. She pointed at Chai and nodded her head, positively identifying him as their quarry.

Colopo came rushing out of her bedroom, hurriedly wrapping her robe around herself as she burst into the room. There was a brief and heated exchange between herself and the intruders and then Chai's arms were trussed up with magnetic restraints and he was dragged from the room.

"What the hell's going on?" he yelled as they led him away.

"You are being arrested for the murder of Councillor Balopop," replied the pale skinned young girl.

Chapter 41

THE TINY TRANSPORTER curved around the huge battle cruiser and slowed, allowing its pilot ample time for a closer look as it passed across the giant ship's upper quadrant. Colopo had never seen a vortex canon before, but she had to admit, the device certainly looked lethal. As much as she had come to like and admire Chai, and despite her suspicions that something was dreadfully wrong about the terrible accusation against him, she was starting to severely regret ever volunteering for this assignment. The aliens were becoming much more trouble than anyone could have ever imagined. She wished they would just go away and find somewhere else to live. Find someone else to burden.

But it was not to be. Even though he had been selected by the Tranian people and not the aliens themselves, the refugees had eagerly put their complete trust in Chai as their spokesperson. Remarkably, he had done exceedingly well so far. Colopo knew it was impossible to walk away now. The lives of seventeen, no make that twenty six thousand beings depended upon her. The future of an entire species rested in her hands.

She had been confident that the other members of the tribunal would have eventually convinced Balopop to accept the will of the majority, and vote accordingly. But now the councillor was missing presumed dead.

A witness had come forward claiming she'd seen a weird looking alien throwing someone into Salin's water purification plant on the outskirts of the city. Her description of the alien and his Tranian victim matched both Chai and Councillor Balopop precisely.

Chai professed his innocence and Colopo had to admit the whole thing sounded implausible. Unfortunately the Law Enforcers did not. In just a few hours he would be formally charged with murder. If convicted, he would spend the rest of his life in the Salin correctional facility. Of even greater concern was the fact that almost every other person in the facility would not only be Tranian, many of them would have been declared criminally insane. They would be rough and dangerous people who wouldn't look kindly upon an alien who had killed one of their own. Colopo imagined the 'rest of Chai's life' wouldn't be very long.

But the trial didn't start until later and that meant this morning Colopo had her work cut out for her. First task of the day was to collect Chai's female mate and bring her to the planet. Tran's legal system dictated that any and all accused had the right to request a person of his or her choosing to observe the proceedings. In this way the accused would be assured that everything would be conducted correctly and according to the law. Chai had chosen Doctor Wawa Shan. She was his choice and so this time the fact she was pregnant didn't matter.

Colopo slowed the vehicle and angled it in towards the main cargo hold hatch, expertly bringing the tiny vessel to rest gently against the battleship's hull. She extended the transfer tube, engaged the magnetic anchor clamps, and remotely accessed the ships woefully inept security system. Quickly she overrode the hatchway locks and slowly the door began to open. There was a slight increase in Colopo's cabin pressure as the air in both vessels equalised and as soon as the pressure had stabilised, Colopo made her way through the tube into the larger ship. The alien they called Admiral Vethil, the creature who was causing all the trouble, was waiting in the hold to greet her.

"Translator Colopo, welcome to our flagship the uh!... the "Hawk," Vethil gushed, bowing deeply and then stepping forward to take the females arm.

Colopo recoiled as if in horror. Many of her friends often took her arm in this way, Chai included. But it was not the act of touching which she found distasteful, but rather the person doing the touching. The knowledge of what this obnoxious little man represented made him repugnant to her and she had no intention of hiding her revulsion.

"Bring the female doctor to me at once," she commanded. Vethil started to do so but then remembered his exalted position aboard the 'War Hawk'. Quickly he motioned to one of the cargo handlers to fetch Doctor Wawa Shan.

"Shan will be here directly," he told his visitor. "In the meantime perhaps I can show you around. This vessel is quite impressive. I'd also like to ask you how things are progressing at the tribunal. For some reason Salang Chai did not make contact with me last night as instructed."

Colopo ignored the vile little man. Chai was in deep trouble and Colopo felt sure that if the angry little admiral got involved, he would only make things worse. She felt it prudent to keep Vethil in the dark as much as possible, at least until she could find out what was going on herself.

In a way that was unfortunate, because Colopo would have enjoyed a tour of the ship. Vethil was correct. The 'War Hawk' was quite an impressive vessel, much larger by a magnitude of fifty than even the largest of Tranian ships. In fact, it was bigger even than Guild Leader Volot's freighter. But whereas the Annuxian's ship was designed to move people, goods and produce from one side of the galaxy to another, Vethil's ship had been designed with only one purpose in mind. It was a war machine, its sole purpose, to bring death and destruction to all it encountered. Colopo found even the concept of such a thing reprehensible and it was all she could do to stop herself from telling the evil little monster exactly what she and the rest of her planet thought of him and his deplorable killing machine.

But yesterday, before he was arrested, Chai had told her of the existence of the vortex canon and of the ten thousand troops. They were scattered throughout the fleet and currently lying in stasis waiting to be revived and any outburst from Colopo would alert Vethil to the fact that the people of Tran were well aware of the threat he posed to them. She knew that in doing so, she might inadvertently force his hand.

Colopo crossed to the other side of the cargo hold, feigning interest in one of the holds' computer terminals. Vethil followed her and began explaining the terminal's function and operation. Rolling one's eyes was not a characteristic trait of the Tranian people, but if it had been, Colopo certainly would have rolled hers. As if she needed someone to explain the workings of something as simple as an automated spatial volume calculator to her! What a fool this man was.

Thankfully Shan arrived at that moment. She had hurried from her infirmary as soon as she'd heard the request, not even bothering to change her clothes. She was still wearing her blue medical isolation suit

"Dr Wawa Shan. You will accompany me to the city of Salin please. Your mate requires your assistance," Colopo advised.

Shan had not been advised of Chai's arrest, nor had she been expecting to be whisked away without a moments notice to the planet's surface. The sudden arrival of Colopo threw her into a bit of a spin.

"Chai? Is he alright?" Shan asked, but Colopo didn't answer, instead she simply turned towards her vessel and marched off, obviously expecting Shan to follow, and ignoring Vethil's demands that he be kept informed at all times. For a second Shan considered asking for a few moments to collect a change of clothes and some other necessities, but the Tran woman was clearly in a hurry. Shan shrugged towards Vethil, telling him wordlessly that she had as little insight into what was going on as he did. Then followed the Tranian translator down the transfer chute and into the tiny space craft.

Unlike the vessel Chai had travelled on, this transporter had two seats. The one on the left, facing forward, was stationed behind a full width windscreen and positioned in front of a complex control panel which had more buttons, dials and switches than the helm of a Galaxy class battle cruiser. The other seat, this one modified to suit Shan's different physiology was positioned directly beside the first, but away from the helm. Shan was slightly perplexed by the control panel. Chai had told Shan all about his journey to the planet's surface ten days ago and had mentioned that the vessel he'd travelled on seemed to be either remote controlled, or piloted by the mechanoid, which had, he thought, integrated itself into the ship itself before the return journey commenced. This craft was obviously designed to be piloted by a living being.

As she had done with Chai, Colopo had Shan disrobe and place her belongings, including her personal communications device, in the receptacle situated in the port side bulkhead. The cabin was once again filled with the pale blue light of the decontamination process, and when that was finished, Colopo handed the doctor a simple blue smock and indicated that once she was dressed Shan should be seated. She then took her own seat at the controls. Shan did as she was asked and once again the fur like covering of the seat grew rapidly, wrapping itself around her and encapsulating her in its protective embrace. Colopo disengaged the magnetic anchors, retracted the transfer tube and manoeuvred the transporter away from the 'War Hawk.' Shan watched in silence, unsure whether speaking would be advisable during what appeared to be a quite complex and precise procedure. Once they were clear the ship increased speed rapidly and turned towards the other vessels of the fleet.

"I wish to inspect the other ships to make sure your assertion only one vortex canon exists is correct," explained Colopo. Then, as the tiny ship crossed silently to the next vessel, she went on to tell Shan of the trials and tribulations which had befallen Chai. Shan could not believe her ears.

"Chai would never murder someone," she proclaimed. "He abhors violence. Besides, what good would killing Councillor Balopop do anyway? They'll just replace him with someone else, won't they?"

Colopo agreed. Although she had only known Chai for a few days, she had to admit such a heinous act seemed totally out of character. Plus, as Shan had just pointed out, murdering Balopop didn't make sense. The councillor's death would only serve to add credence to his claim that the aliens were not to be trusted. Plus if Chai was found guilty there wasn't even the slightest chance Colopo's people would ever welcome the aliens into their society. The whole thing reeked of conspiracy. But by whom? and to what purpose?

For the next half hour or so, the tiny transporter glided silently between the seventeen vessels in orbit around the planet. Colopo piloted the vehicle as close as she dared to the battle cruisers, carefully examining each one for any sign of a second weapon. Eventually she seemed content with her investigation and headed for home.

"It looks like your friend Skillen Chun was correct in his assertion that only the 'War Hawk' carries a vortex canon," said Colopo. Shan agreed. She was quiet for a few moments and then posed a question.

"I have been told that after its initial installation, this type of weapon takes about 30 minutes to charge up before it can be fired for the first time. Is it possible your people might be able to launch an attack on the 'War Hawk' and take out the vortex canon before Vethil can fire it?" Shan asked.

Colopo shook her head. "Not in thirty minutes. Not even in thirty days. We are a peaceful race Doctor Shan. There isn't even a word in our language for war. Such a thing is unheard of. We have no weapons to repel any form of attack should your Admiral Vethil choose to launch one."

Shan felt ill at this revelation. The Tranians were a technologically advanced species, so she'd never even considered for a second that they might not even have the resources to defend themselves.

"Our lack of weaponry, and for that matter our repugnance at using such weaponry even if we had it, is another reason the majority of the members of the tribunal are keen to accept your request to settle on our planet. If we refuse, what then? Will you attack us? Will you invade our home and enslave us as you have done to others so many times before?" Colopo asked her voice trembling with emotion as she spoke. She was clearly becoming distressed. Distressed and obviously frightened.

"Our philosophers have a saying," she continued. "Roughly translated it means, 'Careful investigation at close quarters is always preferable to blind faith.' If you live alongside us, Doctor Shan, we can, as you say, 'keep an eye on you' and make sure you behave in accordance with our laws."

Shan nodded, it was perhaps a bit confronting, but Colopo was right. Shan's own species were obviously creatures to be wary of. But, was this the real reason the Tranians were being so accommodating? Were these peace loving, gentle people, being forced into making a decision they did not really agree with purely out of fear? The answer to those questions were obvious. Of course, they were. They had studied the asylum seekers history and found it saturated with bloodshed, violence, waste and mayhem. Of course, they were frightened. But were they so frightened they were being forced to share their planet with Shan's people against their better judgement?

"I'm sorry," said Shan. "I can see now we have put you in a terrible position. You are a kind, generous and caring people, and I can see it will cause you great pain if you have to turn us away in our time of need. But I want you to know, not all of my species will resort to violence. As with the Tranians, most of my people are peace loving. The problem is, it always seems to be the troublemakers who end up in charge. They mislead the others into doing the wrong thing. I don't understand why Admiral Vethil is like he is. I just hope and pray that one day soon, the more sensible people aboard the fleet will be able to wrest power from him and put him behind bars where he belongs.

Colopo also hoped that would happen, and happen soon, but for now the most urgent thing was to find out what the hell was going to happen to her friend, Salang Chai.

The tiny transporter dropped into the atmosphere and scythed its way across the cloud free, pale blue sky above the city of Salin, dropping rapidly as it approached the space port. Colopo expertly piloted the craft between the long rows of small pleasure vessels moored there and eased her ship into its allotted berth. The magnetic clamps engaged automatically as she shut down the engines, and a transfer tube extended out and attached itself to the side of the vessel, locking on with a loud clunk.

"We need to hurry Dr Wawa Shan," Colopo urged, extricating herself quickly from the tiny craft. "The woman who claims to have seen Salang Chai murder Councillor Balopop will be addressing the law court in two hours. We must get to the other side of the city."

Shan didn't need to be told twice. She leapt from her seat and hurried after her.

Colopo's long legs propelled her quickly along the walkway and Shan had to run to keep up with her. That was something Shan had noticed when the Tranian female first arrived on the 'War Hawk', the real woman was at least a metre taller than her mechanical avatar. She surmised that perhaps the Tran High Council had deliberately made the mechanoid smaller so the refugees would find it less threatening.

The Tranian's tallness was interesting, Shan had studied Tranian physiology quite extensively over the past few days and had been surprised to learn that many centuries ago, the Tranian people had been quite small in stature, smaller even than her own species. But with the passing of each generation, they had grown taller and more robust. Perhaps it was because of better diet or other environmental issues, or perhaps it was simply a natural evolutionary outcome. Interestingly, Shan's own people were also getting larger. Shan was much taller than both her mother and father, and in turn, they were taller than her grandparents.

They reached Colopo's PTV and clambered inside. Shan slid into the passenger side, and as her husband had done, knelt on the seat with her feet curled under her and hung on to the grab rail on the dashboard. Colopo started the vehicle's propulsion unit, raced out of the parking area and hurtled up the street towards the law court buildings. For a while both women were quiet, Colopo concentrating on driving and Shan lost in her own thoughts and her deep concern about what might happen over the next few hours. Eventually Shan spoke.

"There must be some mistake Colopo. You know Chai. You know he could never kill someone!"

"It does not seem likely Dr Shan. Chai has shown himself to be a man of peace. For example, even though it is obvious Admiral Vethil murdered your father, and poses a very real threat to the likelihood of the tribunal accepting your request for asylum, yesterday Salang Chai implored you not to seek revenge and poison him. Those are not the actions of a man who would kill someone to further his own agenda," Colopo answered, but then added sadly, "but unless one of your people has secretly landed on Tran and it was he, not your mate, who killed Balopop, there can be no other explanation. Your species is after all, quite unique in appearance."

"But maybe the woman is mistaken, or maybe she's lying." said Shan. "Perhaps she has her own agenda. Or are you telling me Tranians are incapable of lying?"

"Of course we can lie Dr Shan. But the woman has agreed to submit herself to a shallinop, what you might call a memory scan. It is impossible to fake one's memories. Even if a person is mistaken in their beliefs, lies or false memories are instantly apparent."

Shan shook her head. It wasn't possible that the witness was correct, Chai would never kill anyone. There had to be another explanation.

But there was something else Shan found disconcerting. She knew Chai would never have discussed her plan to poison Vethil, so Colopo's comments confirmed what everyone aboard the seventeen vessels orbiting Tran had long suspected. Somehow the Tran had decrypted Chai's coded surface to ship transmissions and were monitoring all communications between himself and the fleet.

Chapter 42

IT TOOK AN HOUR AND twelve minutes to reach the law court buildings. Six more minutes to find somewhere to park and a further nine to walk to the building itself. They made it with just moments to spare. The area around the courts was teeming with people hoping to catch a glimpse of the evil little creature who had taken the life of one of their own. Some of those attending were there in an official capacity. Law Enforcers, dressed in their distinctive silver and gold tunics and bandoleers, were there to keep the peace and control the crowds. Others were from the news services, reporters who had been dragged away from reporting on the other big story, the largest Nelamine ore discovery in living memory, and who were now hoping to bring the latest drama in the refugee saga to their numerous, loyal and avid followers. But most of the rabble were just members of the public, there to witness the alien vermin receiving the punishment he so richly deserved.

The law courts were on the seventy first floor of a new building known simply as Salin 932. Despite their recent construction, the rooms had been decorated in a manner reflecting the historic significance and importance of Tran's rich legal past. The floor was finished in a facsimile of highly polished timber and the walls were covered with thin sheets of white marble and then adorned with art works commissioned by the High Council from famous artists from all over the planet. They depicted scenes from important legal cases which had been tried by the Tranian judiciary over the past ninety two centuries. The ceilings of the rooms were covered with ornate abstract carvings which swirled in continuous patterns from a central motif, flowing outwards to each of the rooms seven corners.

For some reason, Shan deduced, the number seven held great significance in Tranian society. Not only did most important buildings and structures feature the number seven in their construction, court room number seven had been chosen to host the inquest into the murder of High Councillor Balopop.

When the two females entered and took their seats on the left hand side at the front of the room, Salang Chai was already seated at their table. He was dressed in a basic yellow tunic with some sort of Tranian script printed in large letters front and back. Obviously it was some sort of prison garb. He looked pale and weak and somehow much smaller than he had the last time they'd seen each other. Shan wrapped her arms around him and kissed him. He smiled.

"This is all some kind of mistake, darling" he told her. "But apparently they have some kind of device which proves categorically what actually happened. So I should be out of here by the end of the day. The woman must have been asleep and dreamt the whole thing or something."

Shan began to reassure him that she agreed it must be a mistake, but as she began to speak, the artificial lighting in the room flickered on and off and then became noticeably brighter. A woman dressed in an ornate gold tunic, the integral cape of which was decorated with a huge collar shaped in a graphic representation of a star, took her seat behind a large bench, facing the courtroom. The woman announced something in a loud voice and the murmuring of the public died down completely.

Two other judges entered and took their seats either side of the first woman. She stood, and in Tranian, asked who was to represent the accused. Colopo translated her words for Chai and Shan and then rose to announce that although she had no legal experience, because she spoke the aliens' language and no formally trained lawyer did, she would like to volunteer to assist. The lead judge nodded her head in acquiescence.

"As you have little or no legal training, there are obvious problems with trying this case under strict Tranian law. It is therefore this courts decree that certain protocols normally required, are to be dispensed with for the duration of the trial. Should you require any legal assistance, translator Colopo, please do not hesitate to ask," said the judge. Then she called for the witness who was to tell the court what she had seen the previous night.

The woman entered from a side entrance. She was a security guard at the city's water treatment works a few kilometres north of the city. Her name was V'napolo and she had been employed by the High Council, in her current position, for the last nine years. She was a slim woman, with long, dark hair which she wore in an ornate, curling style, piled high on the top of her head, which accentuated her steep forehead. She stood in front of the trio of judges and in a loud and clear voice told the court how she had seen a creature fitting Chai's appearance, lift the body of a large, overweight Tranian male over the guard rail near the main water outlet, and hurl him into the turbulent water. She finished her report quickly and took a seat on the right side of the courtroom near the front. Colopo rose and approached the bench.

"With great respect to Security Guard V'napolo, she must be mistaken," proclaimed Colopo. "The alien Salang Chai has been residing at my home since he arrived on the planet. He and I were working together on his people's request for asylum the night before last until an hour after midnight. He was arrested less than six hours later. Last night I made some enquires and eventually found out that High Councillor Balopop lives in the eastern hills section of the city. That area is nearly thirty kilometres from my home. Salang Chai has only a very limited command of the Tranian language. I don't see how he could have possibly found out where High Councillor Balopop lived when his command of our language is so poor. Also, even if he had managed to find that out, the distance to Balopop's house, then to the water treatment works and back to my home has to be at least one hundred and thirty kilometres. I am sure you will agree, honoured judges, it would be impossible for a person, without some sort of vehicle, to cover such a distance in just six hours. Salang Chai has no vehicle, nor does he have access to one."

The judges listened to Colopo's comments and conferred, quietly discussing any possible scenarios they could think of.

"Your comments are extremely valid Colopo," stated the lead judge. "But perhaps the alien had assistance from someone else, someone aboard one of the ships orbiting above our planet for example. Someone who was able to hack into Tran's master database and find Balopop's whereabouts. Or perhaps he somehow secreted some sort of miniature tracking device about Balopop's person during the tribunal yesterday."

Colopo nodded. She too had considered this possibility, but as she and a number of others engaged by the High Council were monitoring all communications between Chai and the alien fleet, she knew this was not possible. She told the court just that.

"Also," she continued, "as previously stated Salang Chai does not have any way of covering one hundred and thirty kilometres in just a few hours. He would have to walk, and most of the way he would have to carry the heavy and struggling High Councillor Balopop. Such a feat is impossible."

Once again the three judges conferred for many long minutes. Eventually the lead judge made a decision.

"It is true that there are many unanswered questions concerning the culpability of your charge, Salang Chai. As you know Security Guard V'napolo has already volunteered to submit herself to shallinop. You are also no doubt aware that such a procedure can be quite uncomfortable, sometimes even painful and distressing. I had hoped to spare Security Guard V'napolo the discomfort, but now I believe we need to see some unequivocal proof to back up her statement. The court therefore asks Security Guard V'napolo to submit herself to shallinop for verification of her statement."

The security guard once again rose from her seat and presented herself in front of the three judges. The side door through which she had entered just moments before opened, and a mechanoid brought in some sort of machine supported on a four wheeled trolley. The machine looked like a large coffin and was constructed out of some sort of transparent alloy. It was lying prone on the trolley, with a large complex instrument panel on the side facing the courtroom and a myriad of multicoloured wires protruding out of its side panel. V'napolo faced the judges and solemnly pledged, that she was willingly subjecting herself to the shallinop procedure of her own free will and had not been forced or induced by any other to do so. She slipped out of her tunic, opened the lid of the machine, stepped inside and lowered herself into the opaque viscous gel which filled the machines casing completely. The gel oozed around the woman's body, enveloping her entirely in its gooey embrace, right up to her neck. Shan guessed the semi liquid gel was some sort of neurogel which would detect V'napolo's neurological activity. She had used a similar type of gel herself when testing the brainwave activity and nerve efficacy of accident victims, but never as some sort of lie detector.

Then the mechanoid stepped forward and in a clicking, metallic sounding, disembodied voice asked the Tranian female if she was ready. Nervously V'napolo nodded her head, breathed in a huge lungful of air, held her breath and lay back, immersing herself completely. The mechanoid quickly closed and locked the lid and addressed the control panel.

Through the transparent sides of the machine, Chai and Shan could see the Tran woman floating in the heavy viscous liquid. There didn't appear to be any air inside the container and the woman was quickly becoming increasingly distressed as the air inside her lungs cried out to be replenished. Something had gone wrong, she was drowning. Chai quickly leapt to his feet, attempting to go to the woman's aid, but Colopo placed a calming hand on his shoulder.

She is in no danger my friend," she explained. "The liquid is enriched with oxygen. She will not drown. All mammalian foetus breathe embryonic fluid from the moment their lungs first begin to function during gestation. They do so until they take their first breath of air the day they are born. V'napolo's body has forgotten that breathing liquid is sometimes perfectly natural and she is filled with panic. She will be alright in a moment."

Just as Colopo predicted, seconds later, unable to hold her breath any longer, V'napolo breathed in a huge gulp of the neurogel. Gradually, as her subconscious accepted the reality that she wasn't going to drown, she began to calm. Consciously she slowed her breathing and then, closing her eyes, she crossed her arms across her chest to indicate she was ready. The mechanoid made a few final adjustments and then stepped back.

The lid of the machine doubled as a holographic projector. Above it, a three dimensional scene gradually emerged, taking form in the air above the coffin like mechanism. Everyone in the court room could now see exactly what V'napolo had seen as she sat at her post, in the main security office at the water treatment works, two evenings ago. V'napolo was apparently sitting at her desk. They could see a number of computerised security monitors which seemed to cover almost the entire complex. Suddenly there was an ear-splitting, guttural, scream and the scene before them swirled and distorted alarmingly. Both Shan and Chai felt a wave of nausea wash over them and it took a few seconds for them to realise what had just happened. The Tranian woman's eyes were markedly different to their own. Her eyes were situated on the side of her head, not at the front, facing forward. Not only that, a Tranian could move each eye independently. When V'napolo had heard the scream, her left eye had remained on the bank of monitors, while her right eye had turned outward and backward towards the sound. The distorted vision that Chai and Shan were witnessing was exactly how the Tranian frequently viewed their world.

The vision swung around again, this time both V'napolo's eyes were trained on the door leading out of the office to the vehicle parking area outside. She leapt to her feet and rushed towards the door. She swung it open and hurried outside, pausing momentarily to switch on a bank of lights which illuminated the parking area and the water treatment storage lake beyond.

In the distance, at the far side of the parking area, two figures could be seen struggling. Although it was at least one hundred metres between V'napolo and the two combatants, and even though the lights barely made any impact at that distance, it was still patently obvious that the two figures were Salang Chai and Councillor Balopop. The audience in the court room let out a gasp of horror, as suddenly, the alien took out a knife from beneath his tunic, stabbed Balopop in the heart and then picked him up and hurled him over the barricade into the lake.

For the first time since the day they met, Colopo turned to Chai and regarded him with a look of complete horror, a look which quickly changed to one of total disgust.

Now there could be no doubt. Security Guard V'napolo's memories could not be fabricated. They had therefore substantiated exactly what she had told the court just minutes before. The alien vermin sitting only a couple of metres from her had murdered a respected and well liked member of the Tran High Council.

Murdered him in cold blood and then thrown his corpse into the lake in the hope his heinous crime would go undetected.

Chapter 43

'THOSE DAMN 'FISH HEADS'. What the hell do they think their playing at now?" Vethil raged, cursing the inhabitants of the planet below roundly. Salang Chai had contacted the Admiral every evening since he had been whisked away by the rude translator's mechanoid ten days ago. But last night he had missed their allotted communique and when Vethil had attempted to call him, he'd found Chai's communicator was unreachable. This morning he'd tried again with the same result. Next he'd tried the translator. Her communicator was also switched off.

When the woman herself turned up unexpectedly this morning he'd tried to engage her in conversation, hoping to glean some idea of how the tribunal was progressing. But the arrogant female had simply ignored him. Later, in desperation, he'd contacted the Tranian High Council only to learn that that fool Salang Chai had been arrested for murder.

Vethil picked up the portable navigation relay from his desk top and hurled it at the wall with all the rage driven force he could muster. The device hit the wall and shattered into a hundred pieces.

"Damn that stupid man. How the hell did he allow himself to get caught by a bunch of ignorant 'Fish Heads?" Vethil screamed at the empty room.

Everything was turning to shit. Although he had denied it emphatically, that weedy little cretin Skillen Chun had obviously discovered Vethil's troops secreted away in the converted munitions hold. He had also, no doubt, been in communication with his friends on the other ships, and so now any number of people knew 'War Hawk' wasn't the only vessel harbouring a section of the Admiral's soldiers.

Of course the other seventeen thousand civilians currently in stasis would never have accepted his decision to use military force if he hadn't tried diplomacy first. So he had waited patiently for the damned tribunal to make a decision one way or the other, all the while scheming and plotting ways he could wrest power from the High Council regardless of which way the decision went. The glacial pace at which the Tranian government operated meant Vethil had been forced to play his cards close to his chest for much longer that he had ever anticipated.

Now Salang Chai's incompetence had forced the Admiral's hand. Obviously there wasn't a hope in hell the Tranians were going to roll over and let his people settle on their miserable planet now. The only avenue left open to him was to use lethal force. He opened an internal communications channel to the bridge and ordered the helmsman to prepare to move the vessel to new coordinates. Three hours later the flagship 'War Hawk' moved into its new position. Vethil smiled, now he had a clear shot at his chosen target.

"That'll make the damn 'Fish Heads' take notice," he whispered to himself.

Chapter 44

MANY YEARS AGO, WHEN Chai was just a child, he would occasionally visit his father's brother Sindle. His uncle was twelve years older than Chai's father and worked overseeing and maintaining the mechanoid workforce, at a small textile plant, on the southern side of Riis City. He'd never married or had children of his own, and Chai had always been a well behaved little boy. So for those reasons, plus many others, Sindle adored his young nephew and in return Chai loved his uncle Sindle like a second father. On the rare occasion that young Chai was able to wrangle a visit to Uncle Sindle, the man spoilt the little boy rotten, taking him on many exciting and interesting excursions and outings whenever the opportunity arose and plying him with a wealth of sweets and toys.

But sadly the old man suffered poor health. When he had been not much older than his young nephew was now, he had contracted a particularly virulent virus. A virus which had adversely affected his lungs. After many years of treatment, the virus was eventually eradicated, but not until it had done permanent and irreparable damage. Thanks to expert care and a truck load of pharmaceuticals, Sindle had lived in relatively good health until he reached fifty nine years of age. Then the scar tissue on his lungs began to harden and slowly degrade making it extremely difficult for him to breathe. He eventually died at home, alone, just two months short of his sixty third birthday.

Five days after his uncle's cremation, Chai and his father visited Sindle's home to sort out some minor affair, prior to finalising his will. Of course the nanobot cleaners had cleaned the apartment, digesting every trace of the man's physical existence from his home, at a molecular level. Yet even though this had been done, Chai still felt he could detect the smell of death permeating throughout his uncle's bedroom, the room where Sindle had died. His father had claimed it was just Chai's imagination. The uncle was gone, every single trace of him in fact, had been cleaned away by the nanobots, never to return. There was nothing left to smell. The little boy Chai had been convinced otherwise.

That same, choking smell, the stench of death, once again seemed to assault Chai's olfactory senses as he sat on the hard metal bench, in the holding cell of the Salin's 495 Law Enforcement building. Yesterday morning and last night, before his trial, he'd been held under guard at one of the city's luxurious, temporary accommodation facilities close to the courtrooms. The young slender Tranian girl, the one who had identified him to the Law Enforcers earlier that morning, had explained that unless (and until) a person was convicted by the court, the High Council would always ensure he or she was treated with the utmost courtesy. They would do everything they could to ensure that a prisoner's incarceration leading up to the trial, was as comfortable as possible.

But that was before the trial. Now he had been convicted of murder and his world had come tumbling down around his ears.

To Chai's complete surprise, even with the irrefutable evidence against him, the three judges had deliberated for almost two hours before they'd brought down the expected verdict. Shan had sat beside him, holding his hand and sobbing quietly as the lead judge had risen and delivered her judgement. Colopo translated the woman's words, refusing steadfastly to make eye contact, or to offer any encouragement to, her former friend. Chai knew she believed he had betrayed her trust and proven himself to be no better than a wild animal. No, that was not true. She regarded him, indeed all the aliens as worse than animals. At least animals only killed because they were hungry or felt threatened.

"The court has found you guilty Emissary Salang Chai. Of that there can be no doubt," the lead judge had declared. "However the court is at a loss as to what we should do with you. It may surprise you to learn that even in a peaceful and law abiding society such as ours, there are still those amongst us who would break the law. But very few of our criminals ever act out of self interest. Nevertheless, occasionally we will imprison someone for theft or falsifying documents for financial gain. But these events are rare indeed. However, even on Tran, we still have a few violent crimes and occasionally even murder. But in almost every instance, the perpetrator of that murder is deemed to be criminally insane."

The judge had paused and briefly, consulted with her colleagues for a few seconds and then turned to the screen of her computer. It had displayed a number of cases which had been heard over the past millennium, and she had searched for some sort of precedent to help her make a decision about Chai's future. Finally, she'd spoken again.

"But you, Emissary Salang Chai are clearly not insane. The murder of High Councillor Balopop was premeditated and expertly executed for no other reason than to further your own interest and that of your people. Balopop opposed your request for asylum and you obviously felt that with him out of the way you stood a much better chance of achieving your goal. Despite your deplorable actions, you are as cognisant as any of us, and for that reason we are loath to send you to a hospital for the criminally insane."

The judge had called Chai and Colopo forward and turned the computer screen so that they could see what was displayed. To Chai, the confusing array of swirls and squiggles had meant nothing, but the translator quickly ran her eyes down the page, reading the passage that had been highlighted. As she'd read she'd shaken her head and cursed quietly under her breath. This was even worse than she could have ever imagined.

"We will have to study the legal implications of our intent overnight before we can make a final decision," the judge had told them, "but as far as we can tell, the only option open to us is to place you in stasis indefinitely until someone can figure out what to do with you. As you are no doubt aware, people seldom last in stasis for more than twenty years. That will probably mean you'll be in stasis for the rest of your life."

Then they'd taken him away. Dragged him from the courtroom as he'd fought vainly against the two Law Enforcers who had him gripped firmly by his arms. He'd yelled at them, protesting his innocence in words no one except Shan, Colopo and her student could even understand. They'd thrown him into the back of a large, enclosed vehicle, driven him sixteen city blocks to the holding cell and locked him inside. The cell was cold, uncomfortable and smelt of death. In the morning the three judges would tell him of their final decision. Chai felt sure he knew what that decision was going to be.

As Colopo piloted her PTV back to her home later that day with Dr Shan kneeling on the passenger seat next to her, Shan became almost distraught with grief and confusion at the day's outcome.

"Chai did not murder that woman!" she declared vehemently. "I know my husband. Such an act would be impossible for him to commit."

"Dr Shan, with respect, it is impossible to repudiate what we have just seen. The images produced during shallinop are impossible to fake. What we saw is exactly what happened. There is simply no questioning that fact."

"He's a good man, Colopo," implored Shan. "He doesn't know how to be anything else. You have to believe me. Somehow Security guard V'napolo is either lying or mistaken."

Colopo puffed out her cheeks and made a low, growling noise in the back of her throat, to indicate her derision at her guest's comments. Fooling a shallinop machine was impossible. Everyone knew that. Salang Chai had killed High Councillor Balopop in cold blood, that was indisputable, and now he was going to pay for his crimes.

But even as Colopo told herself these things, something started to nag at her subconscious. Something seemed wrong, dreadfully wrong with the whole incident. Dr Shan was correct Salang Chai was a good man. Colopo knew it without a single doubt in her mind.

So what the hell was going on?

Chapter 45

LIKE SOME DARK AND evil portent to the bleak future on the horizon, the morning of Chai's sentencing dawned overcast and grey. Colopo stood transfixed at the window of her lounge room and gazed unseeingly at the waterlogged city stretched out before her. The rain came down in sheets, teeming out of the black, oily sky and flooding the low lying areas of the city. The mountains to the east of her building were totally obscured by the downpour and the traffic on the streets below crawled agonisingly slowly as a half a million people battled the elements on their way to their place of employment.

Colopo too had a job to do.

"Are you sure you want to do this Sweetheart?"

"Yes......Well no, but I don't think I have any choice."

"Okay." Silpolo handed her daughter her silver bandoleer and watched as Colopo draped it over her shoulder. She adjusted the fall of her mother's silver and gold tunic slightly, so that it fitted more comfortably against her more willowy body.

"So how do I look?"

"Like someone who is going to get themselves into a whole lot of trouble. Impersonating a Law Enforcement officer is a serious crime Colopo."

"Chai is innocent Mum. I know he is. But if I don't do something, he's going to be convicted of a crime he didn't commit and spend the rest of his life in prison or be condemned to an eternity in stasis. I can't let that happen."

Silpolo nodded her understanding. She too did not believe the little alien had committed the heinous crime he had been convicted of. She kissed her daughter goodbye, wished her luck and walked with her to the door.

While Shan continued to sleep on the kneeling mats in the main living room, Colopo quietly left the apartment and travelled down to her building's PTV parking area. She retrieved her vehicle and drove the eleven kilometres, through the deluge, to the Salin 495 law enforcement building. She stopped outside and sat in the vehicle, motionless, her heart thumping so hard in her chest it felt as if it might burst through at any second. Her throat was dry and she felt she might throw up. It took nearly ten minutes before she built up enough courage to leave the vehicle.

"Impersonating a Law Enforcer is a serious crime," her mother had told her. "But not as serious as helping a convicted criminal escape lawful custody."

She presented herself to the front office.

"I've come to collect the alien and take him in for sentencing," she told the officer behind the front desk.

"You're early," she commented.

"Yes. There was quite a crowd outside the court yesterday, and this rain isn't helping with the traffic, so I figured I'd get in early and avoid the crush."

The officer went off, returning a few moments later with Salang Chai in tow. The little alien looked pale and tired, as if he hadn't slept at all during the night, but when he saw Colopo waiting for him, he immediately perked up.

"Hi," he said smiling. But before he could utter another sound Colopo bellowed at him.

"NO SPEAKING. The prisoner will remain quiet and obedient at all times during his transfer to the court."

"Oh! you speak their lingo," said the desk officer. "That explains why they sent you and not one of the regular Law Enforcement officers. I thought I hadn't seen you around here before."

Colopo smiled and nodded, then quickly ushered Chai out the door. She bundled him into the PTV, took her seat at the helm and took off, the tiny vehicle's engine squealing in protest at the rapid acceleration.

Chai noticed they were heading in the wrong direction. The court buildings were over to the south, Colopo was heading north east.

"What's going on?" Chai asked.

"Just be quiet Chai," Colopo snapped, then under her breath she muttered, "I must be insane doing this. I saw that woman's memory of you throwing High Councillor Balopop over the guard rail. There's no way her memory could be false....But it just doesn't make sense. There's something wrong with the whole thing and I have to figure out what the truth is."

She turned down a small side street and parked the vehicle. She threw open her door, clambered out into the rain, went around to the passenger's door and dragged Chai out onto the road. Quickly she unfastened his shackles.

"Okay," she said dragging the alien around to the driver's side of the vehicle. "We're going to take a trip out to the water treatment facility and you're going to drive."

It was nearly an hour and a half later when Colopo and Chai returned to the city. When they re-entered courtroom number seven, the three judges were already in attendance. Once again, the court room was packed to the rafters with sightseers. But except for the trio of judges, Chai recognised only two others. Shan was sitting at their table, her beautiful face still contorted with worry and despair, and her eyes red rimmed from crying. The only other person sitting at the table was the young, female student who had assisted Colopo while she translated Ambassador Iwar's declaration. The exact same woman in fact, who had identified Chai to the Law Enforcers on the morning of his arrest.

Shan looked as if she had been crying all morning, her eyes red and puffy and brimming with tears. She had been worried sick last night, and then woken this morning, only to find Colopo had already left. As Silpolo had no way of communicating with her, Shan had had no idea what was going on. It had been hell.

Chai took his seat between the young Tranian female and his wife. He smiled at her and wrapped her in his arms, kissing her and telling her not to worry. Everything was going to be alright. Colopo asked her student if she would assist by translating what she was about to say and then addressed the bench. But before she could open her mouth, the lead judge had a few comments of her own.

"TRANSLATOR COLOPO," she bellowed. "KINDLY EXPLAIN YOUR ACTIONS BEFORE I HAVE YOU ARRESTED FOR AIDING A CONVICTED FELON."

"Certainly honoured judge," answered Colopo calmly. "To put it as succinctly as possible, the alien Salang Chai is innocent."

"That has not been the finding of this court," hissed the judge. "We have already seen irrefutable evidence to the contrary."

"With deep respect to security guard V'napolo, she is mistaken, or rather I should say, she has been misled. If I may explain."

After some deliberation, reluctantly the three judges all nodded their approval.

Colopo paced back and forth before the three judges, trying to formulate in her mind, the best way of explaining what had happened over the last hour and a half.

"Many of the circumstances surrounding this case have been worrying me," Colopo began. "As stated yesterday, it seems impossible to me that the alien could have travelled over a hundred and thirty kilometres in just six hours, unless he had access to a vehicle. Of course as you yourself stated yesterday, honoured judge, Salang Chai could have stolen someone's PTV. It is quite possible, for example, he had memorised my security code, sneaked down to the parking area in the dead of night and used my PTV without my knowledge. But as I discovered this morning, there is one major problem with that theory. Salang Chai's knees bend the wrong way. It is physically impossible for him to reach the brake pedal if he is kneeling, and if he sits with his knees up around his ears, it is impossible for him to operate the brake pedal because of its vertical orientation. If he slides back so he can operate the brake pedal, it's then impossible for him to reach the steering controls. I assure you honoured judges, this morning I had the alien try every position imaginable. He was simply unable to contort his body in such a way that he was able to operate my PTV."

"That's all very well, translator," replied the lead judge, "but all that proves is that the alien must have used other means to get to Councillor Balopop's residence, abduct him, and take him to the water treatment facility.'

"That's a reasonable assumption of course, but there are other unexplained discrepancies. This morning, after Salang Chai's aborted attempt at driving my PTV, I took him out to the water treatment works and the scene of the crime."

Colopo reached into a fold in her tunic and retrieved a small silver hologram projector. She placed the device on the floor and stepped back as it activated.

"You can see in this vidi, taken earlier today, Chai and I approached the guard rail where Councillor Balopop supposedly met his demise. We made a very interesting discovery."

The two holographic images of Colopo and Chai walked quickly towards the barrier and stopped beside it.

"I am over two and a half metres tall, honoured judges and as you can see, the guard rail is at least another hundred millimetres above my head. Salang Chai on the other hand is not even one point five metres tall. Which means it's impossible for him to even reach the top rail of the barrier, never mind throw someone over it, someone who by the way, weighs nearly twice as much as he does."

"So you're saying some other alien, one much taller and stronger than your friend Salang Chai, killed High Councillor Balopop?" asked the second judge.

Colopo smiled and dropped the bombshell she had been building up to.

"No honoured judge, I'm not. You see Chai's mate, Dr Wawa Shan gave me the clue as to what has actually happened. She commented that the mechanoid which had been built to look like me, and which had brought Chai to Tran ten days ago, was actually much shorter than I am. She correctly guessed that the Tranian High Council had deliberately made the machine smaller so the aliens would find it less confronting."

"Ah!" said the lead judge. "So you surmise it was a mechanoid, a large one built by the aliens, which murdered Balopop."

Suddenly the door to the courtroom burst open.

"NO! The aliens had nothing to do with it at all." The comment came from the back of the court room. Silpolo, temporarily once again operating in her capacity as a Law Enforcer and wearing her spare uniform entered the room. She had Councillor Balopop in front of her. He was very much alive and was bent over at the waist, trying to extricate himself from the extremely painful wrist lock Colopo's mother had him in.

"As you can see, no one murdered Balopop. I found this piece of garbage hiding out at his grandmother's place. He has a very interesting story to tell the court. It makes very enlightening listening. If you have a few minutes to spare, we might even get to see justice done."

Chapter 46

AMBASSADOR IWAR STOOD on the upper level of the massive gantry, beside the towering hulk of Guild Leader Volot's flagship transporter, and shook its head in disgust. For the past six days, the mechanoids had been hard at work in the factory next to the dry docked vessel, constructing and installing the seventeen compression torpedoes. One for each of the alien vessels currently in orbit around Tran. Yesterday, they'd loaded them onto Volot's freighter, but today they were unloading them. To Iwar, the torpedoes seemed incredibly small for such a powerful device. It was hard to imagine that just one of these weapons, a tiny sphere less than a metre in diameter, could have annihilated an entire galaxy class star ship. Not only that but, in doing so, it would've killed thousands of people. All those lives destroyed, and for what? So that Volot wouldn't loose the most valuable freight contract in living memory!

The Tranians had discovered massive Nelamine ore deposits on an asteroid in the Nastalin quadrant. It was estimated that these deposits might even be as much as seventy million tonnes. But the Tranians had no large ships, and so no practical way of transporting the ore to their home planet for processing. Volot had offered, for a price of course, the use of some of the Trader Guild's transport vessels. The deal was worth over ninety million credits, and if it had been announced, the Trader Guild's share price would have quadrupled overnight.

But before the announcement could be made, the alien's had arrived on the scene. They had seventeen Galaxy Class warships, huge ships which could easily be modified to carry the Tranian's precious ore. In fact their Emissary had even offered the use of those ships, should the Tranians ever need them, during his speech to the tribunal. Volot's prospective, multimillion credit contract had suddenly flown out the window.

So Volot and its Tranian co-conspirator, High Councillor Balopop, had hatched a plan to discredit the alien's spokesman. They'd faked Balopop's murder, making it look like the alien, Emissary Salang Chai, had been the perpetrator. They'd tried to force the tribunal to refuse the alien's request for asylum, hoping that they would leave, taking their massive ships with them.

Of course, with nowhere left to go, the aliens might also have tried to force the Tranians to allow them to stay. This was the real reason Volot had implored the Ambassador to allow its ship to be armed with the compression torpedoes. Just in case that eventuality had happened and Volot had been 'forced' to destroy their ships. And in doing so, any potential competitors.

Now both High Councillor Balopop and Guild Leader Volot were under house arrest. Both had been indicted on charges of conspiracy, stock market manipulation, inciting racial hatred and a host of other crimes.

Iwar turned to the factory foreperson at its shoulder and directed it to have all but one of the compression torpedoes disassembled and recycled. Iwar was sure that now that Salang Chai had been cleared of all wrongdoing, and once the tribunal had appointed Balopop's replacement to the panel, the aliens would almost certainly be accepted and allowed to settle on Tran. They had shown themselves to be more than capable of integration into Tranian society. They had, it seemed, just as Iwar had hoped, reached that point in their evolution where they were beginning to realise it was far better to follow a path of peace and harmony and practice the judicious use of the universe's finite resources, than to try to force everything and everyone, to conform to their wishes.

At least Iwar hoped they had. If they hadn't, well then Ambassador Iwar still had that one last remaining compression torpedo.

Chapter 47

AS PREVIOUSLY EXPLAINED, the Tranian word Halinop means 'I am urgent', whereas the derivative word Kalpolo means "I am placid." The two words are coincidently, also the names of Tran's two moons, one of which is designated female and the other male. In fact the origins of these two words, and correspondingly the names of the moons themselves, are almost certainly based on the peculiarities of those two large satellite's unique orbital characteristics.

While it is not uncommon for a planet to have more than one moon, it is rare for them to have two moons which vary so differently in their orbital paths. In many ways Halinop falls into the more regular configuration of a moon, that is to say it not only orbits its mother planet, but at the same time it also follows Tran's track as the planet makes its way around the solar system. But as Tran revolves around an almost vertical axis once every twenty hours, and Halinop itself orbits Tran every sixty two days, the moon Halinop appears in a different part of the sky every night. It's never in the same place two nights running, hence the title Halinop meaning 'I am urgent'

Kalpolo on the other hand, while it also follows an almost identical path around the sun as its larger mother planet, orbits Tran at just a few minutes more than its parent world's twenty hours. It also orbits in the same direction and follows an almost perfectly circular path just a few degrees above the equator. This meant that to the ancestors of the planet's current people, Kalpolo appeared to be almost stationary in the sky, never varying more than one or two degrees from its previous days position. On the other hand, to the ancients at least, the moon Halinop seemed to be moving about the sky continuously.

So while it's smaller sister Kalpolo is actually the speedier of the two, from the planet's surface it gives the impression of being content to stay in just the one spot, moving only slowly, in fact almost imperceptibly over the centuries.

Ironically, although it travels at a much slower pace than its apparently stationary sister, it is the larger, yet slower orbiting moon, which was given the name Halinop, or "I am urgent."

For Admiral Vethil, this meant that the apparently stationary Kalpolo presented itself as the perfect target. He had shown great patience over the past fifteen days. The damn Tranians had been given every opportunity to come to the party and agree to the refugees request, but they had used every delaying tactic known to avoid making a decision. Now even though Chai had been cleared of any wrong doing, Vethil felt sure, even now, they might still refuse to allow the refugees to settle on their dreadful planet. So he felt he had no other choice than to force them to reconsider.

But at the same time, the memory of the destruction of his own planet was still fresh in Vethil's mind, and he knew that were he to fire a full power pulse of the vortex canon at Tran itself, the results could be catastrophic. He might even inadvertently leave Tran uninhabitable. The annihilation of Kalpolo would prove to the 'Fish Heads' that he, Admiral Vethil Wangan, was not someone to be trifled with. Also, the strike on Kalpolo would at the same time, provide an invaluable test of the weapon's capability. If as he hoped, the canon's impact was not as devastating as the device which had destroyed his own planet, if for example the damage could be contained to say just a few kilometres in diameter, he might even be able to use it against Tran itself. The thought of having such destructive power at his fingertips made Vethil shiver with excitement.

He was sure that once the Tranians had witnessed the awesome power of his vortex canon against the moon Kalpolo, they would undoubtedly bow to his will and agree to let his people live on their planet. If not, Vethil would make sure they paid the ultimate price for their disobedience.

He gave the helmsman the order for the canon to be charged ready for firing. There was a momentary and quite noticeable drop in the ship's power as the massive drain on the generators caused them to falter momentarily and then surge. Then, as the vortex canon charged up, Vethil fed the targeting coordinates into the computer and set the countdown for thirty minutes.

Half an hour later the moon formerly known as Kalpolo disappeared in a massive cloud of vapour.

Chapter 48

THE DESTRUCTION OF Kalpolo could be seen quite clearly from the city of Salin, though very few people noticed until the first, huge shock wave hit the planet's atmosphere. When that happened, all hell broke loose. The pressure wave raced across the sky at ten times the speed of sound, destroying almost everything within a one hundred kilometre circle radiating outward from the pressure waves initial point of impact. Thankfully as the epicentre was almost three hundred kilometres from the city itself, Salin was largely spared. But even so, many of the city's buildings were damaged or destroyed, and almost every window imploded inwards when the high frequency vibration which followed the initial shock wave hit. Those buildings in the north east of the city, that is, those closest to the epicentre, suffered the most. Hundreds of people lost their lives that day, and thousands more were injured or lost their homes. Buildings collapsed as huge fissures in the ground opened up. Fires sprang up all over the north east, ignited by the lightning storms, facilitated by the huge and sudden increase in static electricity, brought on by the pressure waves rapid movement through the atmosphere. Some of the fires burned out of control for nearly two days before they were extinguished, and huge clouds of toxic smoke filled the air over the city for much, much longer.

The worst was yet to come. For billions of years, the gravitational influence of the moon Kalpolo had been affecting and controlling the planet's tides. Incalculable megalitres of ocean water had been lifted slightly and held there, by the massive gravitational force of the moon. Now, instantaneously, that force had been taken away. The oceans affected collapsed, dropping just a few centimetres in less than a second. But even that seemingly small change was sufficient to create huge tsunamis, tidal waves hundreds of metres high, which moved at phenomenal speeds, surging towards the low lying landmasses. Huge sections of the coastline on every continent, were washed away and thousands more people perished or were left homeless by the destructive force of the inundation.

Even after the floodwaters had receded, many areas which had previously been dry were now metres underwater and other areas which had once been close to the ocean, were now left many kilometres inland. In fact the shape of every continent on the planet was permanently changed.

While the vast majority of Kalpolo had simply been vaporised, a huge section of it broke free from the main body and disintegrated into large chunks. Most of this shrapnel became entrapped in the gravitational field of Tran itself and for almost a full day after the explosion, the surface of the planet was peppered with white hot meteors, the largest of which struck the ground with a force comparable to a major earthquake.

After the pressure wave hit Tran, the entire planet was bombarded with gamma rays, which rendered all forms of electronic communication impossible for almost three hours. Devoid of any news, at least news which could be authenticated, the population of Tran had simply cowered in their homes and waited for the next devastating blow from the orbiting war ship.

When communications were finally possible again, Vethil opened a channel between himself and the Tranian High Council and laid down his demands. The planet was to surrender unconditionally to him. He would then land his seventeen warships at various locations around the world and set up a number of protectorates. These protectorates would be overseen by one or more of his officers, men and women who would be appointed, by Vethil himself, from within the ranks of his army. When this step had been completed, the seventeen ships in his fleet would land once more and the rest of his people would disembark and take up residency.

If the High Council refused these demands, Vethil told them, his retribution would be swift and lethal. He gave them just thirty hours to comply.

The next communique to the High Council came from the Annuxian Ambassador Iwar. It had some disturbing news. After the discovery of Volot and Balopop's conspiracy, the Annuxian government had decided to decommission all but one of the compression torpedoes previously arming Volot's freighter. It would take at least two Tranian days to build new ones.

"Time will be essence. Annuxians know it urgent. Quickly will work for resolution earlier for dire situation." The Ambassador told the Tranian High Council. What it didn't say was, "Until then, you're on your own."

Chapter 49

CHAI, SHAN, COLOPO and Silpolo spent the day following Vethil's insane destruction of the moon Kalpolo, by helping those in their neighbourhood who had fared worse than themselves. Many of Colopo's neighbours had been injured or were too old or frail to cope without assistance. So everyone who could, volunteered to help out.

Silpolo's apartment had a few shattered windows, some damage to one of the internal, non load bearing walls and some minor water damage from a burst water pipe, but nothing major. In fact the whole building had held up surprisingly well. But while Chai, Shan and the two Tranian women had escaped unharmed, many of their neighbours had been injured, mainly by flying glass and falling debris.

With Vethil's deadline now just twenty six hours away, they all felt sure their efforts were probably futile. At dawn the following day, Vethil would launch his attack. Whether that was in the form of ground troops or another blast from his deadly canon remained to be seen. But whatever happened, at dawn tomorrow, it was almost certain many more people were going to be injured or killed.

Even so, everyone felt it was better to do something rather than just sit at home and wait for what seemed to be the inevitable outcome. Vethil had delivered his ultimatum and no one felt he was bluffing. Both Chai and Shan were certain he would open fire on the city of Salin if his demands were not met. In the meantime, in typical

Tranian fashion, it appeared the High Council were doing precious little.

"The Annuxians have a saying concerning the people of Tran." Colopo had told them earlier, shaking her head in frustration at her governments lack of decisiveness. "The Tranian High Council find even outrage outrageous."

Chai understood what the Annuxians meant. The Tranians somehow just couldn't seem to understand that sometimes a little moral outrage was needed, if you were to elicit positive action, especially when you were looking down the barrel of a gun. A very big and deadly gun. The Tranian High Councils lack of decisiveness was astounding.

With Silpolo's assistance, Shan commandeered some medical supplies from a nearby paramedic station. The medico on duty was totally snowed under, treating dozens of people who had been injured in the attack, and was grateful for any assistance she could get. The paramedic spent a few minutes putting together a comprehensive first aid kit, and sent them away with her thanks.

Shan and Silpolo carried their precious medical supplies back to Colopo's building where Shan up an outdoor clinic, on the street outside the building, erecting a makeshift table by placing Silpolo's broken front door across the top of two waist high storage containers. Then with the help of young Dillip, she set about cleaning and dressing minor wounds and stitching up the occasional deep laceration. Surprisingly, no one seemed to mind that the 'Doctor' treating them was some weird looking alien who spoke only a few words of their language.

Chai and Colopo went door to door checking that each apartment's inhabitants were accounted for, and asking everyone they met if they needed assistance. The building's elevator had been slightly damaged and both Chai and Colopo felt it prudent to give the device a wide berth until it had been checked out by a suitably equipped maintenance drone. That finally happened around midday.

The two friends made it to the fifteenth level before they encountered what they considered their first major catastrophe. The elderly lady in 1506 was lying on the floor of her kitchen with a large, two door refrigeration cabinet, lying across her legs. The two doors of the cabinet had been well stocked with heavy bottles and containers, and when the pressure wave hit the building, both doors were flung open. The refrigeration cabinet had overbalanced and fallen forward, landing on top of the unfortunate woman.

Colopo told her that they were there to help and asked her if she was in any pain.

"Yes," the old woman replied, explaining that her right shoulder had taken the brunt of the impact and that from the pain in her leg, she felt sure her right knee had also been damaged.

Chai climbed up onto the kitchen bench and scooted around to the other side of the cabinet. He took hold of one side of the cabinet and Colopo the other. Together they carefully lifted it back on to its base.

Chai looked at the old woman's right leg. It was sitting at a very strange angle and for a second he thought the woman's knee had been crushed and the leg broken. Suddenly he realised what he was looking at, and before he could stop himself, he burst out laughing. The old woman looked at him as if her were mad. She was in a great deal of pain and was embarrassed at the indignity of being found in such a predicament.

"I'm sorry," Chai stammered. Squatting up and down on his haunches to demonstrate his meaning. "My people, well our legs bend the other way. I forgot that your knees are supposed to bend backwards and when I saw you with your foot sticking out in front of you I thought..... Oh Gods! I'm so sorry."

Colopo tried her best to translate her friend's apology, but although she sort of understood what Chai was trying to say, why he had laughed at the poor old woman's distressing situation was beyond her comprehension. They were strange creatures these little aliens.

Together they managed to carry the woman downstairs and around the corner to the paramedics station where the attending medico confirmed that the woman's knee had been wrenched sideways by the impact and, although there was no broken bones or torn ligaments, the leg would be quite tender for a few days. The paramedic, found her a temporary cot at the rear of the building for her to use until the elevator was fixed, and prescribed a course of analgesics for the pain and two days bed rest. No one mentioned that was two days which she probably didn't have.

By the time they had climbed back up the stairs to level fifteen once more, Chai felt as if he needed two days bed rest himself. Despite the slightly lower gravity on Tran, his short legs and the tall, steep steps were taking a heavy toll on his thighs and calves.

In apartment 6112 they encountered their second major injury. The two year old son of the apartment's owner had been watching some children's vidi show on their viewer when the pressure wave hit. The viewer had been thrown off its stand and the glass screen had fractured. A large section had fallen out and the sharp edge had landed on the little boys left leg, cutting it badly. The child's mother had managed to stop the bleeding, wrapping the leg tightly with some bandages from her first aid kit, but the kid really needed stitches. After Colopo had asked the mother's permission, Chai lifted the toddler onto his shoulders and carried him down the stairs to his wife's temporary clinic with the boy's mother hot on his heels. They lay the little tyke onto Shan's home made operating table and she inspected his injury.

"Yes," Shan agreed. "The cut is quite deep, but luckily all the major blood vessels have been missed. Even so I'd better slip in a couple sutures to close up the wound."

She called Dillip over, and using sign language and mime, tried to get him to understand she needed some form of local anaesthetic to be brought from the plethora of indistinguishably labelled bottles, vials and hypoderms they'd commandeered from the paramedic station. Eventually he got the idea and handed Shan what looked like a thick metal collar festooned with a myriad of coloured lights and a single, solitary switch. Shan shrugged her shoulders and raised her hands, palms up, to show she didn't understand. Dillip took the device from her, placed it around the toddler's neck and locked it shut. Then he threw the switch. Moments later the little boy closed his eyes and his head slumped sideways. He was asleep, or rather unconscious. Dillip lifted the boy's hand a few centimetres off the table and let it fall to show Shan the kid was out cold.

Shan had seen prototypes of such a device on her home planet, but those machines had seemed to cause more pain and discomfort than they'd prevented. She'd seen one such appliance placed around the neck of a laboratory animal. The medical technician had thrown the switch and a series of micro filaments had injected themselves into the animals spinal column. The poor thing had writhed and squirmed in agony for thirty seconds or more before the electrical charge emitted by the device finally rendered the unfortunate beast unconscious. The Tranian device on the other hand, seemed to work perfectly, and did it without painfully intruding into the patients spinal cord.

Quickly Shan inserted four tiny sutures into the toddlers leg and then sanitised and dressed the wound. Then she handed the little boy back to his mother and turned to her next patient. The line was growing inexorably longer with each passing hour and Shan suspected many of those in the line were there for no other reason than to catch a glimpse of the strange alien doctor. She sighed as Dillip led the next injured Tranian to her table. It was going to be a long day.

By mid afternoon the throng of injured or those needing assistance had slowed to a dribble. The elevator had been checked over and pronounced safe, and the city's army of maintenance drones had descended on Colopo's building and were rapidly repairing every pane of broken glass, every damaged apartment and every electrical or water delivery fault caused by the exploding moon's deadly pressure wave.

In many ways the bulk of the drones were extremely similar to those used on the 'War Hawk'. They too were spherical in shape, multi-armed and multi-purpose. But then there was another machine, a mammoth mechanoid almost fifty metres long and twenty metres high, whose sole purpose was to repair the broken windows. The huge machine came trundling down the street outside Colopo's building and stopped, blocking off both lanes of traffic in both directions. It slowly rose up on long spiral pylons which seemed to grow out of the mechanism's underside, lifting the main body up almost to the top of the building. Ports on the machines sides and top then opened up and a couple of dozen long, spindly, tentacle like arms, uncoiled and snaked outwards. The arms pushed their way through the broken windows, and there was a loud clattering din as tonnes of broken glass fragments were sucked up into the machine.

"The mechanoid will collect all the broken glass," explained Colopo. "It will then measure the opening of each window and reuse the broken glass fragments to make new ones."

Seconds later other tentacle like arms extended out towards the building, and as Colopo had explained, each one carried a newly constructed pane of glass, still glowing slightly red from the machine's internal furnace. The four friends watched the machine in action for a while and then turned back to their tasks.

Shan had just picked up a swab with which to clean and disinfect her next patient's minor cuts and abrasions, when a Law Enforcer stepped up to Chai. This time however, instead of dragging Chai away in magnetic restraints, the Law Enforcer asked him politely, through Colopo, if he would please accompany her to the Tranian High Council's chambers, and would his mate, Doctor Wawa Shan and the translator Colopo please accompany them.

Chapter 50

THE MEETING TOOK PLACE in the same building where the tribunal had met just three days previously, but this time everyone gathered in a smaller, more private room on one of the upper floors. The room was sparsely decorated, with plain muted yellow walls, a low white ceiling and a pale grey tiled floor. There were a few vidi images on the walls depicting former High Council members, but the only decoration of any real note was in the centre of the room. It was a large circular mosaic in the middle of the floor depicting the Tranian crest, a gold and black Nary bird, inset into a field of swirling silver. The room had a single, circular table, with twelve chairs arranged around its perimeter. Two of the chairs had been hastily constructed to accommodate the different physical needs of the two aliens. There was no other furniture.

Through a large window looking out over the city to the east, Chai could see the sparkling, pale green serpentine waters of the river Malpo as it meandered lazily through the centre of Salin. Shan joined him at the window, slipping her hand into his and squeezing it gently. She lay her head on his shoulder, quietly told him she loved him and assured him that they would find a solution to the dreadful situation in which they found themselves.

The door opened and the eight most politically powerful women and men on Tran entered. Chai recognised three of them from the tribunal, but the others were all strangers. Not surprisingly, High Councillor Balopop was not among them.

Supreme leader Zilpolo was an ancient, withered old woman, who according to Colopo, had been elected to office nearly one hundred years ago. Her health had deteriorated a little over the past decade, but she still carried herself with remarkable poise and grace for someone her age, and still had a razor sharp mind equal to any on the planet.

The Tranian High Council operated as a true democracy, with each of the twelve elected members, having equal voting rights with the others. So in effect, Zilpolo had no more authority than any other High Councillor, but as Supreme Leader, even if she was in reality just a figurehead, the respect she commanded was palpable.

Everyone took their seats, Zilpolo addressed the meeting and Colopo once again acted as translator.

"Thank you Emissary Salang Chai," she began, "and thank you also Doctor Wawa Shan for agreeing to meet and advise us on the likely actions of the criminal, Admiral Vethil. Please tell us, is there any way in which we can stop this madman from carrying out his terrifying threat?"

Both Chai and Shan had racked their brains continuously to try to come up with a way of thwarting Vethil's murderous intent, but they had been unable to arrive at a single plan. At least nothing practical.

The Tranians had no weapons, nothing more lethal than a kitchen knife. So they had nothing with which to launch a counter attack. They could perhaps send a mechanoid piloted transport vessel, to crash into the 'War Hawk', destroying the vortex canon. But a slow moving craft didn't stand a chance against his deadly weapon.

They had also discounted sending an intergalactic capable craft, through a vortex and crashing it directly into Vethil's flagship. Any wormhole would take at least a full minute to open up, and as soon as that began to happen, Vethil would be alerted and have ample time to prepare for the attack.

There was a slim chance however that if Chai contacted Vethil and told him he was returning to the ship with valuable information, the Admiral might take the bait and allow Chai's transporter to dock. The hope being that Chai might be able to get the jump on Vethil and knock him out.

But Zilpolo put paid to that idea.

"When your armada first arrived we smuggled many nanobots onto your ships. They do two things. Firstly they clean and re-oxygenate your air, and secondly they record everything that happens on board and then relay that information back to us here on Tran," the Supreme Leader told them. "Thanks to the information sent back to us, we now know that Vethil has imprisoned every conscious person on board 'War Hawk'. He has also revived fifty two of his soldiers. These soldiers have been told that our two people are at war and that you and Doctor Wawa Shan have defected to our side. If Vethil lets you come on board, it would only be to capture you or kill you."

Chai felt ill. He also felt deeply ashamed. Once again his people had brought death and destruction to another world. Once again, their violent nature was wreaking havoc on a previously peaceful planet. He hung his head in shame and begged the Council to forgive him.

"You cannot be held responsible for the criminal actions of another, Emissary Salang Chai," said one of the unnamed councillors. "The criminal Admiral Vethil is quite obviously insane and it is also clear he has misled others into believing it is the people of Tran who are the aggressors. You have told us this has often been the case throughout your history. The information we have covertly gathered from your fleet, indicates that not a single person on any of the other ships supports Vethil in his heinous quest to invade our home. Not one."

"That's very gracious of you, honoured councillor, to make such a magnanimous statement," replied Chai. "But as the appointed spokesperson, representing my people, I can't help feeling that this is my fault. I should have seen the danger beforehand. We should have done something to stop him before it became too late. Now we are helpless to stop him and even if the High Council was to agree to his demands, it is certain that more people will die."

He stood and crossed his arms across his chest and bowed deeply. "Please give me the use of a transporter Honoured Councillors. At least let me try to reach the ship. I have to try to stop him before it's too late."

But his pleas fell on deaf ears. Too many people have died already they told him. His attempt would be futile, nothing more than suicide.

But after three hours no one could come up with a better plan.

Chapter 51

EX GUILD LEADER VOLOT, former trader, business person and major share holder of the Trader Clan, considered its life to be over. The aliens had finally attacked the Tranian home world, just as it had always known they would. In the light of the alien's actions, the Annuxian judiciary had found it impossible to condemn Volot. Regardless of the reasoning behind its actions, Volot had after all, been the only one who had predicted the events of the past eighteen hours. Not only that, but it had been the only one who had been prepared to take what it considered the necessary steps to prevent the aliens from attacking Tran. Volot's reasons and intentions had been terribly flawed, but its actions could not be faulted. Volot was released from home detention and told to return to its normal life.

But Guild Leader Volot's normal life could never be the same. Trader Clan share prices had plummeted. In fact a person couldn't give them away at present. Everyone on the planet knew, that until the conflict between the Tran and the aliens was resolved, trade between Annux and Tran would cease. As Tran was Annux's largest, most lucrative trading partner, such an event would obviously have a devastating effect what the clan earned. Share prices plummeted even further.

Now the alien Vethil had declared war on Tran. He'd discharged his deadly vortex canon, destroying one of their moons in a display of such awesome power that the Tran High Council were left floundering, totally unsure about what they should do next. Thank heavens Iwar had managed to convince the Annuxian Government to retain at least one of the compression torpedoes.

Volot knew that its life was over. It would never be able to recoup its losses. Coming back from such a catastrophic financial disaster was impossible. It was also inconceivable that it would ever regain sufficient esteem amongst the trader clan to ever be reappointed to the exulted position of Guild Leader again. Balopop and Volot had, after all, been quite prepared to sacrifice thousands of people, the last remaining souls of an entire civilization no less, in their quest for a few million credits...Okay make that nine million credits.

But if Volot couldn't redeem itself with the Trader Clan, then perhaps it might still make amends with the people of Tran. The Tranian High Council had begged the people of Annux to come to their aid. Admiral Vethil had given them just thirty hours in which to comply to his demands, and only twenty two more hours remained until that deadline expired. Volot would be there in four.

The Trader Clan freighter known simply as number 11, was already loaded with the last remaining compression torpedo. Volot was at the helm, carefully manoeuvring the large, cumbersome vessel out of dry dock. its actions had not been sanctioned by the Government, and vessel number 11 belonged to another guild member. But Volot knew drastic steps had to be taken if a major disaster was to be avoided. If Vethil acted out on his promise and fired the vortex canon at the city of Salin, millions would die. In that light, stealing another guild member's vessel seemed somehow unimportant.

In addition to stealing the vessel in the first place, there was also no time to follow the correct protocols for leaving the dry dock, and no time to disengage the myriad of hose lines, electrical conduits or the walkways leading from the two large gantries positioned alongside the ship. Volot simply fired up the vessel's manoeuvring engines and lifted off. There was a deafening cacophony of tearing and twisting metal as the ship tore itself free from its moorings and a huge crash as the ship burst through the roof, still shut against the heat of the Annuxian midday sun, but once clear, vessel number 11 rose majestically into the air and headed for the heavens. As the ship and it's solo hijacker gained altitude, Volot quickly entered the co-ordinates for the planet Tran. It had one chance of ridding the universe of the scourge of the alien vermin once and for all.

One chance only, and a very slim one at that.

Chapter 52

"I TELL YOU THE MAN is completely mad," this proclamation came from Willish Jhan, 'War Hawk's' primary helmsman. "Last night I heard him pacing about his ready room for hours, ranting and raving at no one, talking about the obligation he had, to make the Tran pay for the devastation they'd inflicted on our home world."

"But the Tranians had nothing to do with our home world being destroyed. That was our own doing. We'd barely had any contact with the Tranians at all until we arrived here and asked them to let us stay!" said one of the cargo handlers.

Jhan held his hands up as if in surrender, shaking his head in despair. "That's exactly what I'm saying. The man's insane."

The remaining six conscious members of 'War Hawks' crew, now locked up in the brig, had decided to discuss what could be done. The first thing of course was to get the hell out of prison. Skillen Chun was sure he could remotely access the cell's locking mechanism and override the locks. He claimed he could have them free in just minutes. But what then?

Everyone on board had of course been horrified by Vethil's recent actions. To launch a completely unprovoked attack on a peaceful species...AGAIN....was totally off the wall. Especially as Tran was quite probably the last safe haven on which they could resettle. Jhan was right, Vethil was totally, bat shit crazy and something had to be done.

"So what do we do?" asked Skillen Chun.

"Hit the bastard over the head with a hammer and lock him up before he wakes up," answered the first cargo handler's offsider. "That way we can explain to the Tranian High Council that the stress associated with the destruction of our planet sent Vethil over the edge and he acted alone. We throw ourselves on their mercy and hope like hell they forgive us and let us resettle."

Everyone agreed.

"I just wish Wawa Shan and I had acted sooner," said Chun and went on to tell the others of the discussions he and the doctor had had a few days ago.

"So who's going to take the bastard down?" asked cargo handler two. There was a long, protracted silence as each person pondered that question. Finally, Willish Jhan spoke up.

"I suppose it had better be me. The squadron of troops he revived are all still in sickbay recovering from their time in stasis, so he's without a bodyguard. He rarely leaves the bridge any more and I know his movements while he's there intimately. The best time would be when he does his hourly navigation check to make sure 'War Hawk' isn't drifting. It requires complete concentration, so I should be able to sneak up on him while his back's turned and take him out. Yea, I'll have more opportunity than anyone else. You guys will have to arrange some sort of diversion to keep his troops occupied I suppose, but I'll be the one who takes Vethil out."

"Maybe we should just stick a knife in his back and be done with him for good. No one here is going to lose any sleep over his death, that's for sure." suggested Gollum Whin, the ship's navigator.

Jhan once again shook his head. "I don't think I can do that. I don't think I can murder someone in cold blood. Besides we still need to convince the Tranians to let us stay. I'm not sure how they'd react to yet another killing. After all, we're trying to show them we've turned over a new leaf and that we're now a peace loving species."

Everyone nodded their agreement. Regardless of the Tranian's take on things, too many people had died already. No matter how mad or evil Vethil was, it was preferable, if not necessary, to prevent any more deaths.

Fortunately, as promised, Skillen Chun was able to spring the locks on their cell and the group split up, promising to meet up again in two hours. Willish Jhan and navigator Whin made their way back to the bridge and after making sure none of Vethil's guards were about, waited outside his ready room for him to come on deck for a navigation check. After the destruction of the Tranian moon, Vethil had moved the 'War Hawk' back into orbit above the city of Salin. Now that the ship was back in position, all that had to be done was the occasional, deft touch on the manoeuvring thrusters if the huge ship started to drift slightly. That was a rare occurrence indeed, but regular checks still had to be made. Such a check was due in three minutes.

Jhan's mind was reeling as he contemplated what he was about to do. Of course he couldn't use an actual hammer. But something heavy and solid was definitely needed. As Jhan glanced around himself, searching for the perfect weapon, Vethil silently crept up behind him and drew his huge, razor sharp ceremonial sword across the helmsman's throat. It appeared Admiral Vethil had been listening to the conversation taking place in the brig and knew he had been betrayed. Navigator Gollum Whin was the next to feel the wrath of their former leader, followed by the two cargo handlers. In fact only Skillen Chun escaped. He got away by climbing up into the ceiling cavity above his workshop and hiding. He quickly scampered through the crawlspace putting as much distance between himself and the Admiral as possible. As he crawled as fast as he could towards relative safety at the rear of the ship, he could hear Vethil bellowing insanely from the level below him. His words were just indistinct ramblings, but there meaning was clear none the less, Vethil was going to kill him and then, if the 'Fish Heads' didn't comply with his requests, he was going to fire the vortex canon on the city of Salin. He was going to keep firing until every last Tranian living in the city was dead.

Then he was going to start on the rest of the planet.

Chapter 53

MOST OF THE TIME, BEING only one point three metres tall and weighing just thirty five kilos, was a distinct disadvantage for Assistant Maintenance Engineer Skillen Chun. If some large, cumbersome, but necessary spare part was stuck up high on the top shelf, Chun had to go and get a ladder, or more likely, have one of the mechanoids retrieve it. Chun's diminutive size also meant he wasn't terribly strong. Heavy objects always had to be moved on a trolley, or by using one of the cargo drones. But sometimes, like now, when Chun had to worm his way through the cramped crawl spaces between the ships outer hull and the internal structures, Chun's tiny size was an absolute boon.

For the last two hours he had been jammed between the false ceiling of the main maintenance workshop and the floor of the upper level. The space was cramped and dirty, with kilometres of electrical conduit, air and water pipes and optic fibre control cables, running this way and that, and all crammed into the tiny crawl space beside him. It was also incredibly hot, and getting hotter by the minute.

Chun knew that the instant he entered the maintenance area, the heat sensors built into the workshop's security system would alert Vethil to his presence. But Chun also knew how to fool that system. By bi-passing the workshop's self regulating thermostat, he'd slowly, little by little, gradually increased the temperature of the room until it was now almost exactly the same as his own body's temperature. Chun knew it wasn't the heat generated by a living being that the sensors detected, but rather the difference between ambient and the higher temperature of that living being. If no difference could be detected, then the alarm wouldn't be activated.

Carefully he slid back one of the ceiling panels and looked down into the darkened workshop. In his mind he plotted out where each device and piece of equipment he needed was stored, working out the quickest, least intrusive method for retrieving them. Gingerly he slid through the hole and dropped silently to the floor. Gods it was hot.

With sweat pouring into his eyes, he crept about the workshop, quietly opening cupboards and sliding open drawers, collecting the equipment and tools he needed to disable Vethil's cursed gun. Now came the hard part.

Of course the easiest way to sabotage the canon was to take it off line. Without instructions from the targeting computer the gun couldn't fire. But to do that, Chun would have to access the computer and unfortunately, it along with Vethil himself, was on the bridge. Plus unless Chun could physically damage the computer link, all Vethil would have to do was reconfigure the computer to make the canon operable once more

Option two was far more lasting and preferable. The optic fibre control cable, which ran from the targeting computer to the vortex canon, passed through a large diameter conduit which ran nearly a kilometre, inside the vessels outer skin, from the bridge, through a sealed fitting on the outside of the hull and up into the firing mechanism on the base of the gun. If Chun could sever that optic fibre near the point where it went through the hull, there wasn't a chance the damn gun would ever fire again. Unless of course, the entire one kilometre length of optic fibre cable was replaced. But that wasn't possible because Skillen Chun had already dumped every spare piece of optic fibre cable on board out the ship's main disposal chute.

Unfortunately, getting to the point where the cable passed through the hull and then cutting the cable wasn't going to be easy. On the bright side, Skillen Chun was the perfect person to do it. Not only did he have an intimate knowledge of the many walkways, crawl-ways and short cuts through the labyrinth of maintenance passages which criss-crossed the entire length and breadth of the ship, he was the perfect size to traverse them. Sadly, even for someone only one point three metres tall and thirty six kilos in weight, crawling a convoluted route of nearly one and a half kilometres in length wasn't going to be easy.

Chun quietly dragged a large square tool box across the floor of the workshop, positioned it directly below the hole in the ceiling, and climbed up. He dragged the ceiling panels back into place and began to make his way towards the front of the ship. The trek would be arduous, hot, and no doubt painful on his poor knees. He would also be slowed by the many hatchways which had to be unbolted to allow access to the next crawlspace.

Chun reckoned it would take him at least two hours. That would leave him a little less than eight hours before that arsehole Vethil trained the canon on the city of Salin, and wiped out nearly three million people.

He desperately hoped he wouldn't be discovered before he managed to cut the cable.

Chapter 54

FORMER GUILD LEADER Volot knew it had only one chance to destroy Vethil's vortex canon, and that it was a slim chance at best. It would take Volot a mere eight minutes to transit through the vortex to the planet Tran. But as soon as it activated vessel number 11's SRS drive, a worm hole would open up between the two planets. The other end of the vortex would form as a huge swirling empty black spiral about five hundred kilometres above Tran's stratosphere. The vortex would be unmistakable and glaringly obvious for the full eight minutes Volot's stolen ship took to race through it. This meant Vethil would have that full eight minutes to target the end of the worm hole and simply wait for Volot to come through.

But even if Volot managed to come out the other side undetected, it still had to contend with the disadvantage of having only one compression torpedo. If Vethil fired off one of those 'Star Burst' mines the alien's had used previously, the impenetrable mesh of lasers would slice the torpedo into a hundred pieces and destroy it even before it reached Vethil's ship. Without a back up projectile, all would be lost. But that eventuality was something about which Volot could do nothing.

Volot laid in the coordinates for Tran, prudently choosing the opposite side of the planet to the one above which Vethil and his armada were stationed. At least that way it had remote chance of making it though unnoticed. Volot engaged the vortex drive and sat back as the aged transporter slowly accelerated towards the massive swirling whirlpool in space the ship's vortex drive had just created. Seconds later Volot felt an incredible surge of power as the ship was sucked inexorably into the worm hole. Time slowed perceptibly then and Volot once again marvelled at the way everything inside the ship, including itself, seemed to stretch and warp out of shape for a few seconds. In many ways the vision was quite beautiful, almost dreamlike.

But once the vessel's trajectory and speed had stabilised and the inside of the ship no longer looked like it was being forced through a narrow, twisting opening, Volot set the auto-pilot and left the helm. The Annuxian quickly hurried forward and began to prepare the compression torpedo for launch. There was no need to make precise targeting adjustments, a direct hit wasn't necessary. As long as the torpedo was headed more or less towards the 'War Hawk' and as long as it ignited less than a thousand meters away, the massive gravitational forces emitted, would destroy Vethil's ship. Volot set the weapon's proximity sensors for eight hundred metres just to be on the safe side and disengaged the safety protocols. The torpedo was now armed.

Eight minutes after first entering the vortex, vessel number 11 burst through into Tranian controlled space and slowed to a halt. Volot quickly opened an all frequency communications channel and listened for any chatter which might reveal if any of the alien ships had noticed its sudden arrival, but there was nothing.

Volot engaged the manoeuvring thrusters and slowly made its way as close as possible to the planets' atmosphere. It hoped the ionising effect of the air would slightly distort any radar scans until the last minute, hiding the Annuxian's presence as it made its way around to the other side. If not, Vethil would be waiting and watching when vessel number 11 rose above the horizon on the alien's side of the planet. In which case, Volot was as good as dead.

The Annuxian entered the coordinates it had downloaded from the latest transmission by the Tranian High Council. These coordinates gave War Hawk's last known position, directly above the city of Salin. Vessel number 11 automatically adjusted course slightly and accelerated. In approximately four minutes, Volot would have Vethil's flagship in sight.

Chapter 55

SKILLEN CHUN HAD LESS than fifty metres left of his trek though the bowels of the 'War Hawk' when disaster struck. The very last bulkhead hatchway had been damaged by a careless drone when it was installed. The drone had used the wrong size fitting to hold the hatch shut, and in typical drone fashion, the stupid machine had simply forced the retaining bolt to fit. The bolt was seized solid and with the simple hand tools Chun had at his disposal, and working in such a tight space, it took nearly ten minutes to get the damn hatch off. Hurriedly he threw the offending hatchway to one side. It hit the floor with a loud bang, which Chun was sure would have been heard back on the bridge, but there was no time to worry about that now. Just a few minutes ago there had been a marked drop and then surge in power, as the ship's automatic power generators surged in response to a sudden, huge increase, in demand. That could only mean one thing. Despite there being still over eight hours until his deadline expired, Vethil was charging the vortex canon prior to firing once again.

Chun unscrewed the conduit directly below the base of the gun and located the correct fibre optic cable. He reached into the pocket of his overalls and pulled out an ancient pair of cable cutters. He was just about to place the jaws of the cutters around the cable when his left foot exploded in a burst of pain. Vethil had finally located him and sent a swarm of tiny, invisible nanobots to deal with him.

The nanobots may have been far too small to see with the naked eye, but the pain and the damage they were doing to Chun's left foot and now left leg, was unbearable. He screamed in agony and tried desperately, blindly, to get away from the excruciating pain. In horror Chun looked down at his left work boot. It was as if it were alive, the heavy leather writhing and squirming as the nanobots quickly took it apart molecule by molecule. Then they started on his foot and leg.

As the tiny robots quickly consumed much of Chun's foot and lower leg, the shock and pain became too much and he began to lose consciousness. But even as he drew his last breath, he knew he had to complete his task. With the blackness of death swirling around him, he thrust out his trusty old cable cutters, wrapped the blades around the cable and squeezed. But just as the hardened Nelamine cutters closed around the optic cable, Admiral Vethil pressed the trigger and the deadly vortex canon fired for the second time. The pulse of energy flowing down the cable sent a shock down Chun's hand and arm, exploding the cutters from his grasp. Despite a valiant effort, Skillen Chun had failed. In just seven hours and fifty three minutes Vethil would fire the vortex canon once more. If that happened, every living being in Salin would be annihilated.

Volot too had failed, and in a far more devastating way than it could have possibly imagined. As soon as vessel number 11 had peeked its head above the horizon, Volot knew it was too late. The 'War Hawk' was bearing down on the Annuxian ship at maximum speed. Volot quickly launched the compression torpedo in the vain hope it would ignite before Vethil fired the gun. But its actions were futile. The projectile had barely covered a quarter of the distance to its target, when Vethil opened fire. The energy wave from the vortex canon raced through space at the speed of light, sweeping up the tiny torpedo in its wake and destroying it. Then the pulsing wave continued on and hit the front of vessel number 11 dead centre, vaporising it in nanoseconds. Volot never knew what hit it.

Ironically, it was Volot's attack that had caused Vethil to fire the gun just as Skillen Chun was attempting to sabotage it.

Now the planet Tran was once again in deadly peril.

Chapter 56

CHAI HADN'T BEEN ABLE sleep, no one had. Earlier that evening, a few hours before Volot's failed attack, he, Shan and Colopo had spent another three hours in the company of the entire Tranian High Council. They had been summoned once again in the vain hope that either Chai or his wife may have been able to think of some useful strategy on how to stop Vethil from launching his diabolical attack. Once again, no one could come up with a viable suggestion that wouldn't be considered simply suicidal. Eventually Supreme Leader Zilpolo closed the meeting.

"I wish you all good luck over the next few hours. If the criminal Admiral Vethil decides to fulfil his threat and fires on the city at dawn tomorrow, many of us will not survive. I hope and pray that by some miracle the disaster threatening us does not eventuate. But if it does, may all of us pass quickly and painlessly into whatever may lie beyond this life."

She crossed her arms across her chest and bowed deeply. Then she left the room. The others filed out immediately after.

That had been over twelve hours ago. It was now just an hour before dawn. The time when Vethil's ultimatum reached its deadline. Only one more hour to go before the entire city of Salin was destroyed.

No one except the very young had slept. Almost the entire city's population had migrated down to the parkland which ran along either side of the Malpo river. They'd set up tables and chairs along the banks, and they'd organised food and drink and music and other forms of entertainment with which to pass their last few remaining hours. No one knew who would still be alive after the dawn and everyone felt that if this was to be their last day on Tran, then they would make it a good one.

Now was the time to say good bye to family and friends and to hold the ones you loved and cherished. It was the time to party, to celebrate the lives lived and not to mourn the lives soon to be lost. Grieving would come tomorrow with the first rays of the sun.

Chai, Shan, Colopo and Silpolo joined the others from their building on the banks of the river. They sang and danced and stuffed themselves full of delicious fruit, and drank heavy, intoxicating alcoholic beverages, until they felt light headed and the world swam and spun around them.

Chai also sat on the grass and wept bitter tears. Despite Supreme Leader Zilpolo's decree that he was not to blame for the actions of that bastard Vethil, he couldn't shake off the terrible feeling of shame which assailed him. This terrible tragedy about to befall them was his people's doing. They were responsible. That meant he was responsible.

When he'd first been brought to the planet, the mechanoid 'Colopo' had shown him the beauty and wonder of what he had hoped would soon be his new home. He'd asked Colopo why the mechanoid had done this and she'd replied, that during the forthcoming hearing, he might be asked what he felt was the most beautiful thing about Tran. His answer, she'd said, might be influential in helping the tribunal to make up its mind.

He'd never been asked the question, maybe they hadn't got around to it, or maybe it simply wasn't really on the agenda. But Chai knew without doubt how he would have answered. The most beautiful aspect of the planet Tran wasn't the spectacular beaches, or the magnificent, towering mountains. It wasn't even the wonderfully productive agricultural lands. It was its people. They had shown him, indeed shown all the refugees, such kindness, such tolerance, such generosity it nearly took his breath away. He couldn't let that bastard Vethil repay them by killing thousands if not millions of them.

Suddenly he made a decision. He asked Shan and his friends to excuse him for a few minutes and made his way up the bank towards a quiet area between two nearby buildings. He reached into his pocket and pulled out his personal communicator. He pressed the button which connected him to the 'War Hawk' and placed the device on the ground in front of him. Seconds later the image of Admiral Vethil rose up before him.

Chapter 57

THIRTEEN MINUTES LATER Chai rejoined his friends on the grassy bank. He sat next to his beautiful wife and wrapped her in his arms. He told her he loved her and always would and kissed her passionately. They sat together, hugging each other, giving each other courage and waiting for the dawn to come. It came slowly. The blackness of night gradually gave way to the rising sun in the east. The stars eventually faded and the heavens turned from black to grey, to white, and finally blue.

In the east, the sky was peppered with a smattering of wispy clouds which slowly lost their grey tones only to be replaced by pinks and reds, before morphing into fluffy, white balls of cotton. It was the most beautiful dawn either of them had ever seen.

Chai glanced at his chronometer, noting as he did so that only seconds remained before Vethil's deadline. But those seconds passed, and more besides. Nothing happened for many long minutes.

Then a cheer went up a few metres further upstream. People began to get up off the grass. They were smiling and hugging and crying joyfully at the news which was travelling through the community like wild fire.

"What's going on?" asked Shan, leaping to her feet and straining to see along the river bank in an attempt to gauge what was happening."

"They've gone," Colopo yelled happily. "Vethil's 'War Hawk' and the other warships, they're all gone." She threw her arms around Chai and Shan and Silpolo, hugging them until they couldn't breathe.

"How? Where?" stammered Shan, barely able to get those two simple words out in her confusion and excitement.

Chai knew the answer to those questions but he wasn't going to say anything. Colopo knew too, and threw her arms around her little friend once more and pulled him close.

"Thank you!" she whispered and began to cry. She knew what had happened and also knew the terrible price Chai had paid.

Chapter 58

IT TOOK TWO DAYS BEFORE the Tranian High Council called upon Emissary Salang Chai and his wife Shan to once again address the tribunal. This time the meeting had been set up to investigate what had happened to Vethil and his armada. Nothing had been heard or seen of the alien's seventeen, galaxy class battle cruisers since the morning of their disappearance. Now, two days later, there were six, heavily armed Annuxian freighters, in orbit around the planet. The Captains of each ship had promised they would stay there as long as they were needed, keeping guard just in case the situation changed and Vethil came back. When the Annuxians had first arrived, just six hours after the alien's battle cruisers had moved away, the entire planet had breathed a collective sigh of relief.

Chai and Shan presented themselves to the High Council tribunal, once again held in the same small room, in the Tranian High Council building, a dozen or more floors above the city skyline. As usual Colopo was there to act as translator. To Chai's surprise, so was the young slender, female student who had assisted after his arrest. Even more surprising was the attendance of young Dillip.

Supreme Leader Zilpolo called the meeting to order and launched into a series of questions. These were predominately aimed at Chai and Shan, and were ostensibly about what had transpired two mornings ago.

"Not that anyone is complaining, Emissary Salang Chai, but we'd really like to find out what happened. At present no one is even sure if the criminal Admiral Vethil has gone for good, or if he's going to turn up again at any second and destroy us. Do you have any idea why he left so suddenly?" asked Supreme Leader Zilpolo.

Chai simply shrugged. "No idea honoured leader. But knowing Vethil, I can't see him ever coming back."

The conversation continued in this vein for a while longer, but both Chai and Shan were adamant they hadn't the slightest inkling about what the hell was going on. In Shan's case at least, that was the truth.

Suddenly Colopo shook her head as if in frustration at the lack of any discernible progress. She and the student both rose, and Colopo exclaimed that she would like to make a statement on her own behalf. The student Drolopo would translate her words so that Chai and Shan would understand.

"Honoured Councillors, my comments will, I believe, clear up a lot of unanswered questions, the answers to which, despite his claims, Emissary Chai is fully able to answer," she began. "On the evening before Vethil disappeared, everyone from my building was down by the river saying good bye and preparing for what we considered to be the end of our existence. A short time before dawn, Salang Chai crept away from our group to a quiet area to be by himself. I was worried about him, so I followed him into an alleyway between two buildings at the top of the river bank. There I witnessed a communique between Chai and Admiral Vethil. Unfortunately, I was unable to record the conversation, but if you will allow me to undergo shallinop, you will be able to witness first hand what I saw and heard. My student Drolopo will translate the alien's words while I am unconscious."

The High Councillors conferred for a few moments, then agreed to Colopo's request. While the equipment was being wheeled in and prepared, Colopo gave everyone a little bit of background history so they might better understand what they were about to see.

"No doubt everyone here has heard of the huge Nelamine ore deposits recently discovered in the Nastalin quadrant. After Emissary Salang Chai's false arrest and the uncovering of Volot and Balopop's conspiracy to have him discredited, it is fair to assume that Admiral Vethil had also become aware of it. It is important that you remember that when witnessing my memory of that night."

Chai got up from his seat. "There's no need to do this Colopo," he implored his friend quietly. "Vethil's not coming back. If he was going to, he would have done so by now. You know that as well as I do. He's gone. That's all that matters."

"NO. You are wrong Salang Chai. I agree Vethil is not coming back, but the people of Tran need to know what happened. They....We...The people of Tran, have a right to be told what you have done."

Chai shook his head, but slumped down onto his seat and buried his head in his hands. He was ashamed of his actions and couldn't stand the thought that everyone would soon know the terrible truth.

The mechanoid indicated it was ready to proceed and lifted the lid on the coffin like device. Colopo shed her tunic and climbed naked into the thick, gooey, neurogel. She lay back, submerging her whole body, including her head and face, into the viscous sludge. The mechanoid then closed the lid and stepped up to the control panel.

Just as V'napolo had done four days earlier, at first Colopo seemed to be in considerable distress as her body and mind fought against the subliminal belief that she would drown. Then she sucked in a lungful of liquid, and after a few moments began to calm. She crossed her arms over her chest and closed her eyes, surrendering herself to the narcotic qualities of the neurogel.

The mechanoid operator made a few minor adjustments to the control panel and moments later the air above the machine was filled with the holographic images of Salang Chai and Admiral Vethil. Both were standing in a darkened alleyway, down near the banks of the Malpo river.

From the images displayed, it was obvious Colopo was watching closely, hiding behind one of the building's walls, peering covertly around the corner into the alleyway. She'd seen Chai standing to attention, his holographic communicator laying on the stone walkway at his feet with Vethil's avatar hovering above it. As he and Vethil began to speak, Drolopo stepped up and began to translate the conversation for the High Councillors.

"It's about time you made contact, Chief Security Officer," sneered Vethil's avatar. "I hope you and your woman have found a nice big rock to hide under. In thirty five minutes I'm going to blast the entire city of Salin off the face of the planet."

"I don't think that would be a very astute thing to do Admiral," Chai answered calmly. "If the information I've recently obtained is correct, such actions could have devastating consequences."

"What the hell are you talking about Chief? What information?"

Chai bent down and pressed a button on his communicator. "I'm sending you the coordinates of a planet called Mogo 3 Admiral. It's a class 1 planet, capable of supporting life similar to ours. It has a breathable atmosphere, an abundance of fresh water, lots of animal and plant life, and huge tracts of arable land on which to grow our crops. But most importantly, it has no sentient life forms. Which means, the Annuxians wouldn't have installed a shield around it."

"You mean, you hope they haven't."

"No Admiral, in fact I'm certain they haven't. You see I've also found out that Mogo 3 is the site of the biggest Nelamine ore deposits, ever discovered. The Tranians made the discovery, and obviously they would never let the Annuxians install a shield around such a valuable find."

Vethil looked down at something, more than likely one of the computer screens on the bridge, which was out of sight of the 'War Hawks' holographic camera.

"I thought that discovery had been made in the Nastalin quadrant? These coordinates are for the other side of the galaxy."

Chai smiled and nodded enthusiastically. "That's right Admiral. That's what the Tranians want us, or rather want the Annuxians, to believe. But their deception is going to work in our favour. You see at present, sovereignty over Mogo 3 is being determined by just a handful of unarmed geologists. They have no way of protecting themselves from us if we decide to eradicate them and claim Mogo 3 as our own. As the Tranians have already claimed publicly that their discovery was made in the Nastalin quadrant and not on Mogo 3, they'll find it extremely difficult to convince anyone that we stole their find from them."

Vethil smiled. He was listening to Chai, but with only half an ear, he was concentrating on the detailed information about Mogo 3 that Chai had just sent him.

"We have a right to live somewhere Admiral, no one can question that," Chai continued. "Mogo 3 is perfect. Not only will it be a wonderful new home world, we will be rich beyond our wildest dreams. You Admiral, as the supreme leader of our new world will be the richest of all.

Vethil nodded. "Mmmmm, yes. Good work Chief. This is very valuable information. Very valuable indeed. As soon as I have dealt with this little problem we have with these Tranian creatures, we'll go to Mogo 3 and uh! investigate further."

Chai saluted once more. "As you wish Admiral," he said, but then continued. "But may I suggest the fleet makes its way to Mogo 3 immediately. You see I have other information pertaining to this wonderful opportunity. Information which requires us to take immediate action. You can always come back later to get me and my wife and to sort out these 'Fish Heads'."

Vethil appeared extremely frustrated at being asked to delay his attack on Tran any longer than necessary, but he nodded his consent and urged Chai to go on.

"As I have already alluded to Admiral, the Tranians want to keep the exact location of their Nelamine ore discovery a secret, particularly from the Annuxians. You see I have also learnt that the conspiracy by the Annuxian Volot and High Councillor Balopop to discredit our intentions to settle on Tran peacefully, had nothing to do with any lucrative freight contract. Balopop has now admitted that the Annuxians want the Nelamine ore for themselves. The don't know the exact location of the deposits, but with time they will surely find out. That could happen at any second..."

Vethil could see where Chai was going with this and interrupted him.

"So the bastards tried to make it look like you killed Balopop, knowing that in all likelihood, such bogus accusations could start a major conflict between us and the Tranians. They wanted us to start a war. Then while we and the Tranians were wasting time on the battlefield, they'd have more time to find this Mogo 3 planet and claim it as their own."

"Exactly Admiral. But Mogo 3 should be ours. We have nowhere else to go. We should go to the planet immediately, and make it our new home world. We can dispose of the few geologists stationed there and simply claim there was no one there when we 'discovered' the planet. Also, we have the vortex canon and nearly ten thousand troops to defend ourselves if anyone is ever foolish enough to try to steal it from us. This is a golden opportunity Admiral, one which will set us back on our rightful path to a glorious future. But every second we wait is one second closer to the possibility that the Annuxians will find out that the Nelamine ore is actually on Mogo 3 is and beat us to our prize."

At this point someone, probably the translator's mother, called out and the holographic image began to swirl and shift as Colopo looked away from alleyway and then began to hurry back down to rejoin the others sitting by the river.

Supreme Leader Zilpolo addressed the mechanoid controlling the shallinop machine, telling it to shut the device down and revive Colopo. There was no need to observe any more of the translator's memories. It was obvious what had happened next. Vethil had left for Mogo 3 in search of a non-existent treasure trove of Nelamine ore and taken the rest of the aliens with him. But that still didn't explain why Salang Chai was so adamant Vethil wasn't coming back.

The mechanoid opened the lid of the shallinop, gently lifted Colopo's comatose form from the neurogel and carried her into the next room. Chai learnt later that the mechanoid washed and dried her and had her lungs purged, by nanobots, of all the gooey gel, before being revived.

While this was happening young Dillip rose and asked if he might be allowed to comment further on what everyone had just witnessed. Zilpolo nodded and the young Tranian stepped forward hesitantly, his voice trembling at the thought of speaking before none other than the Supreme Leader herself. Cautiously he began to explain the significance of sending the alien fleet to Mogo 3.

"I am Dillip, son of Talopan. I am a student of Inter Galactic Navigation at Salin University," he said by way of introduction. "It was I who first told Emissary Chai of the existence of the planet Mogo 3. My hope was that we might find a suitable alternative home for the aliens, but that was not to be. You see the one thing Emissary Chai did not tell Admiral Vethil, was that the atmosphere of Mogo 3 contains a one percent concentration of Wrillin gas."

Here Dillip paused for a moment and consulted the ream of notes he had brought with him. "The aliens call it Argon," he continued finally. "Wrillin or Argon gas is non toxic to all life forms. In fact, it is relatively inert. However, it is extremely corrosive to Nelamine metal and its alloys. I have a friend in the engineering department at the university and he calculated that at a one percent concentration, once the alien's vessels had entered Mogo 3's atmosphere, they would have had approximately two hours before the corrosive nature of the Wrillin gas caused irreparable damage. To put it another way, in all probability the ships made it to the planet's surface, but it is absolutely certain they will never be able to leave. Vethil and his people are trapped forever on Mogo 3."

Every member of the High Council smiled. It appeared what Emissary Salang Chai had said was true, Vethil and the other battle cruisers weren't coming back.

"Of course the existence of Wrillin gas, proves that Emissary Chai's claim Mogo 3 is the site of the largest Nelamine ore deposit ever discovered, has to be a complete fabrication. Obviously he devised the whole tale simply to tempt Vethil into leaving and taking his dreaded vortex canon with him," Dillip continued. "But I assure you honoured High Councillors, everything else Chai said was true. Mogo 3 has everything the aliens need, a breathable atmosphere, fresh water, vast tracts of agriculturally viable land, plus various metallic ores. There is an abundance of hydrocarbons and other raw materials, and much of the planet enjoys a perfect, temperate climate. My estimates based on the information I have concluded, that with judicious use of the planet's resources and with careful land management, Mogo 3 is capable of supporting up to twenty billion people. This is not the end of the aliens, rather it is just a new beginning. Obviously life will be hard for a few years, but I have no doubt that once they are established, the aliens will not only survive, they will prosper. Emissary Salang Chai's actions have saved the lives of countless Tranians, but in doing so he has necessarily condemned his own people to a life in exile. What he did has trapped them on the other side of the galaxy for all eternity. This is why, despite his heroic actions, despite the fact he has saved the lives of millions, Salang Chai feels deep shame and regret for what he has done."

Chapter 59

THE MOUNTAINS TO THE west of Salin city were once again shrouded in snow. Powdery white flurries had fallen on the upper reaches every day now for almost a month, covering the mountain tops with breathtakingly picturesque, blindingly white snow. The temperature inside Chai's multiple person transport vehicle was set at a comfortable twenty two degrees centigrade, warm enough to keep the passengers from complaining, yet cool enough to stop them and Chai falling asleep. Just as well, Chai was driving and the roads beneath the bus's tyres were icy, narrow and twisting.

Ten years had passed since Admiral Vethil had taken his deadly vortex canon away from the skies over Tran. Ten years since the people of his new home had joined together to thank their funny little alien friend for his selfless sacrifice. Everyone on the planet knew what he had done, Supreme Leader Zilpolo had made sure they did. She insisted that every news service on Tran run a story on what had transpired between Emissary Salang Chai and Vethil, just minutes before the criminal's deadline expired. One month later the High Council presented Chai with a medal and unveiled a plaque in his honour in the foyer of Salin Museum. In this way the name Salang Chai was immortalised in Tranian history for eternity.

Of course there had been no question about Chai and his beautiful wife being allowed to stay on Tran. He was a hero, and besides, there was nowhere else for them to go.

Learning the Tranian language had been their priority and with the help of Colopo and her mother, together with the young girl Drolopo, they had immersed themselves in that task. Shan had found the exercise easier than Chai, but even so by the end of that first autumn, both were speaking the lingo sufficiently well to get by without Colopo's assistance.

In the winter of their first year as honorary Tranian citizens, Wawa Shan had given birth to a tiny baby boy. He was, at least in the eyes of his parents, the most beautiful boy ever to have worn a nappy. He had all his fingers and toes, everything worked perfectly, he cried when he was hungry and when he was wet, and did everything all happy and healthy babies have done since the beginning of time. They had called the little boy Salang Shanniwa, after Shan's late father.

The birth had caused quite a stir in Salin. The Tranians, like their friends the Annuxians, were Monotremes, that is egg laying mammals. Though, in stark contrast to an Annuxian, a Tranian female would normally lay only a single, translucent, leathery, envelope shaped egg per season, while an Annuxian might lay a clutch of up to eight silicone shelled, ovoid eggs.

For months leading up to the birth, any number of Tranian medico's had approached Shan, asking if they might observe the special event. There had never been a live birth before on the planet, and every doctor and documentary vidi maker in Salin had been dying to see first hand what such an occurrence looked like.

Being a doctor herself, Shan had no qualms about allowing medical practitioners to observe the birth. But Shan was nobody's fool and figured she'd at least try to get something in return. She'd needed a job. Silpolo and Colopo had told her and Chai that they were welcome to stay and share their home for as long as they wanted to, but both she and Chai had known that the two Tranian women were just being polite. No matter what had been said, the two interlopers had been expected to find their own place as soon as possible. So Shan and Chai had both needed some form of paid employment. Ten days before the 'blessed event', Shan negotiated a deal with the Dean of the medical school at Salin University. At the beginning of the new year, once Shanniwa was old enough to be away from his dotting mother for a few hours each day, Shan would start work as a research assistant in the teaching hospital's diagnostic department. This had meant doing all the boring, mundane jobs like washing test tubes and recalibrating centrifuges, rather than treating actual patients, but at least she was once again working in the health care industry, and earning enough credit to pay the rent on the tiny, two room apartment they'd leased in a building just a stone's throw away from Colopo and her mother. In return for the job, the university had been allowed to record and document the birth.

Eventually Chai had also found a way of making money. Many Tranian business people had approached him about becoming the spokesperson for their company. Ostensibly they wanted nothing more than to take advantage of his fame to promote their products or services. Chai, still racked with guilt for condemning his own people to exile, hadn't been at all happy about their propositions and had told them, politely, to take a hike.

But very few people needed or wanted the other type of expertise Chai had to offer, and eventually he had come to the conclusion that if he was going to earn a living, he would have to establish his own business. Which was how Chai came to be driving a sixteen seat bus through the snow capped mountains to the west of Salin.

He had seen the first of his vehicles for sale, at a very reasonable price, in the car park outside Salin West hover port. With Colopo's help he had approached the Tranian High Council and asked for a small loan so he could buy it. The High Council wasn't in the habit of loaning money to anyone, but Zilpolo had understood that Salang Chai's case was unique, and that no financial institution on the planet was going to loan money to an alien, even one who had saved them from almost certain annihilation. So she had underwritten the money herself and Chai had become the not so proud owner of a twelve year old, nine passenger, multiple person transport vehicle.

He had modified the driving position to suit his 'wrong way bending knees', purchased a tourism operator's licence, and begun taking tourists, predominately elderly men and women, on guided tours around the city of Salin and its environs. After two years he'd bought a second vehicle and employed a middle aged Tranian male to drive it.

Now the company fleet numbered nine buses and Chai was worth quite a sizeable amount.

Half way down the mountainside, Chai pulled the bus into one of the many parking areas and shut the old girl down.

"Okay everyone," he said cheerily, "this is where we stop for our midday meal. At the bottom of that track there," he said pointing, "is a magnificent thermal pool. Normally at this time of year it's about 35 degrees, so if you're going in, and I strongly recommend you do, make sure you stay in for at least twenty minutes. Any less than that and you'll be too tough and chewy for the rest us to eat."

The passengers all laughed at Chai's weak attempt at levity. He'd learnt over the past ten years that the Tranians weren't big on subtle or obscure humour. They didn't understand the nuances of satire either. With a Tranian it had to be obvious and if possible, more than a little absurd.

The passengers gathered their belongings, filed out of the bus and headed down the track towards the pool. Chai stayed back for a few moments to make sure no one had wandered off in the wrong direction, and then began to unpack the food. He then pulled out the portable cooking appliance and the ten folding seats, which he always kept on hand for those passengers who were more demanding of comfort, or were too old and frail to sit on the frozen rocks at the edge of the pool. He grabbed an armful of stuff and made his way down the track. Two minutes later he was back for another load, and then another a little while later.

He set everything up, opened the portable cooking appliances lid and shovelled a small mountain of winter vegetables onto the cooking surface. He sprinkled a good serving of seasoning over the food and set the timer for fifteen minutes.

All but one of his charges were floating about lazily in the steaming pool as he made his way down to the water's edge. Brushing the snow away with a leafy branch from a nearby bush, he climbed up and perched his bottom on top of a large flat rock and watched the tourists at play.

The pool was always popular with his older charges. The heat soothed their aching, elderly joints and loosened their tired muscles. It was situated at the bottom of a shallow ravine, and was almost circular, about thirty metres in circumference and surrounded by a ring of large, granite boulders. It was fed by an underground thermal spring which welled up from deep below the planets surface. Today, surrounded by snow and cloaked in a haze of steam, it looked almost mystical.

He was soon joined by the only other person who had decided not to go swimming. She was an older woman, perhaps close to one hundred and fifty years old. She was taller than Chai, but this time only by a head and had a large, matronly figure. Like so many Tranian people, she had a wonderfully open smile. On her narrow, sloping forehead she had a prominent tattoo of a stylised star. Somehow the tattoo reminded Chai of someone he had met before, a person who had spoken to him many years ago in another time, and on another world.

She greeted him, crossing her arms across her chest and bowing deeply.

"May I join you Emissary?" she enquired in the tinkling bell like voice which characterised so many Tranian women.

Chai smiled. It had been almost a decade since anyone had addressed him as Emissary.

"So you remember my story then honoured Grandmother? You do me great honour by addressing me by my old title. But I implore you, we are friends I trust, in which case I ask that you just call me Chai. Please, be seated and share this wonderful view with me."

The woman nodded and squatted beside him.

"Of course I remember the tale of the great Emissary Salang Chai. Everyone does. Everyone who was old enough to understand the terrifying peril we faced, remembers how the alien Emissary changed the course of history and saved an entire planet with nothing more than a few carefully chosen words. You chose the path of the righteous my friend, and for that, all Tranians will be eternally in your debt."

But even after all these years, Chai still felt a pang of guilt when he thought of what he had done to his own people.

"Yes, I changed the course of history all right, and in doing so condemned my own species to a miserable existence, trapped on a distant world."

The old woman scoffed at his claim. "We are your people Salang Chai. Us. Not the worthless mongrels who left you to die in the middle of the war the insane criminal Admiral Vethil was about to start. Your 'own species' as you call them, had condemned themselves to extinction years before you were even born, young Chai. Their foolishness, their blindness and refusal to see what even a child could see, was madness. Their own actions caused their downfall, not what you did."

Chai knew the old woman was in many ways correct, and yet it still filled his heart with almost unbearable pain to think of what he had done.

A few years ago the Tranian High Council had commissioned an expedition to Mogo 3 to ascertain how many of the aliens had survived their voyage and resettlement on the planet. They had sent a small vortex ship and put it in orbit around the planet, high above the planet's corrosive atmosphere. Then they'd sent an unmanned probe into the atmosphere and had it relay vidi images of any alien settlement it found, back to the mothership.

The probe had been specially reinforced with extra thick Nelamine alloy panels, and the tiny vessel had lasted over three hours before it experienced catastrophic failure. During those three brief hours, it was able to collect enough data to enable the Tranian High Council to estimate there were fewer than eight thousand souls left alive. Of course there may have been more, lots more. The probe was only able to inspect two of the more likely landing sites and surrounding areas before it failed. But the images sent back showed Chai's people were enduring extreme difficulty, and at times were barely able to obtain enough food and shelter to keep themselves alive. Chai had seen those images and although none of the faces were those of people he knew, their pitiful, pleading looks of desperation when they saw the probe looking down at them would haunt Chai for the rest of his life.

The old woman reached out and gently placed a hand on his shoulder.

"Sometimes the path of the righteous is difficult Emissary, but you must accept that your home is here now, with the people who honour and respect you, and with those who love you, not just for what you've done, but more importantly for who you are."

Chai nodded. In a way the old woman was right. His home was here on Tran, he knew that with every fibre of his being, but then he wasn't the only person he had to consider.

Chapter 60

IN THE SPRING OF THE second year, around the time Chai had purchased his third bus, Colopo, who had briefly taken a mate the previous autumn, produced the first of her three offspring. In honour of her treasured friend, she had named the little girl Chaipolo. Two more little girls had followed over the next five years.

But not all the events on Tran had been happy ones. Silpolo died towards the end of year eight, passing away peacefully in her sleep. Chai had been amazed to learn later that his dear friend's mother was over one hundred and sixty years old when she'd died. She was cremated on the banks of the Malpo river, with full Law Enforcer honours, and her sanitised ashes had been scattered over the water, to mix with the ashes of millions of others who had been farewelled in a similar way, over the past few thousand years.

As is the tradition on Tran, the ownership of Silpolo's apartment then passed on to Colopo, and this event had marked the beginning of a new phase in the translator's life. The Annuxian Ambassador Iwar had asked her to join his embassy staff, on Tran, and to act solely on his behalf. The Ambassador had needed someone who not only spoke the language, but also understood the intricacies and protocols associated with it. Colopo, Iwar assured her, was the perfect person for the job. Her new position had commanded a lot more of her time than the University post had done, and over the next few years, Chai and Shan frequently found themselves looking after Colopo's three kids in the evenings, sometimes until well after midnight. Neither ever thought of this task as an inconvenience however, Colopo's three girls were all adorable and the youngest, V'napolo, loved to sing and had the voice of an angel.

But although Chai and Shan loved their life on Tran and had grown to think of the planet as their true home, on the eve of the winter equinox, just nine days before Shanniwa's tenth birthday, and eight days after his discussion with the old, tattooed woman, Chai presented Colopo with some devastating news.

He was leaving Tran and moving to Mogo 3.

"But you can't leave my friend," Colopo demanded, her voice tinged with sorrow. "Your home is here with us. Besides, how will you get there."

"I've sold my business," Chai explained. "The credit I've raised will pay the passage for Shan, Shanniwa and myself. I have already purchased an old ship to surface transport craft and a mechanoid pilot which will take us from the freighter to the planet's surface. I'm having the vessel reinforced with extra thick sheets of Nelamine alloy. With luck that will give us sufficient time to locate one of the settlements and land before the ship breaks up."

"But why? I thought you were happy here?"

"Of course I'm happy here," Chai replied. "Shan, Shanniwa and I love it on Tran, but," he said pointing towards the other room where his son and Colopo's three girls were playing, "Shanniwa needs to be with people of his own kind. Soon he will be entering adulthood. Eventually he will want to take a mate and have children of his own. He can't do that on Tran."

Colopo nodded unhappily. In truth she had known in her heart all along, that this day would come. Her little friend was right. Chai had his wife Shan, and as his mate, she was all he needed. His love for her and hers for him had only become stronger over the years. Colopo felt sure their love for each other would continue to grow until the day they died. Without each other, she knew they would feel incomplete and Chai and Shan both understood that their son Shanniwa would soon need someone of his own.

"I shall miss you, my dear friend," Colopo told him wrapping her long slender arms around him and hugging him tightly.

"Thank you for your cherished love and friendship, my dear, dear friend," Chai replied. Then he stretched his face up as far as her could and kissed her on the cheek. Both her face and his were drenched with tears.

"When do you leave?" Colopo asked, her words catching in her throat as she tried unsuccessfully to keep her emotions under control.

"Tomorrow at midday," Chai replied.

Chapter 61

MILLIONS OF YEARS HAVE passed since Emissary Salang Chai walked amongst us. The well chronicled history of his time on Tran ended the day he left our planet, so it is unclear if Chai and his family survived their resettlement on Mogo 3. Many of the aliens did not. In fact seven of the ships in the armada never even made it to the planet's surface. Just as Dillip had predicted, the argon gas attacked the Nelamine alloy of the ship's hulls with all the ferocity of a raging inferno. The intake vents on the anti-grav drives, the immensely powerful engines which manoeuvred the massive vessels and provided its braking impetus when flying through the atmosphere, had collapsed, causing the drives to overheat and fail. Unable to slow their descent, the seven ships had burnt up in the atmosphere. As a result less than half of the original twenty six and a half thousand souls made it to their new home. Many of those who had survived came to wish they too had been killed as quickly and as painlessly as their counterparts.

Life on Mogo 3 proved to be difficult at first, hellishly so, in fact almost impossible. The argon gas had not only attacked the Nelamine of the ships themselves, but also all the equipment, machinery, nanobots and mechanoids the aliens had brought with them. In less than a week every trace of the precious alloy had been destroyed and the settlers had been left to fend for themselves, eking out a miserable, barely sustainable existence with nothing more than the few simple tools and weapons they had been able to fashion from sticks and rocks. In less than a month the entire species had been hurtled back into the stone age.

The devastation caused by the argon gas had also denied the aliens any possibility of a gradual introduction of those previously interned in the stasis units. With each ship's superstructure collapsing around them, the sleeping men, women and children had to be revived as soon as possible. Sadly, many of the people held in stasis died, crushed by the massive weight of their ship as it had collapsed around them.

By design the fleet had been scattered to all corners of the globe. But it had quickly become apparent that out of necessity, the numbers in each area would have to be reduced even further. It had been logistically impossible to feed over a thousand people from each remaining ship with the meagre amount of food available from hunting and gathering, especially when they had been restricted to an area stretching just a few kilometres from their landing site. The survivors of each ship had quickly formed into smaller, more sustainable tribes and moved to other areas.

With almost all of their efforts restricted to simply surviving, it is little wonder that all cultural, technical and historical considerations had taken a back seat. Within just a few generations the settlers had begun to forget where they had come from. Eventually their true origins were lost in antiquity. In just a few short generations the aliens began to believe they were endemic to their new home and had never lived anywhere else.

Life on Mogo 3 continued to be hard for centuries, but eventually the settlers began to prosper. They introduced new and improved methods of agriculture and animal husbandry, and gradually adopted more advanced farming techniques. They domesticated animals for meat and milk and eggs and learnt to harness the strength of the larger beasts to plough fields and transport themselves and their produce.

Soon they began to build small boats to transport themselves across rivers and lakes. This was inevitably followed by the building of larger ships, which used the power of the wind, to enable them to cross the planet's huge oceans. With time, they began to construct increasingly complex machines which they made from the metal ores extracted from the ground, and learnt to use the energy derived from burning the planet's abundant hydrocarbon deposits to power those machines.

As the centuries passed, the equipment and devices they built became more and more complex. Civilizations rose and fell. Huge cities were built and then destroyed, sometimes by floods, fire or famine but more frequently by war.

With time, science and technology began to improve to the point where once again they had been able to take their first, tentative steps into space. But without access to the precious Nelamine alloy, the aliens would always be restricted to venturing just a few million kilometres from their home.

Though always in secret, we have visited them often over the past few million years. The aliens are wary of strange things they don't understand and we have found it prudent and safer to remain hidden. Long ago the Tranians developed new ways of travelling across the universe, ways which no longer relied on the use of Nelamine alloy, or for that matter, physical vessels of any kind. So it is easier and less dangerous now for us to visit the planet's surface. The aliens have changed markedly over the millennia, as indeed have we. As Wawa Shan predicted all those centuries ago, the aliens have grown tall and slender. They stand more upright now and their skin is smoother, softer and less hairy. Their facial features too have become less harsh, less animalistic than that of their ancestors. In many ways they have grown into a very handsome species.

But sadly, many of their earlier traits are still very much in evidence. They still exhibit a callous disregard for the obviously finite resources of their planet. Their actions and behaviour are still regularly determined by greed and self interest, and worst of all, wars continue to rage almost constantly.

The Annuxians still believe the aliens will one day soon, come to see the error of their ways and learn to live in peaceful harmony with themselves and other sentient beings from across the galaxy. We Tranians share their enthusiasm if not their faith.

But maybe they are right. Maybe this time, before it's too late, the aliens will change their destructive ways, learn to use their planets bountiful resources more sustainably, and live in peace alongside their fellow man. If they cannot do these simple things this time, with no way of reaching anywhere where they might find refuge, their future is more easily determined. This time they will not survive.

Once again the alien's world, the planet they now call Earth, will soon begin to run out of resources. Then the very survival of their new home will once more teeter on the precipice of self destruction. The Annuxians are convinced that this time they will change before it's too late. We are not so sure. But if and when that happens the people of Tran stand ready to welcome them with open arms and open hearts.

The End

THANK YOU FOR READING my novel

A LITTLE OVER A YEAR ago, the plot for *Alien Vermin* popped, uninvited into my head and demanded to be turned into a book. The previous pages are the result.

I say uninvited because I don't really consider myself a Science Fiction writer. In fact if I was to classify myself as an author and nominate a book type as *my genre*, I would have to say I'm a Crime Fiction writer.

At the time of publishing *Alien Vermin*, I had already written seven novels. Six are murder mysteries while the remaining book is a children's/ young adult fantasy adventure in the vein of CS Lewis.

These seven books are listed at the end of the following short story, If you think they might hold some appeal, please visit your preferred on-line book seller and check out my other titles. In the meantime, just in case you're unsure of whether you might like my Crime Fiction writing, here's a CF short story called '*A letter to Oscar's sister*' to whet your appetite.

A Letter to Oscar's Sister

DEAR MISS GONZALES,

Although we have never met, I am sure you know who I am, just as I am sure the first thing you will want to do with this letter, is tear it into a million pieces and throw the bits into a fire. But I implore you, please read the few heartfelt words I have written here before consigning these pages to the flames.

Two years ago when I first met your brother Oscar, I was immediately enamoured by his charm, ready wit and generous nature. It is unnecessary of me to expound on his many and varied virtues and talents, you more than anyone else, will be fully aware of what an extremely special person dear Oscar was. We became great friends he and I, and his death will haunt me until the day I die.

Oscar and I shared a passion for many things, but our greatest love was for surfing. He and I spent many hours together, out beyond the breakers, waiting for the perfect wave. We would sit astride our boards, chatting about everything and nothing, regaling each other with tall tales of our various exploits with women or on the sporting field. It was during one of these happy sessions that he told me about his wonderful sister Elvira.

On many of these occasions he also spoke about his life back in Madrid before he came to live here in Australia. Although he loved his new country, he still missed many things from his homeland. The most important of these was undoubtedly being able to see your beautiful, smiling face. He adored you Elvira, of that I am certain.

Oscar may have told you that I work in the finance industry. He may have also told you that my work frequently has me travelling abroad. In the first instance, at least, he has been misinformed, ostensibly by me. The truth is I work for AATIO, the Australian Anti-Terrorism Intelligence Origination. No I am not a spy, the undercover operatives on our team are far more intelligent, capable and resourceful than I could ever be. But when our government detects a real and credible threat to our way of life, and when, because of international protocols or other considerations the threat cannot be dealt with through more orthodox channels, they sometimes call on me to effect a less legitimate solution. You see AATIO employ me as an assassin.

No doubt you have heard of the recent assassination of Malamud Ben Mustafa, the Pakistani operative and second in charge of that country's Al-Qa'ida. I was the person who put the bullet through his evil black heart. AATIO got involved when they gleaned from some very credible intelligence that an Al-Qa'ida sleeper, living in Sydney, was preparing to launch an attack on the nuclear waste facility at Lucas Heights. Mustafa was that sleeper's contact back in Pakistan and his death meant the sleeper and his associates had no other recourse than to abandon their plans to blow up the Lucas Heights facility.

I was recruited by AATIO three years ago, directly after my time in the Australian Army, where I spent nearly eight years as a sniper with the SAS. Since joining AATIO I have received further training in many forms of martial arts as well as various forms of weapons operation. My speciality however is with a long range sniper rifle. I hold the army record for the highest score over 1000 metres at the 2013 Department of Defence competition and the second highest score over 1200 metres. All this I tell you only so you may better understand how the recent, tragic events came to pass.

Six days ago I returned from an assignment in Afghanistan. The details of that assignment are unimportant other than to say that my time in that country was extremely difficult and stressful. I was so happy to be home again on safe Australian soil.

I caught up with your brother and a few other friends a couple of days later, and remember thinking that Oscar seemed a little over excited and that he kept making strange, veiled comments about the upcoming weekend. When I questioned him about his actions, he simply smiled and told me he was just looking forward to the play on Saturday. As you are aware, Oscar recently joined an amateur dramatic society and they were about to commence their production of Arthur Miller's 'Death of a Salesman' that Saturday. Oscar had been given the lead role and you will be proud to hear he did a wonderful job. His rendition of Willy Loman was totally enthralling. I was spellbound during the entire performance, and completely amazed at how he could so easily hide his normally strong, Spanish accent and adopt the speech and mannerisms of an American from New England so perfectly. Despite his merely amateur status, he was a truly accomplished actor.

Sunday was my thirtieth birthday, a big event in anyone's life. I had arranged with Oscar and a few other friends to meet at the Sovereign Hotel on Sunday evening and was looking forward to the party immensely. But I never got there.

Around midday on Sunday I left my apartment to go to the gym, but as I was about to get into my car, two men, dressed in what appeared to be some sort of military attire, wearing balaclavas over their heads and carrying what looked to be a handgun and a large, vicious looking knife, crept up behind me and threw a black cloth bag over my head. One of the men jabbed his gun into my side and warned me that if I made a sound he would kill me. They dragged me to a waiting van, shoved me in the back, and bound my hands and feet so I couldn't escape. Then one of the men clambered into the back with me while the other climbed into the driver's seat and drove off rapidly. From the semi military attire and heavy middle eastern accents of my attackers, *it seemed obvious to me that my abduction was somehow related to my recent time in Afghanistan.*

As the van made its way through the back streets of Sydney, I lay quietly on the floor listening out for any indication of where my abductors might be taking me. But with my head covered by the bag, unable to see out and trussed up like a turkey, I was blind. Although from our speed and the loud traffic noise I got the impression we had at one stage driven along the freeway, I had no real idea where we were headed.

After about half an hour, the van slowed and slewed around to the left. I could hear from the change in the noise from the tyres that we were now driving along a gravel road. The van stopped a few minutes later and one of my abductors got out. There was the unmistakable sound of a roller door being pulled up and then the van drove inside what I was later to learn was a large abandoned warehouse. The van stopped once again, its rear door flung open and I was dragged out. With my kidnappers holding my arms in a vice like grip, I was marched through the warehouse into a room at the rear of the building.

I was constantly looking for an opportunity to escape, but until that time none had presented itself. But when the two men had bound my arms, I had clenched my fists tightly and kept my wrists straight. In this way, when I relaxed my arms, the ropes around my wrists loosened slightly. I knew that if I had the opportunity, I would be able to get my hands free. That opportunity came a few minutes later.

My captors led me through a doorway into a small room. They pushed me back onto a hard plastic chair and ripped the bag off my head. It took a few seconds for my eyes to adjust to the bright light glaring in my face, but when they did I could see I was being held in a rectangular space about 3 metres by five metres. It had two doors leading off it, the one we had just entered and a second directly opposite. The room contained only the chair I was sitting on, and an old, chrome legged and a timber topped table with a portable CD player on it. A single, unshaded light bulb hung from the ceiling, filling the tiny space with blinding light.

My two captors stood before me menacingly, brandishing large evil looking knives. Both still wore balaclava masks over their faces.

"You are about to die infidel," the taller of the two thugs hissed in an accent I recognised as Pakistani. "How painful that death is, depends upon your answers to our questions. We know who you are Australian dog, and we know what you have done. Tell us the name of your contact in Pakistan and how you reach him, or you will soon be begging your false God to deliver you from unbearable suffering."

I told the man I had no idea what he was talking about. I was just an employee of Granite Financial services and didn't know anyone in Pakistan. But all the time I was speaking, I was working on my bindings behind my back, trying to get my hands free.

The smaller of the two men crossed over to the back wall of the room and picked up a pick handle which had been leaning against it. Then the first kidnapper reached over and pressed a button on the CD player. The room was suddenly filed with loud dance music. I knew what this meant. They had turned on the CD player so that my screams when they tortured me would be drowned out by the music. If I was going to survive, I had to make my move now. As the smaller man approached me I leant back and kicked out with my bound feet, both hitting him squarely in his right knee. He screamed in agony and fell to the floor. The second thug lunged, but he wasn't quick enough. I pulled against my bindings and my hands came free. My right fist shot out punching him in the throat, then I grabbed his knife hand and pressed my thumb into the back of his hand, twisting the blade away from me and towards his stomach. I thrust the blade into his gut and he went down, clutching at his stomach, his shirt front covered in a rapidly spreading pool of blood. I pulled the knife out and quickly slashed the rope around my ankles. I was free.

But then the door through which I had been dragged just moments before, flew open and a young woman strutted into the room. She was dressed in an Australian Army uniform, her shirt open to the waist, the skin between her breasts sparkling with glitter. She had her long blonde hair tucked up into her army slouch hat and her face, which was quite attractive in a sluttish sort of way, was heavily made up with bright red lips and huge false eyelashes. On her feet she wore a pair of black high heels and her nails were long and painted with blood red polish.

Something was wrong, dreadfully wrong.

She froze in her tracks, took one look at the two men lying on the floor and the huge, blood soaked knife in my hand and screamed.

"Jesus Christ," she yelled, then turned and bolted back through the door she had entered just seconds before. As she flung the door open I could see the inside of the next room was decorated with coloured lights and a large, hand painted banner stretched across the far wall up near the ceiling. In the centre of the room was a long rectangular table with twenty or so chairs arranged around its perimeter. The table was laden with food and drinks and in the centre was a large round chocolate cake. I couldn't see what was written on the cake, but no doubt it was the same greeting as on the banner.

"Happy Birthday Alex."

Someone in the other room yelled "surprise", but by that time I was on my knees, trying desperately to staunch the blood pulsing from the horrendous wound I had inflicted on your poor dear brother. I was too late. Long before the paramedics arrived, Oscar had died form massive blood loss.

It was all a prank. All a stupid joke, meant to frighten me witless before the "Australian Army stripper", burst in and "saved the day" and then me and my friends would spend the afternoon and evening celebrating my thirtieth birthday. All a dumb joke, gone horribly wrong. One of my best friends, your poor dear brother, was now dead, and another had had his kneecap damaged beyond repair.

It was my fault Elvira. I should have told them about my past, should have warned them that I had been trained by the army in unarmed combat and was a dangerous man, a man they were better off staying away from. I should have told Oscar that knowing me could quite possibly get him killed. But how was I to know he and my other friends would pull such a prank, and that it would all go so terribly, horribly wrong?

Someone called the police. They came and arrested me, charged me with the murder of your brother and for the assault against my friend Tim who had been taken to hospital with a broken knee. They led me away in handcuffs, took away my belt and shoe laces and then threw me into a cell at the Parramatta Police Station. Later an official from ATTIO came and saw me. He told me there was nothing they could do, that the incident was nothing to do with my employment at AATIO. Not that I had asked them to do anything anyway.

The following morning my lawyer, Mr Albert Pinkerton arrived, and shortly after I was led into an interview room where I gave my statement. When that onerous task was completed, the cops charged me officially once again, this time revising the charge to manslaughter.

My lawyer then accompanied me back to my cell where we discussed my upcoming trial. When we were finished I asked Mr Pinkerton if he might stay for a few minutes while I recorded a letter to you on the small tape recorder he carried with him. The words you have just read are those which I dictated.

I know you can never forgive me Elvira, just as I can never forgive myself. Perhaps I have made things worse by explaining that your brother's death was a freak accident, rather than a malicious act on my part, but I need you to know I loved your brother as if he were my own, and if I could, I would gladly take his place in the grave and restore him to his loving sister. Alex.

Covering letter from Albert J Pinkerton

DEAR MISS GONZALES

The above letter was dictated to me by Mr Alex Randall on the twentieth of this month with the express instructions it was to be translated into your native Spanish and delivered to you as soon as possible.

I am sure you will find the contents of the letter most disturbing and for that you have my deepest apologies together with my sincere commiserations on the tragic death of your brother.

Although I never met Mr Gonzales, in my capacity as Mr Randall's counsel, I attended his funeral on the twenty sixth. You may find a little consolation in the knowledge that he was obviously a much admired and loved young man.

With regard to Mr Alex Randall, it is my duty to inform you that Mr Randall died by his own hand on the twenty sixth of this month. He was found hanged from the bars of his cell, by a strip of cloth he had torn from his prison uniform. His last will and testament bequeaths his entire estate to you. I imagine it will be a few months before his estate is finalised but you should receive a cheque by the end of September.

If I can be of further assistance in this matter, please do not hesitate to contact me.

Yours sincerely

Albert J Pinkerton

Attorney at Law

Other publications by Kevin William Barry

Innocent Until Proven Deadly

A Murderous Addiction

Dead Tropical

Dark Murder

A Pain in the Arts

Lethal Odyssey

And the Children's/ young adult fantasy

Charlotte and the Morthe

Join me on Facebook

Kevin William Barry Author

Don't miss out!

Visit the website below and you can sign up to receive emails whenever Kevin William Barry publishes a new book. There's no charge and no obligation.

https://books2read.com/r/B-A-JODC-PIIJ

BOOKS 2 READ

Connecting independent readers to independent writers.

Did you love *Alien Vermin*? Then you should read *A Pain In The Arts* by Kevin William Barry!

Sally Croft and her unborn son are brutally murdered. The cops have arrested someone, but Sally's husband Daniel is convinced they've got the wrong person.

He tracks the man he thinks is responsible to Far North Queensland, Australia and sets about collecting evidence. But is Daniel seeking justice or just revenge, and what is the secret behind the painting "Miesbach Castle"? a secret so powerful it will cause a seemingly harmless man to commit Murder.

Also by Kevin William Barry

A Murderous Addiction
Innocent Until Proven Deadly
Dead Tropical
A Lethal Odyssey
A Pain In The Arts
Charlotte and the Morthe
Alien Vermin
Murder In The Outback
Murder, Mayhem and Mystery. A Collection of Short Stories
The Rich and The Dead
Fart From the Madding Crowd

About the Author

Kevin William Barry is the Australian author of numerous novels.

He lives on the Atherton Tableands, Far North Queensland Australia with his wife Cathy